"KROYKAH!"
KIRK SHOUTED . . .

Even to the followers of T'Vet, that word, used in ceremonies dating back to the Vulcan Time of the Beginning, meant "stop!"

"You are not on Vulcan now," Kirk said, striding between the two fighters. They rested their weapons with the weighted ends on the floor. "You are on my ship, and here my word is law. There will be no combat with deadly weapons aboard ship. You are welcome to use our facilities for unarmed combat, to practice marksmanship in the—"

"How dare you profane Vulcan custom!" Satat, war-chief of those assembled, said. He turned to the two fighters. "Continue the combat."

The two fighters hefted their weapons again and began moving. Kirk stood still, squarely between them in the center of the mat.

If he didn't get out of their way, they were going right through him.

Look for STAR TREK Fiction from Pocket Books

STAR TREK®
THE IDIC EPIDEMIC

JEAN LORRAH

POCKET BOOKS

New York   London   Toronto   Sydney   Tokyo

Another *Original* publication of POCKET BOOKS

POCKET BOOKS, a division of Simon & Schuster, Inc.
1230 Avenue of the Americas, New York, NY 10020

ISBN: 0-671-63574-3

First Pocket Books printing February 1988

10 9 8 7 6 5 4 3 2 1

Foreword

I would like to thank Gene Roddenberry, the creator of *Star Trek,* which has been an important influence in my life,

William Shatner, Leonard Nimoy, DeForest Kelly, Mark Lenard (Sarek), Jane Wyatt (Amanda), and all the other actors who brought *Star Trek* characters to life,

Star Trek fandom, which over many years has provided a forum for the stories I—and so many other fans—needed to tell,

and the *Star Trek Welcommittee,* who for many years have served to bring fans who love *Star Trek* to know and share their interests with one another.

I have been a *Star Trek* fan since 1966, when the original live episodes first appeared. I learned to write through fanzines, and made many wonderful friends through Trek-fandom. I recommend it to all of you who have Trek stories to tell: get involved in fandom and learn to tell them. Then, if you want to be a professional writer, take workshops and study books on creative writing to learn the procedure of turning from amateur to professional. Don't write to professional writers, asking them to tell you how—they are too busy writing books for you. They haven't time to write letters trying to explain in words something that can only be learned by doing. Books and workshops will get you started; the experience you can only get with practice.

Whether you want to write or not, if you love *Star Trek* you will love fandom. Paramount now sponsors a fan club with a bimonthly newsletter to tell you all the latest news about the movies, the TV series, and the actors and creators:

The Official *Star Trek* Fan Club
P.O. Box 111000
Aurora, CO 80011

But Trekfandom is not limited to the fan club. If you write or draw or make music or costumes or want to interact with other fans, you want the original fandom: friends and letters and crafts and fanzines and trivia and costumes and artwork and filksongs [sic] and posters and buttons and games and film clips and conventions—something for everybody who has in common the inspiration of a television show which has grown far beyond its TV and film incarnations to become a living part of world culture.

The way to that fandom is not through me, or any other author of *Star Trek* novels. You want that wonderful organization, the *Star Trek Welcommittee*. Be *sure* to enclose a stamped self-addressed envelope, as this is a purely volunteer, nonprofit organization of people who love *Star Trek* and are willing to answer your questions and put you in touch with other fans. The current address is

Star Trek Welcommittee
P.O. Drawer 12
Saranac, MI 48881.

In both Trekwriting and my other professional science fiction, I have a strong belief in the interaction between authors and fans. Authors want your constructive comments. They cannot collaborate with you, write the stories you want to tell (you'll have to do that yourself), or critique your novels (they're busy writing their own). All authors, though, are happy to receive comments about their books, and most will answer questions. If you would like to comment on this or any of my books, you may write to me in care of my publishers, or at P.O. Box 625, Murray, KY

42071. If your letter requires an answer, please enclose a stamped self-addressed envelope.

Keep on Trekkin'!

Jean Lorrah
Murray, Kentucky

P.S. *The IDIC Epidemic* is a sequel to *The Vulcan Academy Murders,* which is also available from Pocket Books. Please don't feel that you can't read this book without the earlier one, though. All the *Star Trek* novels are designed like episodes, so that it doesn't hurt to miss some or read them out of order. If you like *The IDIC Epidemic,* you can later find *The Vulcan Academy Murders,* by the same author.

Chapter One

ONLY THE MEMBERS of the Nisus Council were in the refectory, and only computerized food was available. The kitchen was closed for the duration of the epidemic.

Thought Master Korsal dialed up coffee, black, the way Cathy had taught him to like it, and started toward a table where two Vulcans and an Andorian were seated.

"Korsal!" His name was softly hissed in a voice he knew well. It was Borth, the Orion representative to the council. "Come, sit with me." He drew Korsal to a two-person table and activated the privacy shield.

The Klingon reached for the switch to turn it off, saying, "We have nothing to hide from the rest of the council; why make them suspicious?"

Borth blocked his hand. "They suspect us anyway; what difference does it make? I would know what you plan to do about the plague."

"I am an engineer, Borth," Korsal replied. "There is nothing I can do, except vote for stronger quarantine measures. If you are asking whether I will vote to ask the Federation Council for medical aid, yes, of course I will."

The Orion shook his head, thinning his lips in disgust. The flat headdress he wore hooded his yellow eyes. With his green skin, it gave him a reptilian look.

"No, fool. What will you report to the Klingon Empire? Communications records show that you have made no report for sixteen days."

"Under quarantine conditions, scientific progress is halted. There is nothing to report." Korsal took a long swallow of coffee, ignoring the fact that it was too hot. He wondered, not for the first time, why such a bitter brew should be so comforting. Taking strength from that which is harsh, he had long ago learned, was something Humans and Klingons had in common.

"No?" Borth continued his line of thought. "Consider what a weapon this plague could—"

"Do *not* continue!" Korsal told him, getting up from his chair. Heads turned at the other tables. He leaned forward, hands on the table, to keep his words within the privacy shield as he stared into the cold yellow eyes. "A weapon which can turn as easily upon its user as upon his enemy is no weapon at all. Try to sell this virus to my people, Borth, and you will have the Klingon Empire as *your* enemy!"

Korsal straightened, crushing his plastic cup, not even noticing the last of the coffee burning his hand. He tossed it into a receptacle as he stalked out of the refectory.

There was no place to go except back to the council chamber; everything else in the Civic Center, as with all other public buildings, was closed.

The Civic Center containing the council chamber of the science colony Nisus was situated near the gigantic dam and power plant that provided both water and electricity to the valley below. The dam was a product of Earth engineering, a technology centuries old on that water-logged planet, but only a generation old on three Klingon worlds where famine had been conquered by such dams in Korsal's own lifetime.

The Klingon engineer went to stand at the huge window that overlooked the valley. The view of the mountains was blocked by the immense mass of the dam. Some might say that the solid concrete grayness was ugly; to Korsal it held the beauty of power. He watched the tamed river surge through the locks, tumbling downhill in controlled energy. It was divided below into an irrigation system for the fields —designed by Hemanite farmers to prevent erosion —and a water system for the small city where lived and worked scientists from all races of the Federation . . . and a few from outside the Federation as well.

Korsal was uneasy in his position on the Nisus Council, for he was an engineer, not a politician. Not even a social scientist. Certainly no leader among his own people, where strategy—whether in battle or in politics—was the distinguishing feature of those who ruled.

His position on the Nisus Council came by default; every culture represented at the science colony chose a member to sit on the council. And since his colleagues had returned to the empire seven years before, Korsal was the only Klingon on Nisus.

No one else had yet returned to the chamber. Alone, Korsal vented his frustration by pounding his fist against the window: not glass, but transparent aluminum, another Earth invention. Not only could he not break it, but it gave back the feel of solid metal—the feel of futility.

Korsal was not alone in his frustration. The council had taken its break only after four hours of deliberation. The other members finally began filing back into the chamber. The largest contingent were Humans, who had swarmed across the galaxy in the past three centuries, creating colonies so disparate in their gov-

3

ernments and cultures that they could no more be assumed to agree on most issues than Vulcans and Klingons.

Vulcans were the second-largest group, their home planet and each of their colonies having its own representative. Although the colonies were all part of one central Vulcan government, their representatives on the council were not a fair proportion insofar as Nisus' population was concerned. Science was so much the heart of Vulcan culture that the science colony was forty percent Vulcan, thirty-two percent Human, and only twenty-eight percent Tellarite, Hemanite, Andorian, Rigellian, Lemnorian, Orion, Trakeskian, Jovanian . . . and Klingon.

Korsal went back to his place at the table and sat down in the chair that looked like a rather uncomfortable block until a person sat in it. Then it read his size, shape, body temperature, and muscle tension, and molded itself into contours that would prevent muscle fatigue, but—since it was designed as part of a workplace—not allow relaxation into sleep.

Even Keski, the Lemnorian on the council, sat down on an exactly similar cube. It immediately shifted to accommodate his gigantic frame, expanding its back to support the long torso that caused the Lemnorian, even sitting down, to tower over everyone else at the table. Such furniture was an invention of the comfort-minded Tellarites. The tricorders at each place on the table were a Vulcan invention.

At times like these, items usually taken for granted took on new significance. The day-to-day lives of people around the galaxy were improved by these varied technologies. Cooperation among races here at the science colony had in the past century spawned

4

technological advances at a rate never seen before in galactic history.

Only now . . . it had spawned a plague.

Korsal did not want to talk to anyone—did not want to be questioned about his argument with Borth —so he reached for his tricorder. It hurt when his hand closed over it, and he discovered a blister on his palm where the hot coffee had burned him. It was nothing.

He turned on his tricorder and reran his notes. T'Saen, a biochemist, pronounced the words of doom in that flat way Vulcans spoke when they were controlling hardest.

"We are proceeding on the assumption that what we have is a rapidly mutating virus. So far we have been unable to isolate it because of the rapidity of its mutation. It is resistant to all the antimutagens known to science."

Therian, the Andorian epidemiologist, gave statistics on the spread of the disease—too fast, and accelerating.

Korsal shook his head. The biochemistry was beyond him, but the math was plain: within sixty days, every person on Nisus would have the disease. It showed no respect for race; it attacked equally those with blood based on iron, copper, or silicon.

They had closed the schools and canceled all meetings, theatrical performances, or other gatherings twelve days ago, and still it spread. Nonessential public buildings were closed, masks and gloves had become standard streetwear, and still it spread.

And killed.

In its original form, the disease had been only a nuisance. It caused high fever, headaches, abdominal cramps—exceedingly unpleasant, but not deadly. It ran its course in five days, leaving the victim weak but with no permanent aftereffects. The biochemists began working on a vaccine, and no one worried much.

Then a new strain evolved. It started with the same symptoms for three days, but on the fourth the victim suddenly went into kidney failure. The hospital began to fill, but they had the life-support equipment to save these patients too.

Until the day when one of the victims on life support went into convulsions, followed by liver and heart failure. The first was a ten-year-old Human girl. She was so weakened that the most heroic efforts could not save her.

But she was not the last; the mortality rate escalated and total systemic failure was added to the symptomology of the disease. What organs failed differed according to species, but they were always vital.

A number of the early fatalities were doctors and nurses, for the new strain—strains?—also evaded the antiseptic procedures that had previously sufficed to keep it from spreading within the hospital.

Nor did the early symptoms indicate which strain of the disease a victim had. The hospital overflowed with frightened people who didn't know whether the fourth day of their illness might bring death.

Until two days ago, however, eighty-seven percent of the victims of the more virulent version had survived. The disease might have to run its course, but it would not wipe out the colony.

And then suddenly the disease changed again. New victims no longer started feeling feverish and headachy; instead, without warning, the first symptoms were unbearable pain lancing through the victim's head, and an instant, paranoid belief that anyone nearby was an enemy trying to kill him!

Suddenly each new victim was a weapon trained on anyone in his vicinity, even those trying desperately to help him. In only two days, a mother killed her two children, two husbands killed their wives, a staff member killed a doctor and two nurses at the hospital, and fourteen people were wounded by family, friends, or colleagues suddenly gone berserk. It was too soon to be certain whether the knowledge of what they had done undercut the victims' will to live, but almost half of the new victims died within hours of coming out of the violent phase, and the rest remained critical.

Borth's idea of using the virus as a weapon sickened Korsal. Klingons would fight, anytime, and gladly. But they fought fair, enemy against enemy, whether the battle be of wits or of weapons. This terrible plague would not only be a dishonorable tactic; it would be an invitation to those it was used against to retaliate in kind. Let *anyone* use it the first time, and it would be set loose to decimate the population of the galaxy.

Calmer now, Korsal recognized that he had been wrong to walk out on the Orion. The man was not stupid; he had had the plague himself, so he knew Orions were not immune. He would surely listen to reason.

The council reconvened, and the vote to ask the Federation for aid was quickly passed. Unanimously, Korsal noted.

Then one of the Humans, Dr. John Treadwell, took the floor. He was a tall, thin man, a researcher who rarely spoke up in council. "I think," he said hesitantly, "that while we wait for help, we may be wrong in handling this epidemic in the traditional way, by trying to protect those who have not yet had the disease."

"What would you suggest, Dr. Treadwell?" T'Saen asked.

"We are still trying to isolate the virus so as to find both a cure and a means of inoculation. That is standard procedure. Even as our best efforts fail, though, the disease becomes more deadly, and at the same time escapes our antisepsis procedures. Twenty-eight percent of the population of Nisus has had the disease and recovered. Prognosis is far worse for the other seventy-two percent, because of the new strains."

The man swallowed hard, turned deep red, but continued. "In Earth's history, there was a time when smallpox was a disease even more feared than this plague we face. In that time, nothing was understood of inoculation.

"There was another disease, called cowpox, often contracted by dairy workers. Its symptomology was similar to that of smallpox, but it was far less severe. It almost never killed or scarred like smallpox. It was observed that even when exposed to smallpox, those who had had cowpox never caught it. So, out of fear of smallpox, some people exposed themselves to the lesser disease, cowpox."

T'Saen nodded. "Then you suggest that we deliberately expose people who have not had the disease to the lesser strain?"

Again Treadwell swallowed convulsively, his Adam's apple bobbing up and down in his scrawny neck. "I am . . . offering a suggestion for discussion."

Ginge, the Tellarite councillor, spoke up. "The idea

is sound, provided we can guarantee exposure is to the lesser strain."

"Yes," agreed Stolos, in his high-pitched Hemanite voice, the tassel of his flat-topped round cap shaking with the eager movement of his head. "Everyone on this council has had either the first or second strain of the plague, and we have all recovered. With no hope of a vaccine in sight, immunity to the deadly variety is surely worth the pain associated with the first strain."

Korsal spoke up. "You are wrong, Stolos—I have not had any strain of this disease. This latest variation frightens me as much as it does the rest of you . . . more, since I have developed no antibodies against it. Klingons fear no enemy that can be seen and understood—but a disease that attacks invisibly, stealing a person's mind—" He turned to the nervous Human. "Dr. Treadwell, I will volunteer to test your theory."

It felt good to take action, even if only to offer himself in a passive role. In his frustration over the inability to act, Korsal was pure Klingon.

Warner Jurgens, the council chair, sent the request for help to be transmitted, and the council settled down to the logistics of the new strategy. "We'll take specimens from all victims entering the hospital," said Rita Esposito. "Then, when we see which course the disease takes, we'll use those from people who develop the least violent strain to expose volunteers who have never been ill. If it gives them the lesser illness, then their specimens will be used on others, and while it will be an unpleasant experience—"

"No! Damn you to Zarth's lowest hell, Human! You want to kill us all!"

Keski, the Lemnorian, lunged at Esposito, grasping

the startled woman by the throat with one hand while he reached for her tricorder with the other.

There were no weapons in the council chamber, but the tricorder was a blunt instrument, and Keski had more than enough strength to smash Esposito's skull with it.

Everyone at the table moved, but Korsal reached Keski first, grabbing his arm before he could connect.

Keski shook Korsal off, but his swing was broken.

Two Human men were trying to pry the Lemnorian's fingers free from the choking woman's neck as T'Sael came up behind Korsal and tried to reach Keski's shoulder for the neck pinch. He was too tall, so she climbed onto his chair, which had returned to its cubic shape.

The Lemnorian lurched and struggled, and the Vulcan woman missed her grip.

With a mindless roar, Keski dropped Esposito and swung a punch at Korsal, taking both of them out of T'Saen's reach.

The Klingon ducked, saw the tricorder coming at his head, and shifted in the opposite direction.

Keski brought the instrument down on the table-top. It smashed into shards, one piercing Keski's own arm. He screamed, and turned just as T'Saen was in position to nerve-pinch him. He backhanded her, but she managed to land on her feet as she fell off the chair.

Stolos tackled Keski around the ankles and was kicked off like an offending dog.

Keski brought both hands together, readying for a blow that would smash T'Saen's head.

Korsal kicked at the back of his knees, and Keski toppled, falling on top of the Klingon and transferring his fury once more.

Korsal bounced to his feet and blocked the Lemnorian's first clumsy blow with his arm, feeling the jolt numb it. With a speed unnatural to his giant race, Keski swung at Korsal with his left fist.

His back to the table, Korsal couldn't duck. Instinctively, he tried to roll back onto the table to kick at Keski, but the Lemnorian anticipated him, falling forward against his legs, pinning him as he pulled the punch and instead tried to choke Korsal.

Korsal grasped Keski's wrists, managing to hold him long enough that, at last, T'Saen connected, and the unconscious Lemnorian slumped forward on top of the Klingon.

The others pulled him off. Treadwell, the only physician on the council, already had his medscanner out. He ran it over Esposito, saying, "No serious damage, but I want you in the hospital for observation. Someone call for an ambulance—let's get Keski into the hospital before he comes to. Korsal—" He turned, recalibrating his instrument, and ran it over the Klingon's body.

"No injury except for that hand," he said, "but . . ."

The "but" rang in the council chamber as everyone stopped breathing to realize the implications.

Korsal raised his hand and stared at the palm. In the struggle, the blister caused by the hot coffee had burst, and he was bleeding. His hand was also smeared with Keski's orangeish blood. There was no scrubbing down and hoping for the best: he was well and thoroughly exposed to the same strain of the plague that had turned the usually gentle Lemnorian into a raging beast.

But the held breaths were not for Korsal.

"Keski *had* the disease once!" said Stolos. "This means—"

"—the mutation has developed so far from its original form that immunity to previous strains has no force," concluded Dr. Treadwell, his face now a pasty white. "We must all go to the hospital immediately, to the isolation unit, and wait out the incubation period."

"I will call for more ambulances," said Therian.

Korsal got up, thinking of his family, knowing everyone in the room was doing the same.

Almost everyone.

They drew apart, each deep in his own thoughts. Korsal went to the window again.

Borth followed him.

"Go away," said Korsal. "You also have a wife and children to think about."

The Orion nodded. "Yes—and they will be well cared for for life if what I suspect is true. Every member of this council has caught the plague but you, Korsal—for we are all public servants who could not quarantine ourselves in our homes. Your wife had the disease in its earliest form, but you did not contract it, and—living in the same house—neither of your sons has been ill. Now," he said, touching Korsal's injured hand with one blunt finger, "we will know without question whether Klingons are immune."

"That won't do *you* much good, since Orions are not."

"It will as long as I survive—and I am a survivor, Korsal. I don't know what you are. A traitor, perhaps?"

"What do you mean?" Korsal stared at the offending Orion, lips pulled back to expose the points of his teeth.

Borth did not cringe. "If Klingons are immune, you will not inform the empire of this disease."

"Killing off a planet's population with disease is not the way Klingons gain territory. We fight, let them defend their homes."

"Against immensely superior numbers and weaponry," Borth said with an oily smile. "And you, Korsal, do not approve—I can see it in your eyes. You're no Klingon—you're a weakling like the Humans. But I am Orion, and it behooves me to think what certain factions within the Klingon Empire will pay for this virus—if Klingons are immune."

"For the sake of argument, say we prove immune now," said Korsal. "The way this disease mutates, what is to prevent it from developing a strain fatal to my people?"

Borth shrugged. "So long as I am well paid, I will take that risk. I am willing to gamble that this bug would take a long time to figure out how to bite Klingons. By that time, I will be far from the Klingon Empire."

Korsal glared at him. "You make me ill without any virus, Borth. You are no scientist, to base your theory on a single case. But if I do become ill, I won't die. Someone has to be around who knows you for what you really are!"

Chapter Two

CAPTAIN JAMES T. KIRK sat in the command chair on the bridge of the USS *Enterprise,* feeling rested and alert at a single Earth-normal gravity. During the past month on Vulcan, he had become accustomed to a constant nagging fatigue. By his last days there he no longer took notice of it. Now, though, it was a relief to have it gone.

On the other hand, he had acclimated somewhat to Vulcan's summer heat and now felt slightly chilly at the starship's temperature intended for Human comfort. Perhaps he should wear an undershirt, as Spock did, for a few days.

Sitting still didn't help. He decided to tour his ship, glad for an excuse to wander the corridors he had missed while he was away from her. If the activity didn't warm him up, he'd—

"Captain!" the intercom blurted, a female voice he didn't recognize.

"Kirk here."

"Walenski here, sir. Our Vulcan 'guests' are making trouble. There's two of 'em squaring off for a fight, with deadly weapons!" He heard the tension in her voice, and remembered that part of her duty included assigning the use of the ship's physical facilities. She was clerical personnel, not security or combat.

"Where are they?"

"Deck five, gymnasium A."

"On my way!" Kirk told Walenski. "Mr. Spock, you have the con. Call security to the gym."

Damn Sendet and his crowd, anyway! They were not truly guests aboard the *Enterprise,* but political prisoners being transported to an uninhabited Vulcan colony planet, where they would be left to work out their own way of life as they saw fit.

With the exception of Sendet, however, the Followers of T'Vet, as they called themselves, had committed no crimes—because they had been caught before they could put into effect their plans to overthrow the government of Vulcan. The Vulcan High Council had given them a choice of mental reprogramming or transportation off-planet. Under such circumstances, Kirk certainly knew which *he* would choose!

When Starfleet ordered the *Enterprise* to transport the rebels, Kirk had decided there was no reason they should not travel comfortably in guest quarters, as that meant less work for his crew.

As he understood it, while the Followers of T'Vet espoused a belief in racial purity that Kirk found hard to stomach, their philosophy was otherwise a kind of commonsense belief in survival of the fittest, complementary with many of his own beliefs. He hadn't expected trouble—certainly not less than two days out from Vulcan!

Gymnasium A was the large one, with bleachers for an audience to watch the many athletic contests that came up among a young and fit starship crew. It was not intended as an arena for blood games.

When Kirk arrived, two muscular young Vulcan males were circling one another on the mat. Had they been unarmed, Kirk would have simply joined the spectators, but the two held *lirpas,* a Vulcan weapon with one end weighted stone, for bashing, and the other end a razor-sharp curved blade, for slashing. Either end could kill.

"Captain!"

That must be Walenski—a small woman in red services uniform, seated on the bleachers, surrounded by Vulcan women. "Quiet, Human!" one of them said to her. "The combat is not to be interrupted."

"It most certainly *is*!" Kirk exclaimed, striding between the fighters. *"Kroykah!"* he shouted, hoping that even to the Followers of T'Vet that word used in ceremonies dating back to Vulcan's "Time of the Beginning" would mean "Stop!"

It did. Without protest, the two fighters stopped their circling, backed a few paces from one another, and rested their weapons with the weighted ends on the floor.

"How *dare* you profane Vulcan custom!"

A man rose from among the assembled Vulcans—a man as tall and imposing as Spock's father Sarek, of the same generation, and with the same air of being accustomed to obedience. Unlike the other Vulcans, who were dressed in what Kirk recognized from his recent stay on their planet as everyday clothing, this man wore robes of a heavy brown material with panels of green fabric running down the front, bearing designs in gold and jewels.

As the Vulcan spokesman stepped forward, Kirk saw Sendet among the other young men, watching him with the slightest hint of a superior smile. But Kirk kept his attention on the man approaching him.

The Vulcan was nearly a head taller than Kirk and moved close to him to force the Human to look up.

But Kirk had never let that trick intimidate him, from Vulcans, Humans, or anybody else. He stood his ground and replied, "You are not on Vulcan now. You are on my ship, and here my word is law. There will be no combat with deadly weapons aboard ship. You are welcome to use our facilities for unarmed combat, to practice marksmanship in the—"

"Enough!" the Vulcan said with an imperious wave of dismissal. "Continue the combat." He turned and strode back to his front-row seat in the bleachers.

Even though Kirk still stood in the center of the mat, the two fighters hefted their weapons again—it appeared that if he did not get out of their way, they might go right through him.

But he would not ignominiously scuttle out of their reach!

Where was security?

Kirk stood between the fighters, watching their faces. These Vulcans did not believe in Surak's philosophy. They wanted to live like the ancient Vulcan warrior clans had before they were converted to peace and emotional control. Their eyes showed anger—but also uncertainty. The two fighters were young. It was hard to judge a Vulcan's age accurately, but both faces had the unmarked quality of youth on the brink of maturity. The look typical of Academy cadets, physically mature, but still growing mentally and emotionally.

Deliberately, Kirk stepped directly between them, closer to the smaller one, who was wearing a blue loincloth and an amulet of green stones. As he expected, the boy made a lunge toward him, obviously expecting to sweep Kirk aside with the stem of the *lirpa* and continue his charge against his opponent.

17

Instead, Kirk grabbed the *lirpa,* swung under it, and fell onto his back on the mat. He tossed the boy backward over his head in one smooth motion, dealing a strong kick to his midsection.

The Vulcan landed hard, the breath knocked out of him.

Kirk sprang to his feet and faced the other fighter. The second boy, who wore a black loincloth and a headband with a pattern of silver embroidery, did not make his opponent's mistake. He charged, swinging the blade end of the *lirpa* toward Kirk—

"Hold it!"

When the commanding tones did not stop the lethal charge, the air sizzled with a phaser bolt, and the boy flopped to the mat at Kirk's feet, stunned.

Lieutenant Nelson and six other security personnel entered the gymnasium, phasers drawn.

"Well, you certainly took your time!" Kirk commented.

"You seemed to have everything under control, Captain," Nelson replied in his usual laconic style. "What do you want us to do with our misbehaving guests?"

"That," Kirk replied, "is up to them. Walenski, come down from there."

"Yes, sir." The young woman picked her way down to the mat in obvious relief.

"Now." Kirk faced the assembled Vulcans, hands on hips. "Who among you can give a promise that all will adhere to?"

The older man in ceremonial robes rose again. "I can. I am Satat, war chief of the Clan T'Vin. All other clans represented here have sworn allegiance to mine."

"Very well, Satat," said Kirk, "I will give you one more chance—and if you break your word this time, you will spend the rest of the journey in the brig."

"We have not broken our word," Satat replied with unruffled dignity. "We made no interference with your ship or your personnel. Your personnel interfered with *us*."

Damn. Satat was right. That was the agreement, according to Kirk's orders from Starfleet: at the captain's discretion, the Followers of T'Vet could travel as guests so long as they did not interfere with the ship or its personnel. Commodore Bright, who had made the agreement, was a desk jockey who had never commanded a starship. Otherwise he would have added what Kirk had to add now.

"Your breaking the rules of Starfleet or this particular ship interferes with our personnel."

"This combat was scheduled when none of your ship's crew had booked this arena," Satat replied. "All your crewperson had to do," he added with a nod at Walenski, "was to stay out of our way."

"Not when she saw you bringing in deadly weapons," Kirk explained. "The use of such weapons is forbidden in the gymnasium. By restraining Miss Walenski when she tried to stop you, you interfered with her performance of her duty. Now, if you will give me your word that you will abide by all Starfleet and *Enterprise* regulations, you may continue your journey as our guests."

Annoyingly refusing to lose his dignity, Satat replied, "We agree."

The intercom beeped.

Kirk went to the wall unit. "Kirk here."

"Spock here, Captain. Can you come to the bridge to accept new orders from Starfleet Command, or shall I record them?"

"I'll be right there," Kirk replied, and left the gym with a word to Nelson to finish up. If it was Commodore Bright with these new orders, this time he wanted to talk to the man!

Chapter Three

COMMANDER SPOCK TURNED to Lieutenant Uhura, relaying the captain's message. She spoke quietly into her microphone as the bridge crew waited expectantly.

The *Enterprise* was under Starfleet orders to transport the Followers of T'Vet to Vulcan Colony Nine, making two stops along the way. At Coriolanus Spock's parents, Sarek and Amanda, would leave the ship for a diplomatic conference. They would be replaced by the Serbanian ambassador and her party, who were returning home, and at Serbania they would pick up Nurse Christine Chapel, who had spent the time the *Enterprise* had been under repair in a seminar on the latest advances in emergency nursing. Vulcan Colony Nine was only six days at normal warp speed from Serbania.

It was unusual for a starship to know such a detailed itinerary in advance. It was *not* unusual to have plans change at a moment's notice.

Captain Kirk swept out of the turbolift, took the command chair from Spock, and said to Uhura, "Lieutenant, open channel to Starfleet Command."

Captain Henson of Starbase MI-17, a strictly military installation, appeared on the screen. She was a woman of perhaps fifty, with graying hair in a short no-nonsense style. "Captain Kirk," she said, "I have new orders for you from Commodore Bright. An epidemic has struck the scientific colony of Nisus. The *Enterprise* is to return to Vulcan, emergency priority. There you will take on board the healer Sorel, Dr. Daniel Corrigan, Dr. Geoffrey M'Benga, and the xenobiologist T'Mir, along with several assistants and two residents of Nisus.

"From Vulcan you will transport the experts in interspecies medicine directly to the science colony Nisus. You will leave them, along with Dr. Leonard McCoy from your own staff, at Nisus, and then proceed with the rest of your orders. This is an emergency-priority mission. I have transmitted details directly to your chief medical officer."

She attempted a smile, but Spock recognized worry and fatigue behind her brusque façade. "I have other ships to contact, Captain. The *Enterprise* is the closest starship in the fleet to Nisus, and is fortunately also close to Vulcan, where so many medical experts can be found. Your chief medical officer will brief you on the nature of the emergency. Time is of the essence —there are many lives at stake. Henson out."

The screen blanked before Kirk could say a word. But he would not question a medical emergency. "Ensign Chekov, lock in a course for Vulcan."

"Aye, Keptin."

Kirk punched one of the buttons on his intraship console. "Bones, did you—?"

Leonard McCoy's voice responded immediately. "Yeah, Jim, I got my walking papers, along with a report on the epidemic on Nisus. If the best collection of scientists in the galaxy can't stop it, they've got some wild bug on the loose. It's gonna take a while to study this report."

"One hour," Kirk replied. "Then you meet Spock

and me in the briefing room." The captain swung his chair around to face Spock's station. "You know anything about this, Spock?"

"Only what we have just heard," he replied.

"Well, then, please go tell your parents that our arrival at Coriolanus will be delayed. They may want to arrange other transport."

"There is no other ship available," Spock replied, having scanned the schedules of warp-speed vessels to and from Vulcan in their preparations for departure. "However, my father will want to send a message to Coriolanus, explaining the delay."

As Spock entered the turbolift, Kirk instructed Chekov to take the science station. The doors were closing. As he rose, Chekov leaned over and murmured to Lieutenant Sulu, too softly for Kirk to hear, "Last time ve couldn't get *to* Wulcan. This time ve cannot get *avay* from it!"

Spock, of course, was not meant to hear the comment. Humans always forgot the acuity of Vulcan hearing.

His parents were not in their cabin, nor were they in the ship's library or on the observation deck. Having tried the most likely places by intercom, he decided to call the rec room before putting out a page.

Yeoman Kasita answered the rec-room intercom. "They were here earlier," he told Spock, "but then Ambassador Sarek offered to tutor Miss Chong in astrophysics, and the Lady Amanda went down to the gymnasium."

"Thank you, Yeoman," Spock said automatically, but his mind was elsewhere. There had just been a disturbance in the gymnasium—but Captain Kirk had not mentioned Amanda.

Instead of calling, he went down to the recreation

level and asked Ensign Walenski if his mother were there.

"Yes, she's in room six. Don't worry, Mr. Spock —she didn't even know about the excitement in gym A."

Room six was a private exercise chamber. Spock pressed the door buzzer. "Mother? It's Spock. May I come in?"

"Yes—of course." Her voice sounded more muffled than it should just from filtering through the door. Nor did the door open until he pressed the plate beside it.

Amanda was in the middle of the room, upside down.

In a moment he recognized that she was doing a shoulder stand. What he did not know was why. Her recent near-fatal illness had reminded him forcefully of Amanda's ephemeral humanity. Why should she now be forcing her fragile body into such contortions?

After a few seconds, she rolled smoothly out of her inverted position, to lie flat on her back, her blue eyes twinkling up at him as the flush left her face. "No, Spock, your mother has not taken leave of her senses. I'm under doctor's orders to do a series of simple exercises each day, to tone my body after the time I spent in stasis."

"I . . . have never seen you do them before," he said, for she must have started them at home, while he was visiting.

"No, I did them at the Academy gym." She smiled as she sat up, got onto her knees, and began stretching to right and left. "I didn't want my son to see me looking so silly."

"You do not look . . . silly," he replied. As a matter of fact, she looked fit, her dark blue leotard revealing a slender but healthy figure. Spock had never thought of his mother as having a figure, slender or otherwise, for she always dressed in flowing garments of bright colors, not exactly of Vulcan design, but modestly concealing in the same fashion.

"I have a message for you and Father," Spock continued. "Starfleet has ordered the *Enterprise* to divert to Vulcan and then Nisus before proceeding to Coriolanus."

Amanda's blue eyes studied her son. "How late will we be?"

"Six days."

"Not six-point-one-three-seven?"

"Six-point-two-five-two. Mother, is it not illogical to be annoyed when Father or I give you a precise figure yet ask for such precision when we do not?"

"No," she replied with a shrug, "just Human. There." She stood and put on her shoes, then took one of her usual flowing robes off a bench and wrapped herself in the voluminous folds.

With that, Amanda was Spock's mother as he was accustomed to her. With her silver hair piled atop her head, the heels of her shoes giving her added height, and the robe falling in vertical folds, she was once again tall, stately, dignified.

"Sarek is in the computer lab," Amanda told Spock, "helping one of the crew prepare for her astrophysicist's examination."

"I know," Spock said. It was the one thing he understood that his parents had in common. Both were teachers. Give either a willing student, and Sarek or Amanda would work patiently for hours, in perfect contentment.

As Spock and Amanda left the exercise room, she asked, "I suppose you've already checked to see whether there is a way for us to get to Coriolanus on schedule?"

"There is not."

Amanda smiled up at her son. "Then we shall simply enjoy a brief extension of your vacation with us. Why has the *Enterprise* been rerouted?"

When Spock explained the medical crisis, she sobered. "Experts in interspecies medicine? Spock, what's wrong?"

"An epidemic. Dr. McCoy will brief command personnel in forty-one-point-seven minutes."

"Very well," said Amanda. "I will send the news of our delay to Coriolanus. There is no reason to disturb your father until we know more."

Spock's mother was not a telepath, but living on Vulcan she had had to learn to shield lest she broadcast her emotions to everyone in her vicinity.

Even so, as Spock felt her mental shields shut him out, he knew exactly what she must be thinking.

The intermingling of species, people living on planets they were not native to, even living in the artificial environments of starships and starbases, was something still new in the history of intelligent life in this galaxy. No one could predict the long-term effects; many of them were only now beginning to show themselves.

Spock's own mother, today the picture of health, had only a few months ago been dying of degenerative xenosis, a condition associated with leaving her native Earth and living for many years on Vulcan. The precise causes of the disease were not fully understood, but at last there was a treatment for it. Amanda had been cured—permanently, they hoped—by Sorel and Corrigan, the Science Academy's brilliant Vulcan/Human medical team.

Spock had known the Vulcan healer and the Human doctor all his life, for he, the first Vulcan/Human hybrid, had been the occasion of their first working together. They, like Spock, like his parents, like the Federation and Starfleet itself, were examples of what could be achieved when intelligent species learned to work together and rejoice in their differences.

But only too often it appeared that nature objected. How many times had the *Enterprise* found empty outposts, like Psi 2000, where the entire research party had gone mad, killing themselves and one another? When the virus that had destroyed the research party was accidentally brought on board the *Enterprise,* it appeared for a time that they were never meant to go so far from the worlds where nature had first placed them.

But the ingenuity of the *Enterprise* crew had saved them that time, and every other time . . . so far. That crew was assembled from all parts of the Federation.

The silence between mother and son stretched all the way down the corridor. When they reached the turbolift, however, Amanda paused, saying, "Spock . . . you are worried."

"Worry is illogical," he replied automatically.

His mother turned to face him, blocking his way and remaining out of the turbolift doors' sensor range. She gave him a knowing smile. "Concerned, then. But with medical experts from all over the Federation, surely this plague will quickly be contained."

"Mother," he reminded her, "Nisus already *has* experts from all over the Federation—and some from outside it. Even Klingon and Orion scientists are part of the cooperative effort there, as well as researchers in every branch of science from every Federation culture."

"I know," Amanda replied. "Nisus has existed for three generations—I remember learning about it in school when I was a little girl on Earth. 'The finest example in the galaxy of cooperation among intelligent life forms.' There was a time when I thought I would apply to do linguistic research on Nisus—the effects of all those varied languages spoken in one small area—but then I met your father . . . and decided to practice a different form of cooperation between intelligent life forms."

He knew she wished to coax a smile from him —that her statement would easily have won one from Sarek. But Spock's mind was on the connections Amanda refused to make: the scientists of Nisus could not stop the epidemic—for it was probably their own work that had caused it, their cooperation between species that spread it.

The concept at least of tolerance was universal among intelligent species that had reached a certain level of civilization, although some practiced it with greater diligence than others. Spock, grown up on Vulcan, knew the ideal as IDIC, Infinite Diversity in Infinite Combination.

IDIC was a sacred concept to Vulcans—yet logic required recognition of fact. It appeared that just as nature had attacked Spock's mother for daring to live where humans were never meant to, now the scientists of Nisus were suffering for living the ideal of IDIC.

Insufficient data to form a hypothesis, Spock told himself. Surely, as had happened with his mother, the combined medical wisdom of many worlds would unite to preserve Nisus.

Chapter Four

THE HEALER SOREL returned from surgery to his office at the Vulcan Academy of Sciences. He had two more patients scheduled that day: T'Kar and her daughter T'Pina, for routine examinations before leaving Vulcan to return to the science colony on Nisus.

Just as he reached the door to the reception area, his paging signal sounded. He continued inside, asking T'Sel, "Why are you paging me?"

"Vulcan Space Central is calling."

Space Central? "I'll take it in my office."

All Vulcans practiced emotional control, but Sorel now knew from long experience what he had been told when he began his training many years ago: "A healer," his master teacher Svan had explained, "is a paradox. While he must keep the strictest emotional control of any Vulcan, for the sake of his patients' health and his own sanity, he has also chosen a profession which, above all, provokes the universal Vulcan failing: curiosity."

Indeed, by the time he reached the console in his inner office, Sorel was nearly consumed with curiosity. His daughter was safely home now; there was no member of his family off-planet. So his curiosity was unmixed with concern as he wondered what Space Central could possibly want with him.

The moment he pressed the switch, his screen was filled with the image of a Human male in the uniform of a Starfleet commodore. "Greetings, Healer. I am Vincent Bright, director of Starfleet activities in this sector. Vulcan Space Central is patching this message through to you. Starfleet Command requests the aid of you and your associate, Dr. Daniel Corrigan."

Long years of training automatically suppressed Sorel's concern that the *Enterprise,* which had left Vulcan only two days previously, had a medical emergency. If Dr. Leonard McCoy, whose skills he had recently come to know and respect, had to call for help, the situation must be dire indeed.

With complete calm he replied, "I am here to serve, Commodore. What aid does Starfleet seek?"

"There's an epidemic out of control on the science colony Nisus. The residents request medical personnel with knowledge of interspecies medicine. You and Dr. Corrigan are specifically named in the request, as is your daughter, the xenobiologist T'Mir. The USS *Enterprise* will return to Vulcan for you in two-point-seven days. I have been able to contact all Vulcan medical personnel that Starfleet has requested, with the exception of Lady T'Mir and Dr. Corrigan. Do you know their whereabouts?"

"I do."

"Excellent. Please give me their communications codes."

"That is not possible," Sorel replied.

"What? It has to be possible! Corrigan's a doctor; he has to be reached in emergencies. And surely you can contact your daughter."

"My daughter and Dr. Corrigan are recently married," Sorel replied. "They are in Seclusion."

"You mean honeymooning?"

Someone off-screen grabbed Bright's arm and tugged. He shook off whoever it was in annoyance. "I'm afraid this emergency takes—"

The hand was back on Bright's arm, followed by a body in a blue Starfleet uniform. It was a Human female, middle-aged, wearing commander's stripes. A protocol officer, Sorel judged as he watched impassively, using his strongest controls to curb an inappropriate amusement.

"Commodore!" the woman whispered sharply, pulling Bright away from his console. "Nothing can take precedence when married Vulcans are in Seclusion!"

Sorel, accustomed for many years to judge Human abilities by Corrigan's, realized that a Human could not have overheard the woman's voice.

Bright frowned at her. "Dammit, Miss Frazer! I don't care what planet it is, vacations don't take precedence over medical emergencies!"

"It's not—" She gave a quick glance at the screen, and must have remembered Vulcan hearing, for she tugged Bright right out of the picture.

Sorel could no longer hear her words, but after a pause he heard Bright's blustery protest, "But this Corrigan is *Human!*"

The man's obtuseness irritated Miss Frazer enough to make her raise her voice, for Sorel heard her whisper angrily, "We don't know *anything* about how these things affect Vulcan *women,* sir! And with Vulcans, when it comes to biology, you *don't ask!*"

Then both voices were too low for him to hear, although there was a soft hum as words were swiftly exchanged.

Finally Commodore Bright appeared on screen again, red-faced and sweating. He cleared his throat.

"Is there any way to get a message to Dr. Corrigan and the Lady T'Mir?"

Nisus, a colony of the best scientists the galaxy had to offer, would call for medical aid only in the gravest emergency. So, "Yes," Sorel replied. "I can do so. And," he added, "Daniel and T'Mir can travel in two days' time, should the situation warrant it."

"Thank you," Bright said in obvious relief. "If you will set your console to record, I will send you the information we have on the Nisus plague."

The screens of data flashed by too quickly for even a Vulcan to follow—but the last one lingered for a moment, burning itself into Sorel's brain.

The mortality figures.

Quickly, Sorel called up the summary of the disease and its pattern of spread. What he saw told him why he and Daniel were needed.

When Commodore Bright reappeared on the screen, Sorel said, "We will come, Commodore. In this situation I can speak for my partner. Although I cannot speak for my daughter, I expect her to be honored to be requested. I will verify with them, and notify you within the hour."

"Thank you," Bright repeated, and gave Sorel the communications code.

There was, of course, no biological reason for Daniel and T'Mir to be in Seclusion, but Sorel had no intention of enlightening that officious Human. He doubted such a one could comprehend the imperatives of privacy and tradition. As soon as the commodore left the screen, the healer punched in the code of his partner's home, along with the privacy-override sequence that he alone knew.

Chapter Five

KORSAL SHARED A ROOM in the isolation wing of the Nisus hospital with Therian, the Andorian epidemiologist. Ordinarily, each patient would have a single room in this area, but the hospital was so badly overcrowded that it was impossible to put any but critical patients in private rooms.

Both men had requisitioned computer terminals and had spent the past two days trying to keep their minds off their own danger by plotting the progress of the plague. Korsal put Borth's threat out of his consciousness and concentrated on helping Therian search for clues to the cause of mutation of the virus.

The Andorian's blue skin was pale with fatigue, for neither man had been able to sleep. The incubation period was almost up—provided, of course, that the new strain followed the pattern of the old at least in that respect. Dr. Treadwell had begun exhibiting the new symptoms yesterday—but as a physician he had been in contact with other victims before the council meeting and, thinking himself immune, might not have exercised complete caution. All the weary hospital staff could tell them was that the Human doctor had not injured anyone, and was now critical. So was Keski.

Therian entered data on every newly reported case, his antennae drooping as more cases of madness were reported, fewer of fever and headache. He plotted everything on graphs that meant nothing to Korsal.

"They mean nothing to me, either," Therian said sadly. "I cannot find a common factor of race, age, location, or previous illness. Here," he added, pulling a data cartridge from his computer and handing it to Korsal, "please check the math on this while I try something else."

Korsal inserted the cartridge into his own terminal and began graphing the equations, knowing that once again Therian would be proved accurate.

The Andorian, meanwhile, asked the hospital computer for family records on all victims of the latest strain. Then, almost as an afterthought, he asked for family statistics on everyone reported to have *any* form of the disease. Soon he was busy figuring again.

The room-to-room intercom buzzed. Korsal, who had found Therian's graph as accurate as he had expected, flipped the switch. "Korsal here."

Rita Esposito's image appeared on the screen. "Bad news, I'm afraid."

Therian left his work to stand beside Korsal. "More victims?"

"No end," she replied. "But also, John Treadwell just died, and Keski has gone into systemic failure and is on total life support."

"Has anyone yet recovered from the new strain?" Therian asked.

Esposito glanced away from the screen. She was a floor nurse here at the hospital; Korsal was sure she was getting regular reports from her friends on the staff. Then she looked back at them and replied, "A few cases are now listed as critical but stable. But no one has come off the critical list."

"Thank you for letting us know," said Korsal. "Has anyone else on the council . . . ?"

She shook her head. "The next six hours are crucial. God help us all."

The screen blanked. Therian turned away, his antennae so wilted they almost disappeared into his fluffy white hair.

"All your figures are accurate," Korsal said in an effort to encourage him.

"But meaningless!" Therian replied. "Why can't I find the pattern?"

"There has to be one," Korsal said. As an engineer he believed in patterns. "We just haven't found the key factor yet."

Therian made a small hissing sound that was the Andorian equivalent of a sigh. "Let me see what happens when I add family data to the equations."

Korsal watched as Therian programmed in his instructions, and the computer computed. It was slow today; monitoring dozens of people on life support, keeping records on the largest number of patients the hospital had ever held, it actually had a perceptible lag between entry or request, and the time items appeared on the screen.

Finally the results began to appear. Family size was not significant, nor ages of family members. No area of the city produced more cases per capita except for the hospital complex—

"Compute according to occupation," Therian instructed.

Korsal studied the figures coming up on the screen. Nothing new; the largest percentage of victims were doctors and nurses, exposed to patients despite all antiseptic procedures. The next largest number were students and teachers—the perfectly ordinary course of any epidemic on any planet.

"Now compute only for victims of Strains B and C," Therian told the machine.

The figures told Korsal nothing. There were fewer students and teachers because the schools had been closed; otherwise, there seemed little difference in the figures.

Therian pulled at one of his antennae—an act that hurt the sensitive organ, indicating the degree of frustration the Andorian was experiencing. "Take every individual factor in the data files on victims," he instructed the computer, "and compute for it separately."

"Memory drain," the computer announced. "Programming overload. Time factor for completing program under current conditions is three hours, fourteen-point-seven-three minutes."

Korsal estimated that such a program would normally run in minutes, not hours; the hospital computer *was* badly overloaded.

"Let me get a terminal patch to the engineering lab computer," he suggested.

"Go ahead," said Therian, "but I'm going to start this program running anyway; it could easily take three hours to get set up on your lab computer."

That was true. However, Korsal called and got one of his colleagues to start the process of patching through to his terminal, then turned to watch what Therian was doing.

The program was running, but so slowly that each line could be seen coming onto the screen and crawling upward to disappear off the top. Therian studied them as they passed, and Korsal did not interrupt his concentration.

Soon he had his connection to the lab computer and began entering the changes necessary to adapt the hospital computer terminal to work with it.

"Great Mother Andor!"

Korsal was jolted out of his concentration by Therian's exclamation.

He turned to see the Andorian staring intently at the lines crawling by on his computer screen, his antennae raised up almost straight out of his head. "It's the children!" Therian gasped. Then, almost a sob, "Oh, Great Mother—it's the *children!*"

"What children?" Korsal demanded, crossing to where he could read the screen.

Therian turned on him, teeth bared. "No!" he cried. "You traitor—*twice* you have desecrated the purity of species as the Great Mother made us! No more! *No more!*"

"Therian—it's the plague," Korsal said softly, backing away from the Andorian's fury. He held his hands up, palms open, hoping Therian would recognize that he was not attacking. "You're ill, Therian. Let me call—"

"*Laskodor!*" Therian raged. "Seducer of the Daughter! Destroyer of the Children!"

The room was monitored for sound level—Korsal didn't have to shout for assistance; Therian's shouts already had orderlies on the way. He could hear their running steps in the hallway, but Therian was leaping for his throat!

The Andorian had far less strength than a Klingon, but the rage of madness gave extra power to Therian's slender body. Trying not to injure him, Korsal pushed him away, but the thin arms snaked out to grasp his throat.

Korsal fought, bending Therian's fingers back—but

Andorian joints bent naturally that way! He would black out in a moment! Where were those orderlies?!

Getting his elbows under Therian's arms, Korsal broke the Andorian's hold, flinging him backward against two orderlies in contamination gear charging in at the door.

Therian bounced off them, shrieked wordlessly, and lunged for Korsal again.

The Klingon caught him by the arms and started to turn him toward the orderlies when the Andorian went limp. "He's passed out," he said, lifting the light form and laying it down on Therian's bed. "Better get a gurney."

One of the orderlies left, but the other switched on the life-function display over the bed. None of the indicators moved, except the one for body temperature. It rose, but then began to drift slowly downward.

"He's dead," said the orderly, his voice muffled by his suit.

"He can't be!" Korsal exclaimed. "Call for life support! No, I will—you resuscitate him!"

"Sir," the orderly said, "he was Andorian. He cannot be resuscitated."

Korsal had never known whether that was a fact of Andorian biology or one of their religious tenets. Either way, there was nothing he could do; Therian was gone.

He sat dejectedly on his own bed as the orderlies removed the body.

Gone. And his knowledge with him.

Or had it been only the madness?

Korsal stared at Therian's computer screen, where the lines of data still crawled obediently upward and disappeared. Whatever the epidemiologist saw had long since scrolled by, and Korsal had no way of determining which lines to call back.

Was it just the madness that made Therian think he had found the answer? Or to his statistician's mind had the screen actually given a clue to the mutation of the plague—a clue that somehow involved the children of Nisus?

Chapter Six

SOREL'S PATIENTS WERE right on time. Physically, both T'Kar and T'Pina were in perfect health.

"Are you certain it is wise to return to Nisus now?" Sorel asked the two women. "You have no family there—"

"It is home," T'Kar replied serenely. Had he allowed himself such an emotion, Sorel could have envied her serenity. T'Kar had returned to Vulcan two months ago, to return her husband's *katra* to his ancestors, as was the Vulcan way.

"Nisus is the only home I can remember," T'Pina added. "Now that I have completed my education, I am eager to begin working."

"But you will expose yourselves needlessly to a deadly disease," Sorel reminded them. "Surely the epidemic will be under control by the time the next transport is available."

"I am a nurse," T'Kar replied. "Nurses are desperately needed. You have not refused Nisus' call for aid, Healer."

"So that information is already public," he commented.

"Sorn told me," replied T'Pina. "He also wished to persuade me not to go home."

"Sorn would wish T'Pina not to return to Nisus at

40

all," said her mother, "but his family has not contacted me."

Sorel caught the unspoken warning to the younger woman. He did not know Sorn, but he gathered that the young man must come from one of the Vulcan families who took great care about what families they married into.

T'Kar and her husband came from Ancient Families—those who could trace their ancestry back to original followers of the philosopher Surak.

Their daughter, however, was adopted.

T'Pina had been one of twenty-four children who were the only survivors of an attack on Vulcan Colony Five. No one lived on Vulcan Colony Five today, for Vulcan had other colony worlds farther from the Romulan Neutral Zone.

It was assumed Romulans had destroyed the colony, which had been there just a few years and was only seven hundred strong, but there was no way to prove it. So far was the colony from the regular space lanes that their call for help had reached Starfleet more than a day after the attack. By the time a starship got there, nothing was left but devastation, and twenty-four children under the age of three.

All adults and older children were dead, all buildings destroyed, and all records along with them. The other children were identified by retinal scans, but one infant girl was only days old, her birth as yet unrecorded. None of the other children could tell who her parents were, and so no one knew what Vulcan family she belonged to.

T'Kar and Sevel did not care. Having no children of their own, they joyfully adopted the little girl and took her with them to Nisus. She grew up bright and healthy, earning her own place on Nisus by placing first in her class at the Vulcan Academy of Sciences.

All of that was in T'Pina's medical records. What the records did not show was the young woman's serenity, so much like her mother's. There might be no blood kinship between them, but the bonds between mother and daughter were stronger than those between many "natural" parents and children.

Sorel found judgment according to bloodlines rather than accomplishment incomprehensible. Few Vulcans were unable to rejoice in people's differences, as Surak taught. Unfortunately, those few could do great damage. He remembered Sendet actually attempting to disrupt the bonding between Daniel and T'Mir, and recalled for the first time that the young man was aboard the *Enterprise*. He hoped Captain Kirk was transporting Sendet and all his kind in the brig!

Suppressing that unworthy thought, Sorel returned to the subject of Nisus. "Daniel and I have been requested—but we have experience at treating not only Vulcans and Humans, but many other intelligent species here at the Academy."

"Our friends are on Nisus," said T'Kar. "We cannot stay here when every hand is needed to care for the sick—even to keep the power plant and the fields attended!"

T'Pina added, "Healer, Nisus' self-sufficiency could be destroyed. Or the colony could die—for the want of one pair of willing hands."

"For want of a nail, the shoe was lost," Sorel said without thinking.

T'Kar looked at him curiously, but T'Pina nodded. "For want of the shoe, the horse was lost. It is an Earth saying, Mother. I learned it from some Humans here at the Academy."

"And I learned it from Daniel Corrigan," said Sorel. "The point is the ultimate consequences of apparently trivial events: eventually the kingdom is lost because of a nail—a small, nearly worthless item. But people are not small or worthless, T'Pina."

"Exactly why we must not let any more be lost."

"I agree," added T'Kar. "Healer, logic does not apply. There is no way to know whether our return to Nisus will mean enough help to conquer the plague, or our own deaths. We understand that the disease is increasingly contagious, but Nisus is taking stringent precautions to prevent its spread. To save our home and our friends, we will accept the risk."

"Then I will make no further attempt to dissuade you," said Sorel, admiring their courage. "T'Par is waiting to do the final test of your psychological healing."

T'Kar's eyebrows rose. "Not you, Healer?"

So—she did not know. Possibly T'Pina did; those who knew how the stasis chambers worked might deduce that only time could heal Sorel's broken bonding.

"I bear the same wound from which you are recovering," he said flatly. "However, my wife was taken from me unexpectedly, our bonding torn asunder. I could not return her *katra* to her ancestors."

T'Kar paled visibly, but the cause was certainly sufficient. Although she had completed the mourning cycle, and Sorel was certain T'Par would find her healed, she understood as her unbonded daughter could not.

Sorel's was a wound from which some Vulcans never recovered; sometimes he had to force himself to maintain his body from day to day, his only sense of purpose in his work. He reminded himself that T'Zan

43

would insist that he go on, but it became harder every day. He poured all his energies into his routine at the hospital, resisting going home to the empty house they had once shared.

The mission to Nisus was welcome to Sorel. After T'Zan's death, Leonard McCoy had suggested he leave Vulcan for a time, but he had had no reason then. He did not want T'Kar going to Nisus for the same reason he was—to feel that his life was worth something, even if he died for it.

To his shock, he saw in her eyes that T'Kar understood his motives. She had blue eyes, rare among Vulcans, hard to conceal emotions in. Sorel had been told that his own black eyes were unreadable—yet T'Kar, who hardly knew him, had discerned his feelings as easily as Daniel did. But his associate had known him for forty years and, being Human, was always alert for signs of emotion.

He saw sympathy in T'Kar's eyes. Then she looked down, her lashes concealing the inadvertent exchange. "We understand, Healer," she said formally, "and grieve with thee. Come, T'Pina. T'Par will be waiting."

Chapter Seven

JUST BEFORE THEY reached orbit around Vulcan, Captain James T. Kirk called Sendet and Satat to the *Enterprise* briefing room. "Gentlemen," he said, "we disagree about a whole galaxy of things, but I believe we share one thing in common. If I give a man my word, he can count on it. Is that not also true for you?"

"It is," Satat replied warily.

"Very well, then. I'm going to explain our emergency and ask your word that you will make no trouble while we are transporting medical personnel to Nisus."

"Nisus?" asked Satat. "I have distant relatives there—Sern and T'Pren and their children."

"I am sorry. There is a medical crisis on the science colony," Kirk explained. "It's a disease, an epidemic, spreading and mutating. No race seems to be immune to it, and some strains are deadly. The *Enterprise* will be transporting medical aid."

"Of course we will not interfere, Captain," said Satat.

"Sendet?" asked Kirk. "You should know that Sorel and Corrigan, and Corrigan's wife T'Mir, will all be aboard."

The young Vulcan squared his shoulders. His aristocratic features took on a look of disdain that Kirk should even need to ask. "I cannot approve of T'Mir's choice of husband," he replied, "but I would never hinder a medical mission."

"Good. Satat, please inform the others in your party."

"Certainly—and I can speak for all of the Followers of T'Vet in this instance. We wish to maintain the ancient strengths of Vulcan, but we are not barbarians, Captain. Not only will we not interfere in any way, but if we can be of assistance, please feel free to call upon us."

Well, thought Kirk as he left the briefing room for sickbay, *that was certainly easier than I expected!*

His meeting with McCoy, though, was not nearly as satisfactory. The pockets under the doctor's blue eyes showed that he had spent a sleepless night. Spock was with him, analyzing data on the sickbay computer.

They left the Vulcan absorbed in his task and stepped into the next room. "We just got some new information, Jim," said McCoy. "It's bad."

"Another mutation?"

"Probably not—just that they've learned that antibodies to the first strain of the plague do not confer immunity to the third. They'll know in a couple of days whether having had the second strain protects from the third. Right now the whole Nisus Council is in isolation."

"What happened?"

"Everyone on the council had had one of the two earlier versions of the disease, so they felt it was safe to have a meeting. Shoulda done it by communicator."

"And?" Kirk prompted.

"After they sent the call to Starfleet, they reconvened for other business, and the Lemnorian representative went berserk—first symptom of the most recent mutation of the plague. He'd had the first strain; now everybody on the council's been exposed to the third. Spock is rerunning his computations with the new data. They sent us analyses of specimens from victims of the new mutation, but—"

"—but we may want to run further tests once we arrive," came Spock's voice from behind Kirk. The Vulcan joined them, adding, "Thus far, I have found no clues in the new data, and only time will provide more information."

"And you two want to get down on that planet and gather data yourselves," observed Kirk. Then, knowing both men were frustrated, even if McCoy was the only one who would admit it, he added, "You know, in a situation like this one, Bones, Spock, you are two of a kind!"

As he had hoped, his friends could not resist the bait. Spock and McCoy looked at one another, and then back at Kirk, saying in perfect unison, "Really, Captain, I see no reason for you to insult me."

Kirk grinned—he had succeeded in breaking the tension. But his elation was brief. "Wait just a minute here! Spock, Starfleet's orders don't include you —medicine isn't your specialty."

"Research is," the Vulcan replied. "And who is to keep Dr. McCoy proceeding logically if I do not accompany him?"

"Logic's not the answer, Spock," McCoy retorted. "Nisus is crawling with Vulcans, and *they* haven't found a cure. What it's going to take is the experience and human intuition of a few old country doctors!"

"In which case," Spock said with unruffled dignity, "I will return to my post and leave *you* to analyze the data." And with that he walked out of sickbay.

McCoy watched him go without protest. "That means he's sure the clue we need is not in that new data. Damn!" He went to the dispenser for coffee for Kirk and himself. After taking a swallow, he admitted, "Jim, I sure could use Spock's help on Nisus."

"Sorry, Bones—it may be months before that plague is under control, before the *Enterprise* can come back for you." He refused to voice his fears that McCoy might fall victim to this organism that outwitted all quarantine attempts. "I'm already losing my chief medical officer for that time; I can't give up my science officer as well."

"Yeah," McCoy agreed sadly. "I know."

"You'll have plenty of other Vulcans to work with. And how about Sorel and Corrigan? You sure got along with them on Vulcan."

"Right," the doctor said. "We'll find the cause of this disease, Jim—and that'll give us the cure." He paused, then added with a wan smile, "Besides, I *have* to find it fast and get back aboard before Chapel rearranges my sickbay so that I can't find anything."

Chapter Eight

KORSAL LEFT THE hospital feeling more alone than he had since the first day he had set foot on Nisus. Unlike other Klingon scientists who had participated in the experiment of scientific cooperation, he had found a home here.

On his home world he had been a misfit. Myopia and astigmatism had kept him from military advancement. Wearing thick lenses before his eyes, he could see well enough—but an enemy would instantly recognize that to deprive him of that external aid would be to blind him. Therefore he never got past the required basic term of service at the lowest rank.

That had satisfied Korsal, though; his interests had always been in research and technology, particularly engineering, where he could apply the theories that fascinated him in practical ways. He had used his right to minimal education earned in his military service to make a mark as a scholar. First in his class, he had been admitted to his planet's Academy of Engineering, where he continued to dominate his classmates intellectually.

With their father's enthusiastic encouragement, his brothers rose slowly through the military ranks. Korsal, meanwhile, soaked up the knowledge available at the Academy and was chosen to study on Klinzhai itself, at the most prestigious university in the empire. His father gave grudging approval. "If you cannot succeed in the military, you might as well do something useful."

Something useful was exactly what Korsal wanted to do, and on Klinzhai he found his opportunity. He studied and he built. He invented an antenna that would draw in subspace radio messages from twice the distance formerly possible and eliminate the distortion caused by ion storms. He moved from student to teacher. Eventually, despite delays caused by political maneuvering—or rather his refusal to participate in it—he became the youngest thought master on record.

But Korsal's scientific career brought him little fame or glory, because he had no interest in designing weaponry. His colleagues found his attitudes incomprehensible.

He grew thoroughly tired of being asked, "Do you not believe in the Perpetual Game?"

"Only when I can get outside this universe to gain a perspective," he would reply, "will I know whether there is a Perpetual Game. All one can know for certain is that in *this* world the only game is the Reflective Game."

The Reflective form of *klin zha* was played with only one set of pieces, a man and his enemy as one. It was the great game of the greatest Klingon strategists, yet few allowed themselves to admit that it represented the futility of war. It was the game of entropy in which both sides lost—for at the end, the winner triumphed over an empty board.

In a society founded upon war, Korsal's attitude did not win him many friends. Thus when the invitation came for Klingon scientists to join Federation scientists in an exchange of knowledge on Nisus,

Korsal was one of the first to apply. There was no reason not to let him go; he might not be an enthusiastic inventor of military technology, but he was certainly no traitor.

He was, to most Klingons' way of thinking, nobody.

Korsal's family was not of the Imperial Race, nor had any member distinguished himself greatly. By the time he left for Nisus, two of his brothers had died honorably in the Space Service and the third had achieved the position of squadron leader. Their father took pride in his soldier sons; he never quite understood the scientist he had produced.

One of the first things Korsal had discovered on Nisus was that the Federation had a simple, painless, chemical treatment for eye problems like his. When it was offered to him, he accepted the risk, assuming the Federation would not invite a Klingon scientific mission to join them only to begin by blinding one of its members.

After interminable allergy testing, he was given the treatment in one eye—and in three days had gained perfect vision! They made him wait thirty days more before they treated the other eye—and for the first time in his life Korsal woke in the morning to a clear world, rather than a blur that would not focus until he had groped for his glasses.

That was the first time Korsal had served as a guinea pig for Nisus' medical personnel. Now he was doing so again—would that the results turned out as sanguine as the first time! The eye treatment Korsal had undergone was now as routine in the Klingon Empire as in the Federation.

Unless the plague underwent an unusually long incubation period in Klingons, they were apparently immune to it. Before releasing him, the doctors had taken what felt like at least half Korsal's blood to study. Now he was free to go home, for so far as they could tell he was not a carrier.

But what if the doctors were wrong? What if, despite all the precautions, despite being bathed in the same sterile rays that surgeons used, what if Korsal were even now carrying the deadly disease home to his family?

Were his sons immune? They were half Klingon, and neither had contracted any strain of the disease, although they had both attended school every day until it closed. He wanted them to be immune—to be safe.

But if they were, what about Borth's plan to sell the disease to the Klingon Empire?

Korsal might defend Klingon honor to his last breath, but he knew as well as any Orion that even if no one in official channels would purchase such a dishonorable weapon, it would not take a wily Orion trader long to discover someone who would make the purchase through unofficial channels.

He felt as if he had been coerced into a game of *klin zha* known as the Final Form, where to take an opponent's piece was not merely to set it aside, but to destroy it utterly—burn wooden pieces, smash or melt those made of stone or metal. There was no victory—when only one set of pieces was left the game reverted to the Reflective Game, and the weaker player's mistakes resulted in the destruction of the stronger player's pieces.

Only Klingons, Korsal thought, could conceive of such a game—but only an Orion could force a Klingon to play it.

Yet if Nisus' biochemists could isolate and duplicate the factor in Klingon blood that gave them immunity—

He could hope for that. Biology was not his field, however; he had to rely on the Humans and Vulcans now studying his blood samples to find an answer.

Korsal's home was on the distant outskirts of the city. The public transport system was still running, although he saw no one else on the slidewalks as he worked his way from the slow-moving outer bands to the high-speed inner ones. With the skill of daily practice, he switched lanes so as to be carried along C-belt, out to the suburb where he owned a home.

His own home. Land, a garden. It was something he could never hope to gain as a scientist in the Klingon Empire. His title of thought master meant little there if his science was not military strategy.

It had rained that morning. The air was fresh and moist in his nostrils as he stepped off the slidewalk into his own neighborhood. In the whole trip, only three lonely figures had slid past him on the bands designed to carry thousands. No one was on the streets, either, although a few children played in their own fenced gardens.

Those gardens might look normal at first glance, except to a resident of Nisus. Here two Vulcan girls played under the watchful eye of a *sehlat*. There five Hemanite children of the same litter tumbled happily on the grass beside a small pond. A few houses further on, another Vulcan child, a boy, practiced alone with an *ahn-woon*, while across the street Caitian children used a huge movidel tree as a gymnasium.

What was unnatural was that the children of each family were confined to their own home ground. Ordinarily they ran the streets or gathered in noisy groups in various gardens. The unnatural quiet did nothing to improve Korsal's mood.

He reached his own house and found his sons in the cheery main room. Kevin, now fourteen, was on the couch, frowning over a problem on the screen of his tricorder. He had inherited his father's eye problems, which could not be treated until he was sixteen—but knowing that he would be able to discard his glasses then, Kevin did not resent them. They were sliding down his nose now, and he shoved them back into place with a gesture so familiar that it made his father smile. He noticed, too, that Kevin was succeeding in growing a mustache, although he did not yet have enough facial hair for a beard. Nonetheless, his Human heritage was plain in his appearance, his hair light brown, his skin lacking the swarthiness of his father's.

Korsal's other son, Karl, who was nine, was playing *klin zha* at the communications console, his opponent a Vulcan schoolmate, Sonan. When Korsal entered, Kevin set his tricorder aside and rose, saying, "Father!"

Karl turned from his game and also got to his feet. "Welcome home, Father. I am pleased that you are well. You have a message from Ms. Torrence, asking that you call her as soon as you get in. She missed you at the hospital."

"Thank you, Karl," he said as his younger son turned to freeze his game and sign off contact with Sonan so his father could use the console.

His sons' formality might be appropriate in a high-ranking Klingon family, but that was not the reason for it here. A few years ago, both boys would have thrown themselves into his arms when he returned after several days' absence. Kevin, though, was now at an age when demonstration of affection for parents was considered embarrassing—a stage both Klingon and Human adolescents exhibited, and so perfectly natural to Kevin.

Korsal understood Kevin—it was Karl, the same fusion of Klingon and Human as his brother, who was the family enigma. It often seemed to Korsal that his younger son was trying his best to turn out Vulcan.

Ordinarily, Korsal would have hugged his sons despite their protest, but today he would not touch any member of his family until he had showered and changed clothes. He did not *think* he could have become contaminated on his way home from the hospital, but he would take no risk with their health.

"Where is Seela?" he asked as he crossed toward the communications console.

"Gone to the market," Kevin replied.

"Did you not offer to go instead?" Korsal asked. He would be equally concerned if one of his sons were risking exposure, yet with every passing day their immunity to the plague seemed further assured.

"I did offer," Kevin said. "Seela said no one on the council who had had the second strain of the plague caught the third."

That was true; Korsal had told her that when he called to say he had been released. Seela had had the second strain of the plague and recovered.

Kevin continued, "She also said I would not know how to choose either meat or vegetables."

"A sad lack in your education," said Korsal. "Seela must teach both of you—and you must learn how to cook as well. I would not wish my sons to marry too soon, or to choose consorts merely because they are hungry."

Kevin grinned. "Or starve our own sons one day?"

"Kevin," Karl said flatly, "you should have more respect for our father. He always provided adequate nutrition."

"And you, Karl," said Korsal to his younger son, "should stop being so serious! Kevin is quite right: I married Seela for her cooking."

Karl was too young to comprehend the humor in that, but Kevin choked on his laughter, pleased to share an adult joke with his father.

"Kevin," said Korsal, "take your brother out into the fresh air. The rain is over. I'll come out and play ball with you as soon as I see what Torrence wants. I need some exercise after being cooped up in the hospital!"

But Korsal was not to have the game of rough-and-tumble he had looked forward to sharing with his sons.

Torrence's face did not come onto the screen when he keyed in the woman's code. Rather, he heard the hollow ring of someone speaking into a hand-held communicator, and the sound of rushing water in the background. "Korsal! Thank God there's one engineer not on the sick list! Get up here to the dam right away. We've got trouble!"

Chapter Nine

T'PINA WAS FASCINATED by the USS *Enterprise,* the largest ship she had ever traveled on—at least that she could remember. She had no recollection of being taken to Vulcan as an infant, and only hazy, fragmentary images of the transfer from Vulcan to Nisus.

Once, during her secondary education, she had made a three-day journey with four other outstanding students aboard a survey ship mapping the uninhabited planets in Nisus' system. Later, she had traveled to Vulcan to take up her classes at the Academy aboard a Vulcan trading vessel. A Federation starship was far more interesting than either.

She found herself surrounded by legends.

Of course the current situation was unusual. On an ordinary voyage Sarek, the famous Vulcan ambassador and scientist, would not be aboard with his equally famous wife Amanda, one of the foremost linguistic scholars of the Federation. Nor had the renowned medical team of Sorel and Corrigan ever left Vulcan together before—and here they were in the same room with Sarek and Amanda!

But the crew of the *Enterprise* itself was headed by the legendary Captain James T. Kirk, and his first officer was Commander Spock, rapidly outshining his famous parents as scientist and explorer.

Having grown up amid people of all Federation

races in close cooperation, T'Pina did not take conscious note of the fact that each legendary pair consisted of one Vulcan and one Human. She saw the chief medical officer of the *Enterprise* approach Sorel and Corrigan, who were talking with a Human male of the race they called black, dressed in the blue sciences uniform of Starfleet, but with no insignia to indicate his current assignment.

Curious, wondering if they were already working on ways to conquer the plague devastating her home planet, T'Pina drifted closer to the group. The *Enterprise* doctor—McCoy, she remembered—was saying, "It's a pleasure to work together again, although I wish it weren't under these circumstances."

"Let us hope we can quickly change the circumstances," said Dr. Corrigan, a short, portly, balding man.

"Has Starfleet sent any new information, Leonard?" Sorel asked.

"Yes—but I don't think it'll do us much good, and I don't want to discuss it here. Kinda touchy."

"Touchy?" asked the Vulcan healer.

"Likely to create controversy," his Human partner interpreted. "In which case," he added, "we'd best not create questions by all going off together. May we join you in your office when the reception's over?"

"By all means," McCoy replied.

"When healers confer in whispers," a male voice spoke behind T'Pina, "patients must beware."

T'Pina turned, horribly embarrassed to be caught trying to overhear a private conversation. *Two days away from Vulcan, and I have forgotten all my control.*

Even worse, when she caught sight of the man who had accosted her, her throat tightened so she could not reply.

Vulcans were not supposed to react to physical appearance, and T'Pina could not recall ever in her life before feeling as she did now. The man was Vulcan, tall, only a few years older than she was . . . and beautiful.

"Handsome" was not a powerful enough word to describe his face, although it was completely masculine. It was as if the greatest artist who ever lived had set out to portray the ideal of Vulcan male beauty —thick, straight, shining dark hair falling in a perfect cap about a skull of ideal proportions; oval face, straight nose, strong jaw, high cheekbones; and his eyes—eyes of brilliant brown touched with amber, wide and thickly lashed, set under winging brows.

Only the mouth escaped classic perfection—and that only because its neatly sculpted lines were set in an expression of disapproval.

T'Pina grasped hold of her emotions, determined to give this man no further reason to disapprove of her.

And only then realizing that he had no right to approve or disapprove, unless she gave it to him.

He was not old enough to have the right by seniority; he was not her teacher, her healer, or her superior. Nor was he a member of her family—not that that would give him such a right, since they were of the same generation.

Armed with that realization, T'Pina found control easier to maintain. "My name is T'Pina," she said. "I am a biotechnician."

The man looked her over almost clinically, but his mouth softened from disapproval almost to the hint of a smile. It set her pulse to racing. "My name is Sendet," he told her, "of the clan T'Deata. I am a neurophysicist."

"A neurophysicist?" T'Pina deliberately focused on

what they were saying lest her unwelcome physical reactions become apparent to Sendet.

He offered his clan name upon first acquaintance! What could that mean? Both of them were unbonded. It was not possible to have this kind of reaction to a bonded male.

"I know little of the plague on Nisus," she continued, "but I thought it was a virus. Does it then attack the nervous system?"

Sendet blinked, glanced over at the healers deep in conversation, then back at T'Pina. "You are going to Nisus? Surely they have enough biotechnicians. Forgive me, but you do not seem old enough to be called as an expert."

"I'm not," T'Pina replied. "Nisus is my home. I have just completed my training at the Vulcan Academy."

"Ah—I am also a graduate of the Academy, and have spent the past few years on the staff of the hospital there. T'Pina . . . I have heard your name. Did you not graduate first in your class?"

"I had that honor," she replied, irrationally pleased that he had noticed and remembered.

"Daughter."

T'Pina had not heard her mother come up behind her. With careful control, she turned to T'Kar. "Mother, this is Sendet, a neurophysicist from the Academy. Sendet, this is T'Kar, my mother."

"I am honored," said Sendet with impeccable politeness. T'Pina saw his eyes light on T'Kar's clan badge worked in gold and silver, which she wore in honor of the formal occasion. "Your daughter does you great credit, T'Kar."

"She has never disappointed me," T'Kar replied. Wondering if that were a warning not to disappoint her now, T'Pina glanced at her mother's face. But T'Kar was studying Sendet's clan badge of gold with red and green stones. T'Pina had never studied clan heraldry; she would not have recognized the symbols if Sendet had not spoken his ancestral name. His emblem apparently meant nothing to T'Kar, either —except that the right to wear one meant the ability to trace his ancestry to one of the ancient warrior clans.

She glanced around, curious. Sorel wore his clan badge, but neither Sarek nor Spock wore theirs. Sarek wore only ambassadorial ribbons; he was neutral of all personal or factional claims when he acted for all of Vulcan. Starfleet regulations, though, could not preclude an officer from wearing such a token with his dress uniform—otherwise Mr. Scott, the *Enterprise* chief engineer, could not be dressed in tartans.

Spock, however, instead of a family emblem wore an IDIC. Infinite Diversity in Infinite Combination —more than merely the union of opposites, the Vulcan symbol of triangle piercing circle to release a brilliant jewel represented the ideal blending of diversity. The triangle was offset on the circle to represent motion and change; nothing alive remained static. Vulcans respected life—and that meant respecting change.

T'Pina's gaze returned to Sendet. She wondered whether T'Deata were one of the Ancient Families. Since she would never know whether she belonged to one of them, she had never bothered to study them beyond the standard information in her history lessons. T'Deata was a matriarchal lineage designation, but it did not tell whether that clan had become converted to Surak's philosophy during the great leader's own lifetime, or in later generations.

Sendet was asking, "T'Kar, T'Pina, have you seen the stars from the observation deck? Motion is discernible at this warp—it is a unique experience."

T'Kar looked from Sendet to T'Pina. "Indeed, one that I have appreciated often. The observation deck will not be crowded at this time. It is something you should see, my daughter. Will you escort her, Sendet?"

"I am honored," the young man repeated, and T'Pina struggled to control her joy. Her mother approved! She lowered her eyes, lest either her mother or Sendet see her undisciplined delight, and started to leave with Sendet.

"T'Kar!" It was Sorel. He left the group of other healers. T'Pina hid her concern. Obviously the healer did not want her mother to leave.

"Come, T'Pina," said Sendet. She followed him, wondering what the healer could have to say so urgently to T'Kar. Perhaps something to do with her nursing skills.

T'Pina and Sendet were not alone on the observation deck—but when they stared out at the hurtling stars, they might as well have been. Only by biting her lower lip did T'Pina suppress a gasp at the sensation of falling into eternity. Out there, before her, was utter coldness, absolute zero. Despite the layers of her clothing, she had to control a shiver.

And then she felt, at her back, Sendet's warmth, a shelter from the cold, the night. He did not touch her.

But one day, she thought, when the time was appropriate, they would touch.

Staring into the reflectionless glass that separated her from the depths of space, T'Pina allowed herself to smile.

Chapter Ten

THE SLIDEWALKS STOPPED at the cluster of government buildings at the foot of the dam, so Korsal took a two-wheeled power cycle and rode up the steep, winding trail to the dam entrance. He ran inside, grabbing up a utility belt and communicator from the toolroom.

"Torrence, I'm at the dam. Where are you?"

"Turbine three," her voice answered tightly. "Hurry!"

Every sound at the dam was dominated by the noise of rushing water, but as Korsal followed the orange lines that would take him to the turbines he heard another sound—a muffled clunking that shifted the ground beneath his feet, as if some giant machine were shaking itself apart.

Outside the entrance to the turbine chamber, the status lights showed turbine three off-line. That did nothing to account for the deafening clangor. Korsal pushed the door open and was assaulted anew by the noise.

Emily Torrence was a member of one of the dark races of Humans, skin as deep brown as coffee beans, hair black and springily curled—frizzed up tight against her skull now from the flying spray in the turbine chamber.

With a pair of waldos, she was maneuvering one of the gigantic cranes in an attempt to capture something spinning in the whirling water—something that showed a bit of itself above the water every so often, even though it shouldn't.

Korsal recognized the underwater turbine blades —the wheel had shifted partly off its axle and was undulating wildly off-center.

"How did this happen?" he shouted as he fitted his hands into a second pair of waldos, putting another crane into operation.

"Ice!" Torrence replied.

Ice?

It was impossible to converse amid the deafening combination of rushing water and clanging, clanking runaway water wheel, so Korsal simply added his efforts to Torrence's.

They clamped two cranes onto the recalcitrant wheel to stop its gyrations. Then, while Korsal watched both sets of waldos lest the raging water tear it loose again, Torrence released the turbine wheel from its axle, rejoined Korsal, and together they maneuvered the gigantic, dripping wheel over onto the concrete at the side.

Once they had captured the water wheel, the infernal banging and clattering stopped, but the rushing water was loud enough in itself to prevent conversation while they recalculated the control functions.

Two other wheels were off-true, hit by pieces of the same ice that had torn number three apart, but they could keep those turbines on-line until each could be repaired, by manually rebalancing the system. Temporarily, the power system could work with one turbine missing.

Toggling the control unit shut, Korsal and Torrence

walked over to the useless water wheel. It wasn't wheel-shaped any longer. Several blades were twisted outward, others shorn off. How could ice have done that much damage?

They left the turbine chamber for the plant status office before Korsal could ask his question. By that time, Torrence was having a reaction he had seen in Humans before: she was shaking, her skin turning gray beneath the brown.

Humans had a gland that poured a chemical into their blood during emergencies, to make them alert, strong—and in battle, supremely dangerous. When the situation passed, however, Korsal had discovered, they often had withdrawal symptoms.

Torrence wore a waterproof jumpsuit, unlike Korsal, who had not stopped to change clothes. He was soaked to the skin from the spray, but it was Torrence who was chilling.

There were towels in a top drawer. Korsal handed one to Torrence, who mopped her face and began scrubbing at her hair.

Korsal stripped off his soaked shirt and toweled the water out of his hair and beard, keeping an eye on Torrence. She was coming out of the shock reaction, her skin texture and breathing returning to normal. He draped a dry towel around her shoulders, and she looked up at him gratefully, then poured them each a cup of steaming coffee from the machine that was ubiquitous in offices frequented by Humans.

"Now," said Korsal, taking the other chair before the status console, "what's this about ice?"

"The early thaw," she replied. "Up in the mountains the ice broke loose in huge pieces this spring —too big to melt away before they reached the reservoir."

Korsal said, "There are supposed to be safety sluices above the dam, to prevent anything too big for the system to handle from getting through until it's melted down to size."

"Apparently," Torrence said grimly, "the safeties have stopped working." She turned to the computer and logged onto the inspection schedule. "Look here —Dekrix and T'Lin were scheduled to fly an inspection tour five days ago, but there's no log notation that they did so."

"Check the hospital admissions," Korsal suggested.

The names were there. T'Lin was a fatality. Dekrix was on the critical list.

Torrence bit her lower lip. "Both pilot and backup out of commission—and we're so understaffed that we're running with only one person on watch out here. I plead guilty. My last shift was over by the time I had run all the status checks; I didn't call up the logs. And this shift I hardly got started before that ice hit the turbine. You realize what would have happened if that wheel had gotten away from us?"

"It probably would have spun down and knocked out all the turbines below it," Korsal replied. "With only one and two operating, Nisus would have lost three quarters of its electrical power."

Torrence nodded and started to get up. "I've got to do the rest of the status checks."

"I'll do them," said Korsal. "You check the logs."

"The hydroelectric plant's not your job," Torrence protested.

"Give me the checksheet so I don't miss anything," he told her. "Emily, all I have to do is watch for yellow or red lights! I'll call you if I find any."

She looked up with a smile. "Thanks." Hunting around under various tools and printouts, she found an electronic tablet, which lit up with the checklist. As she handed it to Korsal, she put her hand on his arm. "Thank you for coming today without asking questions first. I couldn't have—"

"Take your hands off my wife!"

Korsal turned. The man in the doorway was someone he knew only slightly, Torrence's husband. "Charlie!" she was saying. "What are you doing here?"

"What are *you* doing?" the man countered. "I heard there was some kind of emergency, that you were calling all over town for help—but when I get here I find my wife half naked—"

"Charlie, shut up!" Torrence exclaimed, getting up and pulling the towel off her shoulders to show that she was fully dressed. Korsal, of course, was not—his shirt was hanging over the back of the chair, still dripping, while his soggy trousers clung uncomfortably to his legs.

"I *won't* shut up!" the man replied, moving face-to-face with Korsal. The two were close in height, but Charles Torrence was built like an athlete; he was head athletic coach at the school, and Korsal remembered that he had an Olympic gold medal in some form of hand-to-hand combat. Torrence taught many forms of the martial arts, including Kershu. Korsal had encouraged his sons to take lessons with this man.

"Ms. Torrence was calling all over town," Korsal said calmly, "for any engineer who could handle the waldos in the turbine room and help her rebalance the system afterward. I happened to be the first one she found."

"Yeah—and now you're trying to take advantage of her." Torrence moved closer. "I don't know why we ever let you stay on this planet, Korsal. You weren't satisfied with white and green—now you got a taste for black—"

"Charlie!"

The anger in Emily Torrence's voice cut through the man's own. "You stop right now, and you apologize! What is the *matter* with you?"

Her response seemed to pull her husband out of his rage, and Korsal felt a breath of relief. It was not another attack of the plague.

Then he realized how absurd his relief was—the stress of the plague on the science colony was bringing out hidden prejudices. Perhaps . . . he wasn't really at home here, after all.

Charles Torrence was looking from his fully dressed wife, her wet hair, to Korsal's also-wet hair, his dripping shirt hung over the chair. "The emergency was in the turbine room?" he asked with tremulous calm.

"Yes, the turbine room," his wife replied acidly. "You've been in there, Charlie. No one can work in there without getting soaked."

The man looked stricken. "Oh, man—I am *sorry!*"

"You should be!" his wife told him.

"I *am*, Emmy. Korsal, listen, man—you've got a beautiful wife. If you caught her with another man, his clothes off—I mean, you'd think—"

"I hope," Korsal said, trying hard to curb his anger, "that I would trust her enough to ask questions before I accused her."

The Human looked thoroughly chastened. "I'm sorry. Both of you—dammit, Emmy, if I didn't love you so much—"

"We'll talk about it later," she said wearily. "Right now I have work to do, and Korsal has volunteered to check the status boards. There are clean jumpsuits in the locker room," she added to Korsal. "You'd better put one on. I hear Klingons may be immune to the plague that's going around, but it wouldn't do to have you catch pneumonia!"

"No, and it won't do to have more ice hit the turbines," he told her. "I've got a hoverer license, and my son Kevin just got his. Round me up some maps of the safeties, and we'll fly upriver tomorrow to see what's happened."

"I'd be happy to," she replied. "Thanks."

"And set the computer to run the logs daily and report any tests not done."

"Someone should have thought of that a week ago!" Torrence said.

"No one is thinking clearly on Nisus," said Korsal, "not even the Vulcans."

Chapter Eleven

ON THE *Enterprise* observation deck, T'Pina stared out at the passing stars. "Nature has such beauty to offer," she said at last, "and we see so little of it. Most people never leave the planets on which they are born."

"Perhaps that is what nature intended," Sendet replied—not at all the answer T'Pina had expected. She turned, looking up into his face, but he was as controlled as a healer. "I have never before been off Vulcan," he added.

"Then I hope that after the epidemic has been stopped, you will be able to spend some time on Nisus," said T'Pina. "It is very different from Vulcan. Nisus is a watery planet, very humid by our standards. There are oceans—you must take a sea voyage while you are there!"

"A . . . sea voyage?"

T'Pina was amused to see him slightly disconcerted at the idea, a common reaction among Vulcans. Travel by water was not in the heritage of their desert-born people, and the first experience of the deck of a boat shifting beneath one's feet was as strange as free-fall. She wondered if Sendet had ever known that sensation, either, and determined to find out if the *Enterprise* had a zero-g recreational facility.

"Wide experience increases wisdom," she quoted

70

Surak, "provided the experience is not sought purely for the stimulation of sensation."

"Sensation is necessary," Sendet replied, "lest the spirit die."

It had the sound of an oft-quoted saying, but T'Pina had never heard it before.

"Not every Vulcan has always agreed with Surak's precepts," said Sendet in response to her raised eyebrow. "Surak's philosophy brought peace to Vulcan's warring tribes, and made civilization possible. However, the complete suppression of emotion will kill a civilization as certainly as the complete denial of rules or authority."

"Complete suppression of emotion?" T'Pina asked. "No, I have never desired to seek the disciplines at Gol. However, my teachers have always warned me that my curiosity quotient is extremely high, even for a Vulcan."

She was rewarded with a slight quirk of Sendet's lips as he controlled a smile. "As is mine."

"Then why do you say that nature intended us to remain on the worlds where we were born? Intelligent beings grow by seeking what lies over the next hill, on the other side of the mountains—or beyond the farthest star."

"There is growth," he said, "and there is corruption. On the other side of the mountain may be other people—weak but seductive people who leach away one's strength."

Now T'Pina was thoroughly confused. "What are you saying, Sendet? Many on Vulcan opposed our joining the Federation—but after all these years, the benefits of interaction with other cultures have been well proven."

"T'Pina—look what it has done to us. Once the

only Vulcans to interact with other cultures were those who left the planet, like the scientists who went to Nisus, and the traders. We did not permit aliens on our world. Now they overrun it. Nearly a quarter of the students at the Academy—"

"Sendet!" T'Pina exclaimed. "Surely you cannot believe it is an error to educate all those who have the ability and the desire. As for offworlders 'overrunning' Vulcan, statistics prove you in error. Fewer than one-hundredth of a percent of Vulcan citizens are of other races; less than one-half percent of the population, whether temporary residents like students and researchers or the few who have sought citizenship, are non-Vulcan."

Although he kept control of his facial muscles, Sendet's eyes showed surprise.

T'Pina could not understand why he would expect her to accept his assertions when they were patently untrue.

At the same time that her mind rejected Sendet's false assertions, she regretted her sharp reaction. The conversation had begun pleasantly. Why was it deteriorating?

"In the past generation," Sendet said flatly, "outworlders have gained a strong foothold. What is more serious, their influence on Vulcan grows daily."

"How can that be detrimental?" T'Pina asked. "Do you not believe in IDIC? The combinations of diversity have produced only good. On Nisus, where everyone is different from everyone else, scientific progress occurs at a rate never seen before in the history of the galaxy." She searched his face. "Sendet, I fear you and I have a basic disagreement in philosophy which neither is likely to overcome. If you will excuse me, I shall return to my quarters."

"You will not stand your ground and fight?" Sendet asked.

". . . fight?"

"With words," he explained. "I do not suggest the *lirpa.*"

The *lirpa.* Today it was a ceremonial weapon, although every Vulcan male was trained in its use because of the possibility, however rare, that he might one day face a ceremonial challenge.

But the heavy, awkward *lirpa* was not a woman's weapon. Between a man and a woman it had no function today, but historically it had been the method used by a male warrior to strike off the head of a woman who betrayed him. During the Reforms, sisters, daughters, even the occasional wife who followed Surak against the will of male clansmen, were sometimes executed thus.

Sendet's words drew a chill up T'Pina's back . . . and yet there was something paradoxically pleasant in that chill. For all her experience of people of widely varying cultures, T'Pina found Sendet like no one she had ever met before.

"Will you abandon the field," he challenged her now, "or stay and refute my contention?"

"I have no need to refute it," she replied. "The people assembled on this very ship refute it. The captain and his first officer—Human and Vulcan, and it is said that they command the finest ship in Starfleet. Sarek of Vulcan and his human wife Amanda; Sorel and Corrigan—"

"And Daniel Corrigan's wife, T'Mir," Sendet interrupted, his voice so cold T'Pina did shiver—and this time there was no pleasant aspect to the chill. "There you see the hidden vice within the virtue of IDIC," he continued. "Vulcans intermarrying with outworlders, polluting our blood—"

"I will hear no more of this," said T'Pina, carefully controlling a growing anger. "I did not think any person trained in logic, as surely a scientist must be, could so easily deny fact. Good night, Sendet."

T'Pina left the observation deck, fighting down an illogical sense of loss. How could someone so young, healthy, attractive, be so *wrong?* And, when he was so determinedly wrong, why did she feel such an attraction to him?

It was true she had not managed to terminate the discussion with courtesy and dignity. Perhaps that was why she was dissatisfied with herself.

She must meditate. Therefore she did not go back to the reception, but took the turbolift to the deck where quarters had been assigned to the passengers.

She palmed the plate outside the room she shared with her mother, and the door slid open.

But the room was not empty, as she had expected. In the outer office area, with its desk, terminal, and two chairs, sat T'Kar and the healer Sorel.

T'Pina grasped control. "Good evening, Mother, Healer. Do you desire privacy?" The open-work screen between the work area and the sleep area did nothing to prevent voices from being heard through the entire cabin. "I shall return to the reception."

"No, T'Pina—stay," said T'Kar. "Sorel has been telling me about the man you met at the reception."

"Do not be concerned, Mother. I know what Sendet is." For a healer to feel compelled to warn them, as surely Sorel had been doing, something was badly amiss—and that suddenly caused T'Pina to put together facts she had known, but not connected before. "He is not part of the medical mission. He is a Follower of T'Vet."

"He told you?" asked Sorel.

"There was no need. His philosophical beliefs told me. We . . . have nothing in common. When I discovered that, I left him on the observation deck."

"You did well, my daughter," T'Kar told her.

Then why do I feel as if I've done wrong? T'Pina wondered, shielding her thought—but not strongly enough. Sorel's head lifted slightly, and those unreadable black eyes rested on her.

"T'Pina," said the healer, "I can answer your question. Shall I speak before your mother, or would you hear in private?"

T'Kar's blue eyes revealed surprise as she looked from Sorel to T'Pina, knowing that Sorel had read something with his healer's ESP that could be shielded from any other Vulcan.

T'Pina had never hidden anything from her mother. In fact, she had intended to confide her ambivalent reactions to Sendet if her meditations did not resolve them. She had often found that private meditation left her mind ever cycling through a problem, while discussing it with her mother would clarify and resolve it.

"I know I have done nothing shameful, Healer," she replied. "Speak."

"No, T'Pina, nothing shameful at all," said Sorel. "What you are experiencing is perfectly normal. Your physical examination revealed the first signs: you are fully matured."

His meaning, to Vulcan ears, was clear. She was already legally an adult, a citizen, and her graduation from the Academy had admitted her to the ranks of those who shaped the future. Now her physical growth matched her intellectual achievements: she was ready to marry and bear children.

"It is nothing to fear, my daughter," said T'Kar.

"I do not fear it," said T'Pina, only half lying.

Sorel said, "You are unbonded. So is Sendet. The attraction you feel is normal, but you have learned to control your desires with rational thought, as do all intelligent beings. Proceed as you have begun, and you will not err."

"Sorel," T'Kar said hesitantly, "do you think I should actively seek a husband for T'Pina?"

"I do not think that will be necessary," Sorel replied. "I predict that eligible males will quickly present themselves once T'Pina sets foot on Nisus."

Marriage. Bonding. That would resolve these unsettling feelings. Now that she understood what was happening, T'Pina recognized her reaction to Sendet: it was normal for Vulcans to bond, husband and wife sharing a mental intimacy unknown among nontelepathic species. When she met an unbonded male of appropriate age, there was an instinctive attraction.

Her parents had chosen not to bond her in childhood, although there had been several offers. Now she wondered if T'Kar and Sevel had been wise; the ancient tradition of bonding at age seven meant that when the pair reached their maturity they already had one another to rely on.

With sudden insight, she recognized that of the three Vulcans in that room, she bore the least discomfort.

Both her mother and the healer had lost bondmates; T'Pina yearned for some unknown that she had never had.

T'Kar had had the presence of Sevel through all the years until his death. It was certainly worse for her, knowing what was lacking in her life.

And Sorel—his wife had been torn from him unexpectedly, without the chance for farewells or healing rituals. His lack must be an agony compared to the pleasure/pain of T'Pina's vague yearnings.

Was it possible, she wondered, that Sorel and T'Kar might find what they needed in one another?

"Thank you, Healer," she said. "Knowing what is happening will enable me to control it. It is still early. I shall return to the reception if—"

"I must leave," said Sorel. "Dr. McCoy has some new information to share with the medical personnel."

"Thank you for your help, Sorel," said T'Kar.

The healer did not give the standard reply: "One does not thank logic." It was not logic that had led him to speak to her mother, T'Pina knew. Instead, he said, "I am here to serve. Do not hesitate to call upon me."

Chapter Twelve

WHEN KORSAL STARTED home from the power plant, the clouds had closed in again and it was pouring rain. Since he now wore a waterproof jumpsuit, he didn't get soaked again, but the cold rain on his bare head made him shiver.

Leaving home hurriedly, he hadn't been able to find the helmet that should have been hung on the cycle's handlebars. One of his sons was due a scolding: Kevin if he had misplaced the helmet, and Karl if he had been riding the cycle. Karl had inherited the Klingon early growth pattern. He was big enough and well coordinated enough to handle the cycle, but Nisus law prohibited anyone less than ten standard years old, no matter what his species, from driving a powered vehicle.

Oddly enough, that frequent argument with his younger son was reassuring to Korsal: it proved that the boy was Klingon. In the empire, he would have been operating such equipment for over a year by now.

And, Korsal reminded himself, be well begun in his primary military training. There was no military training on Nisus. Korsal had not protested when Kevin had taken the examinations for early entry into Starfleet Academy, for he did not expect him to be accepted. Would the Federation teach its military strategies to someone with dual citizenship, when one of the nations was the Klingon Empire?

Well, if they did, the boy would certainly get adequate training in combat and weaponry, and an excellent general education along with it. If they did not . . . Kevin would have to decide within the next three years whether he would go to the Klingon Empire and perform the required minimum military service, or renounce his Klingon citizenship. The boy knew he would have to make the choice; Korsal kept painfully silent on the subject, although he hated the thought that either of his sons might renounce his father's heritage.

Korsal had trained both his sons in small-arms self-defense himself, and insisted that they enroll in all the martial-arts classes offered in school. Should they choose their Klingon heritage over their Human, he would not have them defanged.

The encounter with Charles Torrence had unnerved Korsal more than he cared to admit. After the first year or so of mutual distrust, the Klingon delegation and the other scientists on Nisus had become accustomed to one another. Nisus had many children of mixed heritage, and when Korsal married Cathy Patemchek they had not hesitated to have children of their own.

Korsal's sons were competitive—something they had inherited from their mother as much as from himself—but that was the norm on Nisus. All children were "advantaged" here—all had well-educated parents who encouraged them to learn, to participate, and to judge people by accomplishment rather than origin. He could not imagine a better place for his sons to gain the foundation of their education. That, and his Human wife, had been the primary reasons Korsal had not returned to the Klingon Empire when the rest of the delegation did.

But now . . . would this plague bring an end to the cooperation that characterized life on Nisus? Unbidden, he recalled Therian raving obscenities at him with his dying breath. The same things Charles Torrence had said, focusing on his marriages to women who were not Klingon.

He hadn't intended to marry twice. He had been content with Cathy—but she was career Starfleet. She had thought her assignment to Nisus permanent; Korsal was certain that she would not have married —certainly not borne two children—if she had known she would be unexpectedly promoted and reassigned to a starship.

Korsal could not go with her, nor could the boys. And . . . Cathy refused to resign. The opportunity was too great: science officer on a Constitution-class starship, the rank of commander.

They had fought bitterly, made up just before she left. There were promises of meetings on leave, of requests for reassignment to Nisus at the first opportunity. There were message tapes every few days, then every few weeks, and finally . . . divorce documents, with a message cassette of a tearful Cathy telling Korsal and her children that she had no right to bind them when she could not be with them. She gave up her sons' custody to Korsal . . . and none of them had seen or heard from her since, although Korsal had heard she was climbing steadily through Starfleet's ranks.

Korsal left the muddy mountain trail for the smooth pavement of the town. He now rode on a slick cushion of water, not daring to speed up as he longed to, to get out of the cold rain and away from his morbid thoughts.

But the thoughts would not be denied. When Kevin was born, Korsal had decided to stay on Nisus until his son was old enough to decide between the Federation and the Klingon Empire. Karl's birth had extended the length of his intended stay. Now—was the plague going to force a premature choice upon all of them?

Was there a choice? "Fusions," children of mixed heritage, were regarded with scorn in the empire. There was only one way to overcome it: military glory. His sons would be forced to fight—often against Humans like their mother—or endure being second-class citizens.

Korsal had traveled in the Federation, experienced the fear and hatred of Klingons that prevailed everywhere but on Nisus. He had thought Nisus a safe haven. Was he wrong?

Was that what Therian had meant when he cried out, "The children!" the day he died? Was his last lucid thought the realization that if this plague released pent-up prejudices, large numbers of Nisus' children—all those of mixed heritage—would suffer the consequences?

No . . . surely even oncoming madness would not lead from that thought to the uncharacteristic attack on Korsal.

Then what? Korsal's scientist's mind suddenly fastened on an idea: suppose there were a connection between Therian's discovery and the particular form of his madness. What if he had indeed seen something significant in those statistics scrolling up the screen, certainly something about children, but . . . perhaps children like *Korsal's* children?

All that data was still available—the engineering computer was still linked to the hospital computer system, still taking part of the overload. Korsal could call up the statistics from his home terminal. Now that he had some idea of what he was looking for—

Korsal stored the power cycle and entered the house. His shoes squished, and he was dripping water.

He stopped in the utility room, kicked off his shoes, and looked for towels, eager to get to the computer, suddenly sure the answer was there. Cause? Pattern of spread? Every piece of information was a step toward either finding a cure or stopping the spread of this *khesting* plague.

But as he began drying himself off, the door to the kitchen opened, and his liver turned over.

He didn't have to look at her. Her scent, delicate, almost unidentifiable as such, embraced him before she arrived herself, taking the towel from his suddenly unsteady hands and mopping his face, murmuring, "Korsal. Oh, my husband, you are home at last."

Seela. Orion and female, she was enough to suspend any man's thoughts, but when she focused her attention on him it sometimes seemed he forgot to breathe. His liver turned over.

Like all females of her race, Seela had emerald skin, black hair, and vivid blue eyes. Her body was lithe and sensuous, her fingers gentle but strong as she unfastened his jumpsuit and pushed it off his shoulders, rubbing her face against his neck. "I am so sorry I was not home when you arrived this afternoon," she whispered.

"It was fortunate you were not," he managed, "as I had to go out again immediately."

It was days since he had touched her. He had no resistance. Coherent thought fled, and his next lucid moment was sometime later, in their bed upstairs, with no memory of how they had gotten there. Memories of their loving, though, were keenly sweet. Smiling, Korsal traced Seela's face with one finger. She caught it between her teeth, nipped it gently, her eyes offering—

Korsal's stomach rumbled, and Seela laughed. "Come, my husband; I will give you dinner. What happened at the dam?"

Satisfied now merely to be in Seela's presence, Korsal told her about the ice and the turbine as he ate. He did not tell her about Charlie Torrence, but the memory brought his train of thought back to his inspiration on the road. Finishing his meal—Seela's excellent cooking even more delicious after the hospital food he had been subjected to for the past few days—he poured a cup of coffee and told her with regret, "I have work to do. It's early."

In his office, he had to chase Kevin away from the computer terminal. The boy stared at him in astonishment. "I thought you'd be, uh, occupied for the rest of the evening."

"You think too much—about the wrong things," his father told him. "Why don't you give some thought to what happened to the power-cycle helmet?"

"Oh . . . I forgot to put it back. It's in my room," Kevin admitted. "I wore it yesterday, out at the airfield."

"What were you doing at the airfield when you were supposed to be observing quarantine?"

"They needed hoverer pilots. People started getting sick out at the geology camp, so they had to be evacuated. They needed every qualified pilot who wasn't sick, Father."

Korsal stared at his son. Kevin had been called on in his father's place. No, he realized, if he had not been stuck in the hospital they'd both have been called—but still, his boy was taking his place in the community as a man. "You did right. I am proud of you, Kevin. And tomorrow you and I have a job to do by hoverer—you pilot, and I'll navigate."

Kevin grinned, exposing his teeth in the Human way. He must have seen something in his father's eyes, though, for he pulled his lips down before the grin faded. Then he said, "I'm sorry I forgot to put the helmet back. I'll do it now."

Korsal turned his thoughts to the computer. Yes, he found, the engineering computer was still tied in with the hospital computer; probably it would remain so until the emergency was over. He began searching for the statistics Therian had been working on just before his death, statistics, he guessed, that had to do with the progress of the various strains of the disease in children.

The information was there, the computer willing to sort it out any way he wanted it: age, sex, race, even body weight. There was no pattern that he could see.

Then he played his hunch, asking for statistics on children of mixed heritage only. There were nearly four hundred on Nìsus. Almost all of them had had some form of the plague, but Korsal could still find no pattern.

Frustrated, he added in adult fusions, knowing in his gut that somehow the answer lay with those whose ancestry included people of varying races. Still the figures would not give him any useful information.

What had Therian seen? Was the Andorian's outcry merely the first ravings of madness? Why did Korsal persist in hearing it as his last statement of lucidity?

He strained to remember everything else Therian had said, the kinds of information he had been calling up. Occupations, locations—

"Computer," Korsal said suddenly, his guts tightening as if he were bracing for battle, "show me the pattern of spread of the three strains of the disease among all Nisus citizens of mixed heritage, their families, supervisors, teachers, students, partners, colleagues, and anyone else with whom they would have daily contact."

"Working," replied the cold mechanical voice.

And then the pattern appeared—undeniable, lethal. It took no Vulcan logic to perceive the deadly pattern. What glared at Korsal from the cold screen negated the entire purpose of Nisus.

Chapter Thirteen

ON BOARD THE *Enterprise,* Spock divided his time between his normal duties and the sickbay computer. He skipped his sleep periods until he had gone over everything Nisus or Starfleet's medical records had to offer. Then he gave in to Dr. McCoy's assertion that if he did not rest while there was nothing to do, he would not be ready to perform at optimum efficiency when they received new data.

There were times when McCoy could be annoyingly logical.

So Spock took his rest in sickbay . . . until he was wakened by whispered but vehement swearing. He swung off the couch and went to McCoy's office.

Leonard McCoy stared at a multicolored display coming to a halt on his computer screen. "Oh, God," he whispered. "Oh, no—that's too dirty a trick for even a virus to play!"

"What have you discovered, Doctor?"

"I didn't discover it—some engineer on Nisus did. Look at this spread pattern, Spock." Then he spoke to the computer. "Transfer to wall screen and replay."

The large wall screen used for monitoring surgery came to life. At first there was nothing but endless lines of statistics such as they had seen a dozen times before.

"Here's what happens when you color-map those

statistics for the victims' species," said McCoy. The names and numbers disappeared from the screen, and a multicolored grid appeared. "Blue for Andorians, green for Vulcans, red for Humans, and so forth. At first there's no particular pattern—until you look at a group of people who don't fit any species: those of mixed blood. There are hundreds of such people on Nisus, most of them under twenty standard years old."

Spock frowned. "Biologically, such a disparate group of people should not exhibit the same medical profile."

"Exactly why none of the medical personnel thought of them as a homogeneous group. Our engineer friend didn't know any better. Proceed to next screen," McCoy told the computer, and suddenly masses of multicolored specks all turned white. "Those are Nisus residents of mixed heritage," the doctor explained.

"Now," he continued, "this grid is by association —colored dots near the white dots represent family, neighbors, close friends, classmates, and colleagues of those of mixed blood. The varieties of the plague are circles around the dots: purple for the first, fairly harmless Strain A; gray for Strain B; and black for the deadly Strain C. Time analysis," he instructed the computer, and the screen began ticking off days in the upper-right-hand corner.

Circles appeared here and there around dots. The dots were of different colors; the circles were all purple.

As the chronometer ticked away the days, more and more dots were encircled, the white dots as often as the colored ones. Then the first gray circles representing Strain B began to appear . . . always around colored dots in close proximity to purple-circled white ones.

McCoy looked up at Spock, who schooled his features lest he betray anxiety. The pattern continued. White dots that had never had purple circles acquired gray ones—and near them the first black circles appeared, as often as not around circles of purple.

"The mutations to more deadly strains," Spock forced through the tightness in his throat, "appear to take place . . . in the systems of people of mixed blood."

"That's what it looks like," said McCoy. "It gets worse, though."

"Worse?" Spock wondered peripherally why McCoy had the sickbay temperature set so low as he controlled a shiver.

"In medicine you look for the solution in the problem," McCoy told him. "Vaccination uses disease against itself. It would be . . . logical to look to those people in whom the disease mutates for immunity to the mutated strains."

"I understand, Doctor," said Spock. "Their blood ought to develop antibodies against the new strains."

"Exactly," said McCoy. "Such people should exhibit an immunity that could be cultured from their blood and passed on to other people."

"Of course," Spock said with a hopeful nod. But even as he said it, the screen showed why that was not a solution. Some of the white dots began to be circled with black . . . including some already circled with purple.

Those in whom the disease mutated were no more immune than anyone else. "Whatever antibodies they develop," said Spock, "give no protection against advanced strains. The disease mutates in hybrid people, but we will not be able to produce a vaccine from their blood."

The screen faded to blank silver. McCoy rested his head in one hand, rubbing at his temple. "That certainly settles one thing, Spock. You're not going down to Nisus."

Chapter Fourteen

DESPITE SEELA'S BEST efforts, Korsal spent a restless night after he had transmitted his discovery about the plague's pattern of spread to the hospital's epidemiological section. That his own children were apparently immune to this disease did not quell his anxiety. What new and grotesque variation of the plague might appear tomorrow, possibly attack his sons —and turn them into incubators of new horrors?

He longed for a physical enemy—something he could see, take a disruptor to, or a knife, or even his bare hands. Then he could *do* something to protect his family!

Seela had finally fallen asleep, curled up against his side in animal abandon. As dawn broke, he looked at her soft green skin, her sweet, innocent face, and remembered how badly she wanted children. Hers and his.

It would take a great deal of help from the geneticists; Klingon and Orion were far more different than Klingon and Human. But it had been done before, and Korsal had had few qualms about starting a second family before the plague.

Now . . . was this plague a message from nature that the Klingons were right to consider fusions somehow inferior? He could not believe that—not in the face of Kevin and Karl.

Almost at his thought, he heard movement in the hallway. Kevin was up, eager to be off to the airfield. Korsal got up and dressed, too, and joined his son for breakfast.

Seela, so perfectly domestic that sometimes Korsal wished for some flaw in her housekeeping, had left coffee ready to brew at the touch of a switch and two meals in the stasis bin. All they had to do was heat them for a few moments.

That was nothing new to Korsal or Kevin; before Seela, they had warmed up preprepared meals as often as not. The difference was that even before Cathy had left, the meals were usually commercially prepared. Seela's were her own cooking.

And never since he had married Seela had Korsal had to dial blandly inoffensive nutrition from the kitchen console. He wondered if it was even stocked anymore.

They ate quickly and took a jug of fresh hot coffee with them. The spring weather had disappeared again. It would be cold in the mountains. They put on boots, sweaters, and heavy jackets, and Korsal tossed Kevin the helmet. "We'll have to get another of these," he said. "Now that you've got your hoverer license we may both be flying, like this morning, or have one of us flying and one using the cycle."

"We can borrow a spare helmet at the field today," said Kevin. "When they called me the other day they asked me to bring one because they'd lent out all the extras. I guess I was at the bottom of their list of pilots."

"You were *on* it," Korsal reminded him, "and you performed responsibly. I doubt that you will be at the bottom of the list the next time pilots are needed."

The dispatcher at the airfield echoed Korsal's sentiments. She already had a craft booked for them, telling Korsal, "Your son proved himself quite a pilot on that evacuation mission. But it's a good thing you're with him today. A storm's brewing in the mountains—you could run into rough weather three or four hours from now."

"Dangerous?" Korsal asked.

"Shouldn't be for a pilot with your experience," the Lemnorian woman replied. "Still, you know how unpredictable these mountains can be. Turn back if it gets too rough."

Korsal's expectations of his son's skill proved true. He had never flown with Kevin before, for Kevin's lessons had been with a licensed instructor, and the day he had come proudly home with his license had been only one day before the closing of the airfield for all but priority flights.

Hoverers were small aircraft that skimmed across the terrain, ten or twelve meters above the ground. Since they operated on a combination of air cushion and antigravs, it was a rough ride, rising and falling as did the ground below.

The skill in piloting a hoverer came in compensating for terrain: the craft responded differently to water, trees, plowed land, buildings. An unskilled pilot would let the craft jolt and buck each time the terrain changed—and it was quite possible to crash into a mountain or a tall building if he misjudged how quickly the craft's sensors could react.

Kevin proved a smooth pilot. Korsal gave his son the left-hand seat, but there were dual controls; he could take over if they met up with something beyond Kevin's experience.

The navigation tricorder led them across the dam

and along the river fed by mountain tributaries. Korsal was pleased at the way Kevin maintained altitude. When he said it aloud, the boy grinned. "I had to come up this way on the rescue mission. I'd practiced over the dam for my license, but that was the first time I flew the river. I took some jolts that almost shook my teeth loose, till I got the hang of it. But carrying evacuees, on the way back, I didn't shake them up much at all."

"And you didn't shake the bolts loose in the hoverer, either," said Korsal with his engineer's respect for complex machinery.

Although clouds gathered on the mountain's peak, here on the lower slopes it was a beautiful morning. The mountains near the city still had native plants and small animals, but among them were pine and movidel trees, wild roses starting to put out leaves and buds, and wildlife from a dozen planets.

Startled deer, drinking at the water's edge, fled at the approach of the hoverer. A family of *sehlats,* allowed to go wild, reared up and challenged as they sailed by.

"Here's where we turned off before, up to the geology camp." Kevin pointed left along one of the tributaries. "It's new territory to me from here on."

"Just keep your eyes on where you're going," Korsal told him. "It winds even more as we get higher."

There was snow on the ground and ice here and there in the river, although Korsal saw nothing large enough to damage a turbine. Besides, these small pieces would melt away before they got so far.

But the higher they climbed, the more ice there was. Some bigger pieces indicated that the screening system was indeed not working. There were clouds overhead now, and a fine mist of rain reduced visibility.

The hills on either side of the river grew steeper, until they flew within a twisting canyon, with rapids below. Radio contact with the airfield was lost—too much solid rock between them and the city now.

Spits of snow mixed with the rain. Wind buffeted the hoverer, and Korsal grasped his controls to help Kevin hold it steady. Had the boy been alone, Korsal would have expected him to turn back at this point; he would have done so himself if they hadn't been so near their goal.

"We're almost there," he told his son. "It has to be the lowest one that's not functioning—"

They swung around a curve, and saw it.

The safety sluice was a shambles of cracked concrete and twisted metal supports. "*Khest!*" exclaimed Kevin—the first time Korsal knew his son knew the Klingonaase obscenity. Even a Vulcan, Korsal judged, would have decided that the cause was sufficient.

Obviously the piece of ice that had crushed the turbine had been much larger when it smashed through here. What was left of the screening system wouldn't hold anything back. This had to be repaired at once.

"Activate the cameras," Korsal told his son. "I'll maneuver in as close as I dare. Get as good shots as you can; this repair must have emergency priority."

Korsal brought the craft in low over the smashed safety sluice, fighting the gale until Kevin said, "Got it!" then letting the wind lift and spin the hoverer like a leaf tossed in a whirlwind.

"Father!" Kevin gasped, reaching for the controls.

"Let be!" Korsal ordered. "I fought that updraft all

the way down, and deliberately let it lift us again. You'll learn those tricks, Kevin." He leveled off at normal maneuvering height. "Now—do we go up and see if the safety sluice above this one is also damaged, or do we go back?"

"I've never flown in this kind of wind and snow," said Kevin. "I don't know how to judge it, Father."

"Neither do I," Korsal admitted. "If we can manage a few more kilometers, we can see whether there's more ice ready to break loose. If not, and if the safety above this one is undamaged, the repairs are not so urgent that we have to risk a party out here when winter is still brewing up storms."

They decided to continue as far as visibility continued adequate—and flew out of the storm around the next bend. "Good," said Korsal, eyeing the weather sensors. Walled in as they were, the sensors had little to work with; right now they proclaimed all clear ahead as far as they could reach.

The wind remained treacherous. Several times Kevin had to stop scouting for problems below in order to help Korsal fight the controls.

They swung around another curve and faced a wall of pure blizzard.

The weather sensor began whistling loudly.

"Time to go home!" said Korsal, and swung the hoverer around on its vertical axis.

"I think I had that figured out for myself!" said Kevin.

"You were looking for a senior science project, weren't you, Kevin?" Korsal asked.

"Yes."

"Why don't you try designing a system to send a warning to the dam if anything breaks through these safety sluices?"

"If it were possible, why didn't you design it years ago, Father?"

"Because I never thought of it until today!"

The boy was silent as they sailed through the clear curves of the canyon, alert to the ever-changing wind. Then he said, thinking aloud, "It would have to withstand weather and animals, yet go off when something was really wrong. That's the problem, isn't it? Any system sensitive enough to sound a genuine alert sends too many false alarms."

"That's the problem," Korsal agreed.

"It has to include a computer capable of judgment —but computers are too sensitive to cold and dampness."

Smiling to himself, Korsal listened to his son reason out the problem. By the time they got home, he would probably have a prototype design in mind.

His smile wrenched into a snarl as they swung around the bend that concealed the shattered safety sluice and found that the storm had closed in behind them.

They faced a wall of whirling snow and ice, completely blocking the narrow canyon. Korsal fought the hoverer to a standstill and stared at the deadly whiteness. "Unforgivable!" he said. "We have allowed the enemy to surround us."

Out of the corner of his eye he caught the sharp movement of his son's head as Kevin turned to look at him. "It . . . it's a storm, Father," he said uncertainly. "It isn't sentient."

"I know—but remember what you learned on Survival?"

"Nature is more dangerous than an acknowledged enemy, for it so often appears one's friend that one never expects the moment it turns and casually kills."

He heard the tightness in the boy's voice. Kevin had passed his Survival at age six—and had obviously never given a thought to the lessons again.

I have failed as a father, Korsal thought. *My sons do not think like Klingons.* "Suggestions?" he prompted.

"Always assume Nature is an enemy," Kevin replied. He immediately reached out to change the setting on the weather scanner, having it search behind them. A faint trace indicated that the blizzard that had caused them to retreat was pursuing them. "We are cut off forward and rear. We cannot scan to the sides because of the canyon walls, but our only chance is up and out."

Had the situation not been so grave, Korsal would have taken pleasure at the way his son responded.

"Will the craft do it?" he asked.

"Equipment capable," Kevin responded instantly. "I took one up and over the dam."

"You *what!*"

"I told my instructor I had calculated that—"

"Never mind! You'd better remember *how* you did it."

"The wind was steady over the top of the dam, providing lift," Kevin explained. "I don't know if we can get over the canyon wall here, unless we can find an updraft, but . . . that's our only way out."

"Alternatives?"

"Set down—but where?"

Where, indeed? Below them the river was already spring-swollen, filling the canyon from one side to the other. The hoverer was not watertight, and if it had been it was never built to be a raft. The river would simply carry them into the rapids and smash them on the rocks.

While they held their hasty conversation, both

fought the bucking controls. "Visibility deteriorating," Kevin noted.

It was not news to his father. "Let's go, then." He let the craft slew left, then right, feeling for rising wind. When he found it, he rode it toward the right-hand canyon wall. "Friend or enemy?"

"If the enemy provides an advantage," Kevin replied, "take it and use it against him. There. Up that rockslide! It'll take that angle, Father."

They rose rapidly until they reached the limit of the thrusters against the canyon floor. Now they had only angular momentum, tilting the small craft crazily to thrust against rocks, ice, canyon wall. Korsal applied more power until the engines wailed in protest. The snow closed in around them.

"Visibility zero," Kevin reported.

The hoverer's instruments were not meant for this kind of flying, but they were all Korsal had to go by as he flew "by the seat of his pants" as his Human instructor had once called it.

Tossed by the wind, they couldn't tell whether they were rising at all. "Altimeter on barometric!" he told Kevin. It had been reading their distance from the nearest surface below them. Now it registered a slow but definite climb. "Good," said Korsal, peering through the flying snow.

"Antigrav warning," Kevin said suddenly. "Overheating!"

Korsal saw the red light flashing, but he had no choice now—it was either up and out, or crash into the river.

They were still climbing, but yawing and heaving until he did not know which direction to steer. If he leveled off too soon, they would crash into the canyon wall; if he did *not* level off soon—

Its warning light ignored, the antigrav malfunction siren began to sound. "Altimeter relative to surface!" Korsal ordered, eyed it as he urged the craft toward the horizontal—they were safe, some two meters above solid ground!

He leveled off, blind, intending to settle on the canyon lip and wait out the storm.

But he had not reckoned with the overheated antigravs.

He heard the warning sizzle as they settled on layers of snow and ice. "The thrusters!" he exclaimed. "They've melted through their insulation! Kevin —jump! Run!"

Cold air swept into the tiny cabin as Kevin opened the left-hand door and vaulted into the snow.

Korsal thrust open the door on his side—just as the explosion came.

He was lifted, tossed through the air like just another snow pellet, and slammed against something huge and hard. He heard ribs snap, then felt the pain, but for a moment he was still able to think as his body slid bonelessly to the ground.

Kevin! He wanted to shout, but had no strength, no breath. Had the boy jumped far enough from the craft? Or had the explosion caught him too?

Korsal tried to move, but could not. He tried to shout, but produced only a muffled gurgle. Then blackness and cold shut out all thought.

Chapter Fifteen

WHEN SPOCK EXPLAINED the new findings on the Nisus plague to Captain Kirk, he saw his friend's face pale. But immediately the Human's natural optimism reasserted itself. "It's a clue, Spock. Medicine's not my field, but it's McCoy's, and all these other experts'. They'll build on this information to find a vaccination or a cure."

"What security classification do you want placed on the information?" asked Spock.

"Need to know," Kirk replied, "and continue to code all reports to Starfleet. Bones will brief everyone on the medical mission, but there's no point giving this information to the rest of the crew . . . or any of the other passengers."

"My parents—" Spock suggested, but Kirk cut him off.

"There is no reason to worry them, Spock. *You* are not setting foot on that planet."

Spock nodded wearily. Vulcans were realists, basing their lives on facts and logic. Nevertheless, he found it troublesome that his hybrid nature was now a physical liability. Many times in his life he had blamed illogic or emotion on his Human blood—but those things were still his choice, under his control. This mutating plague was not.

A puzzle like this plague was irresistible. Until the new information had come in last night, he had been determined to find a "logical" way to beam down to Nisus with McCoy.

As happened only too disconcertingly often, Kirk had followed his train of thought. "I'm frustrated too, Spock," the captain said. "No, not over as serious a matter, but I can't beam down to Nisus, either—and that means I have to deliver by viewscreen a message I'd dearly love to deliver in person."

"And what is that?" Spock responded.

"Seems there is a young man on Nisus who has just pushed me out of the record books for youngest admission to Starfleet Academy." Kirk did not appear at all unhappy to have his record broken.

"A Vulcan?" Spock suggested.

Kirk grinned. "Not unless Vulcans have changed their pattern of naming. This young man's name is Kevin Katasai."

Katasai! Spock felt his eyebrows rise involuntarily.

Kirk saw, and frowned. "What—you know him, Spock?"

"No. However . . . the engineer who uncovered the spread pattern of the plague is one Korsal Katasai, presumably a relative of this successful candidate."

Kirk's frown grew even deeper. "Korsal? That sounds like—" He broke off with a laugh. "Come on, Spock; it's just a coincidence! Starfleet's certainly not going to admit Klingons to the Academy!"

"You are probably right, Captain," Spock replied. It did seem a most unlikely thing for Starfleet to do.

They left the briefing room, but Kirk was in no hurry to return to the bridge. He accompanied Spock to the large mess hall, where most of their passengers were having breakfast. There they joined Sarek and Amanda, who were eating breakfast with Daniel Corrigan and his wife, T'Mir.

Spock sat down with his tray just in time to hear his mother say to T'Mir, "I have always found that there is a far greater difference in ways of thinking between male and female than between Vulcan and Human."

Daniel gave his wife a grin that spoke volumes, but T'Mir looked demurely down at her plate, then back to Spock's mother. "I am beginning to understand that," she said softly.

Sarek arched an eyebrow and said to Daniel, *"Mulier est hominis confusio."*

The Human doctor's grin turned to helpless laughter. T'Mir stared from her husband to Sarek and back. "What did he say?" she demanded.

"Woman is man's joy and all his bliss," Daniel choked out.

Amanda gave Sarek a look compounded of amusement and annoyance.

T'Mir caught it, saw that her own husband could not meet her eyes, and said, "Daniel, that is not what it means!"

"It is," he replied, "according to an ancient authority from Earth, one Chauntecleer."

With that Spock, whose Latin was good enough that he had recognized the true meaning of the saying, remembered where it came from. Chaucer. Trust Sarek to cast his jokes in literary obscurity! Glancing at Kirk, he saw his captain smothering a grin, and remembered Kirk's passion for ancient books.

T'Mir cocked an eyebrow at Sarek and said, "I shall have to look up that reference."

"Precisely what you should do," Spock's father

replied, exactly as if he were speaking to one of his students.

It had occasionally occurred to Spock, since he had reached maturity, that possibly his adolescent decision to apply to Starfleet Academy rather than the Vulcan Academy of Sciences might have been influenced by a desire not to have either of his parents as a teacher, especially his father. Sarek professed not to understand the concept of humor, but was reputed frequently to produce the same reaction in his non-Vulcan students that he had just created in Dr. Corrigan.

When the thought occurred, though, Spock quickly suppressed it, as he did today.

As the small commotion at their table faded, Spock became aware of something at the food console. A young Vulcan woman was waiting for her choice to appear in the cubicle when Sendet came up to her. Spock could not hear their words, but he saw the woman give a negative movement of her head.

The cubicle door slid open and the woman removed her tray and started away. Sendet followed.

As they approached the table where Spock sat, he could hear Sendet saying, "You must listen to me, T'Pina. You have the strength, the intelligence to be one of us. Let me show you what comes of practicing this grand ideal of IDIC."

"Sendet," T'Pina said flatly, "I do not wish to speak to you further. Please go away."

By this time Kirk had noticed, but even as he shoved his coffee aside and started to rise, another voice spoke loudly. "Sendet! Let the woman hear, along with everyone else. Then she will have facts with which to make her choice."

Satat stood just inside the door, flanked by other Followers of T'Vet. Now he strode forward, toward Kirk.

The captain rose, and so did Spock, automatically assuming a position behind him and to one side, where he could defend his back if necessary. From the other side of the room, Lieutenant Uhura, the only other line officer there, got up and moved to a similar position on Kirk's other side.

Satat looked over the group at the table with a sneer. "I take it you have not told them, Captain Kirk. Surely these practitioners of IDIC"—he spoke the words as if they tasted bad—"would not sit calmly eating breakfast if they knew the secret data supplied to your medical unit during the night."

"What do you know about such data?" Kirk countered.

"You are a fool, Captain. Do you think because we practice the ancient philosophies that we are technological savages? There are computer experts among us. We have been monitoring all data relayed to the *Enterprise.*"

Their monitoring had never been noticed because no one had ever considered that the Followers of T'Vet might do such a thing. Kirk looked to Spock for an explanation. "Any computer technologist could program one of our standard monitors to interface with the sickbay computer," he said. "Why did you do it, Satat? You gave your word not to interfere with the operation of the *Enterprise.*"

"Our monitoring did not interfere—but it gave us the justification for all that we stand for. This unnamed plague is irrefutable evidence of what happens when Vulcans forget their true heritage, turn from warriors into philosophers, and pollute their bloodlines with alien genes! Infinite diversity exists—no one can dispute that. But infinite combination is against nature. You see the results on Nisus!"

"Captain Kirk," said Sarek, "do you know what this man is talking about?"

"Yes, I know," Kirk said grimly. "The latest discovery concerning the Nisus plague. We knew it kept mutating, becoming more severe with each new strain. What we have just learned is that the deadlier strains develop . . . when it attacks people of mixed heritage."

Sarek and Amanda looked at one another and then at Spock. Sarek raised his hand, and Amanda touched her first two fingers to his. Daniel Corrigan also reached for his wife's hand, but gripped it in the Human fashion.

And Satat continued triumphantly, "This disease is only the latest symptom of the corruption spread from Earth and Vulcan to every world which has allowed high-sounding ideals to overpower fact. Give the plague its proper name now, for its true source. Call it the IDIC Epidemic!"

Chapter Sixteen

KORSAL AWOKE TO bitter cold and pain. He did not know where he was. Everything was a white and gray blur. When his eyes focused, he recognized that the white was snow, falling all around him so thickly that he could make out nothing more than a few meters away. The gray shapes were rocks and trees.

Memory returned. Kevin!

He tried to sit up, and pain stabbed through his right side. He tried to take a deep breath, to call his son's name, but again the sharp pain stopped him.

"Father?"

The voice was faint, blown away by the wind. But Kevin was alive!

Despite the pain, he drew breath and tried to shout. It came out a croak. "Kevin!"

"Father? Are you all right?"

Again he tried to answer, managing only a gasping wheeze.

But there was a faint shape out there in the whiteness now. Was it just a tree branch blown by the wind? No! Something moving toward him—

"Father!" Kevin knelt beside him. "You're hurt!"

"Just . . . broken ribs," Korsal got out.

"Lie still, then," said Kevin, and delved into Korsal's pockets for his gloves, which he had taken off inside the hoverer. Kevin helped his father put them on over shaking hands. "The antigrav engines exploded."

"I know. Are you hurt?"

"No. I was thrown clear. Lost my glasses, though. Don't try to talk. I know what to do; we just have to survive till the storm's over. They'll send a search party. The fire in the hoverer is almost out. In this snow it'll cool off quickly, and then I'll see what I can salvage."

"Not . . . in the blizzard," Korsal gasped. "Lucky you found me."

"We make our own luck," Kevin said. It was a Human saying, but it could as easily have been Klingon. "You can't move around to keep warm, so I'm going to build a shelter and start a fire." He took off his jacket and laid it over Korsal. "Exercise will keep me warm till I get the fire going."

Kevin and Korsal both wore heavy utility knives inside their boots—badge of manhood, earned at Survival, but also an all-purpose instrument that served as well in a fight as it did now. Kevin cut a low-hanging limb from a pine tree and used it first as a broom to clear the snow away from where Korsal lay.

He made a bed of pine boughs to insulate them from the frozen ground, and with great care helped his father onto it. Korsal felt odd, being supported and cared for by his son—as if they had suddenly changed places. He was deeply proud of the boy. In a genuine emergency, Kevin was reacting calmly and competently. Because of that, they would probably survive.

Kevin constructed a lean-to, Korsal unable to contribute more than the effort of putting points on the limbs before Kevin drove them into the packed snow.

Fortunately, the boy did not have to search far for

wood, as the snow was falling ever more thickly, the wind howling. Korsal watched him strip wet bark back, shred the dry inside of a limb into tinder. "Now," he said, "how do we light it? I have a magnifying glass but no sun, steel but no flint—there will be firestarters in the hoverer's emergency kit, if it wasn't blown up."

"There've been no secondary explosions," said Korsal. "I think you dare go to the hoverer to get the kit."

But the snow was now falling so thick and fast that although it was noonday, darkness had settled over them. Korsal peered out of the shelter and decided, "No sign of stopping. In that you could get lost and freeze to death not ten meters away. It's getting colder. We'll have to start the fire by friction."

It was not an easy task in the cold, damp air, but Kevin worked diligently, spinning a stick amid the tinder he had created. "At least my hands are getting warm," he joked. "I can't feel my feet anymore."

Nor could Korsal feel his. In fact, his whole body was getting numb. Perhaps the best thing would be just to go to sleep, let his body heal—

"Father! Father, wake up!"

He was hauled to a sitting position, gasping at the pain in his broken ribs.

"Wake up!" Kevin demanded. "I won't let you freeze to death!"

"Snowing . . . not cold enough—" Korsal muttered.

"The wind chill is!" said Kevin. "Stay *awake*, Father. Talk to me!"

"What?" He cracked open one eye, to find his son peering myopically at him.

"Talk to me!" Kevin demanded again. "Tell me

. . . tell me about the empire. What if I go there someday? What will I have to do to be accepted?"

"Fight," Korsal said groggily.

"In the military. Yes—but what else? I want to be a scientist, like you, not a soldier."

"They want . . . weapons."

Kevin picked up his tinder and spinning stick again. "Tell me about families. What was it like growing up in the Klingon Empire?"

"Like here. Passed Survival . . . went to school. Always good in school, better than my brothers, but they were bigger, stronger. Krel—he was the oldest. I remember . . . he taught me *klin zha*. By the time I was eight I always won. And he always challenged again. . . ."

"Father?" sharply from Kevin.

"I couldn't win at wrestling, shooting, running. None of the others would game with me. But Krel —he always . . . always gave me the chance to do what I was good at."

"I'll remember that," said Kevin. "Karl's much better at *klin zha* than I am. I should play with him anyway."

"No need," Korsal said softly. "He's better than I am too—and I taught him." He opened his eyes as a smell of smoke teased his nostrils, saw Kevin leaning over, gently blowing on a tiny wisp of flame.

"Stel says that's the sign of a good teacher—when the student outperforms him."

Korsal's foggy mind had to grope for the name. His eyes drifted shut again. Stel. Kevin's mathematics teacher. Starfleet. Kevin's score on the Academy entrance exam must have been higher than his teacher's.

"Stel is wise," said Korsal.

"Lots of Vulcans are—or seem to be," said Kevin. "Sometimes I think it's because they never say very much, so what they do say sounds profound."

Korsal smiled at his son's astuteness. Warmth was beginning to coax him back to life, and he opened his eyes to see Kevin feeding a cozy little fire.

They talked, and Kevin packed snow up the sides of their shelter, the fire creating a little ice cave for them. "Kai Kevin," said his father. "We can hold on until rescue comes."

After a time there was a break in the whirling snow, and Kevin said, "I'm going to see if I can get the emergency kit out of the hoverer. Then I'll get some more firewood."

"It's warm in here now," said Korsal. "Put my jacket over yours—and my gloves too."

Kevin accepted without protest and went out into the snowy dimness. Korsal watched him go, hoping the thick low clouds would not start dumping their burden again before Kevin could finish his tasks. He fed the fire sparingly, hoping Kevin would soon have the hatchet from the emergency kit. The threatening snow would not allow the boy to forage very far, and at the same time it was covering fallen limbs and making walking nearly impossible.

It seemed a very long time before Kevin returned with an armload of snowy branches, breathless from the effort simply of struggling through the knee-deep snow.

Hunkering down before the fire, Kevin took off his gloves and spread his fingers to the flames. "I'll go back for more wood as soon as I warm up," he said. Then, "Father . . . the hoverer is gone."

". . . gone?"

"The heat of the thrusters must have melted

through the layers of ice and snow on the canyon rim, and that tilted it. The wind probably helped it along. You can see the path where it slid, and fell down into the river."

Korsal's broken ribs stabbed as he drew a sharp breath. No emergency kit meant no hatchet, no food, no blanket, no light, no medical supplies. "It's all right," he said. "All we have to do is stay alive until rescue comes—and surely that will be by morning."

"Yes, Father. Surely by morning," said Kevin. Korsal realized he was being humored. "I'll get more wood now," said Kevin, "so I can make another trip before night falls."

Again Korsal looked outside, up at the sky. The clouds were solid, black, snow-filled. The snow began again before Kevin returned, and a raging wind had the blizzard howling around their shelter until long after night fell. Kevin could not go out again for wood, even if there was a chance of finding it under the layers of snow. They fed the fire as sparingly as possible to try to make the wood last until daybreak, melted snow in one of the helmets, and drank the hot water in an attempt to keep warm from inside.

But the temperature was falling, penetrating into their small haven. They layered their clothes back on and huddled together to share body warmth as the cold seeped in.

"Tell me more about your brother Krel," Kevin said. "Maybe someday I'll get to meet my uncles."

"He died," said Korsal. "Died in a battle with the Federation, six years ago. I never got to tell him I knew . . . he gamed with me when I was a boy . . . so I could . . . win . . . at something."

"Father?"

Korsal heard the word, but could not find the

energy to answer. Anything else Kevin said he did not hear.

He sat down before a board set up for the Reflective Game. Across from him sat his brother Krel. He smiled without showing his teeth and gestured to Krel to make the first move.

Chapter Seventeen

CAPTAIN JAMES. T. KIRK sat on the bridge of the USS *Enterprise* as she entered orbit around Nisus at last. Leonard McCoy stood at his left shoulder, watching the viewscreen.

The planet was Earth-like, with vast oceans surrounding one large continent and a number of good-sized islands. The science colony occupied only one small area of the continent; there was plenty of room to spare if the population increased.

It appeared deceptively peaceful and beautiful. McCoy echoed his thought: "Looking at it from up here, you'd never know they had all that trouble."

"Well, it's your job to go down and solve the problem, Bones," Kirk said, swinging his chair around so he could look into the weary blue eyes. "We're gonna miss you, you know."

"Just don't get into too much trouble while I'm gone," McCoy replied, never one for fond farewells.

As he turned to climb the step to the turbolift, Spock left his station. "Doctor," he said, "I trust that one of your noxious potions will quickly destroy that virus."

"You better believe it, Spock," McCoy replied with a grin. "But if it doesn't, maybe I'll try beads and rattles."

"However you do it," Spock said solemnly, "please protect yourself. It would be a great inconvenience for the *Enterprise* to have to break in a new chief medical officer."

"Oh, I certainly wouldn't want to inflict *your* anatomy on some other physician," the doctor agreed, and turned to the turbolift. The doors opened. "See you soon."

"Good luck, Bones," said Kirk.

To his surprise—and McCoy's, he saw as the doctor's eyes widened—Spock echoed, "Indeed, Doctor. Good luck."

Then the turbolift doors closed, and the reports began coming in from the transporter room as the medical experts were beamed down to Nisus.

As soon as the transporter reports ended, Kirk called the Starfleet liaison officer on Nisus. There was no military installation here, but there were always numerous Fleet scientific staff on the planet. At the moment, senior officer was Commander Carmilla Smythe. He took a moment to check her file, as he had never met her, and discovered that her specialty was ethnography. What in the world was an ethnographer doing at the science colony?

He called her office, where an assistant told him, "Dr. Smythe is at home, recovering."

"Recovering?"

"Yes, sir. She was very fortunate—she is one of very few to survive the most recent strain of the plague."

"Perhaps I shouldn't bother her," said Kirk. "Who is next in command?"

"Command?" the young man asked in obvious confusion. "Oh—you mean Starfleet personnel. Uh, Master Thorven died a few days ago. Dr. Chang was taken to the hospital yesterday. I'm sorry, sir, but I'm not Starfleet. I don't know the line of command on Nisus. If it's not classified, could you tell me what you need to talk to Dr.—uh, Commander Smythe about?"

"A young citizen of Nisus has gained early admission to Starfleet Academy."

"Oh—*good* news! Let me give you Dr. Smythe's home code; it'll do her good to hear that."

For a few moments, Kirk thought he was not going to get an answer, but then his screen filled with an extreme close-up of a woman, backing off after pressing the answer switch on her own console. "Smythe here," she said. Then, studying him, "Captain Kirk? The *Enterprise* has arrived? Thank goodness!"

Now that she was in proper range for the scanners on her console, Kirk got a good look at her. She was standing, leaning on a cane, and he could see a cast-brace on one foot that peeked out from under her robe.

Even though she wore one of those one-size-fits-all flowing garments favored by women whose privacy might be intruded on even in their own quarters, he could see that she was too thin, too pale. He wanted to put an arm about her frail shoulders . . . but she was just an image on a screen. A very attractive image, actually, the youth of her face belying the premature gray of her hair.

"Please sit down, Commander," was all that he could do about making her comfortable. "I see that you've been injured."

Her dark eyes narrowed for a moment as if the memory pained her. "Yes. It seems that I attacked one of my assistants. This new version of the plague often starts that way. He was able to evade and subdue me, but I sustained a broken ankle. However, I am lucky: I did not kill anyone. Not all victims have been so fortunate."

"So we hear," said Kirk. "I am glad that you recovered, and I have news that I hope will speed your recuperation. You recommended one Kevin Katasai for early admission to Starfleet Academy."

"You mean they actually—?" For a moment her face lit with a smile, but then it clouded again.

"Yes," Kirk assured her, "he's been admitted."

"I hope it's not too late," was her strange reply.

"Don't tell me he's ill with the plague?"

"Kevin?" She looked at him with a puzzled frown. "Surely the doctors transmitted the information on immunity. Kevin's not going to get the plague, but right now we're not sure he's still alive."

"What do you mean you're not sure?"

"We've had some trouble with ice hitting the power plant at the dam. Yesterday morning Kevin and his father took a hoverer up the mountain to check the safety sluices, see where the ice was getting through. They haven't come back; there's a storm raging up there now. The automatic emergency beacon from the hoverer is on, but we can't get search parties into the area. There are two possibilities: they landed and turned the beacon on . . . or the hoverer crashed."

"Damn!" said Kirk. Then, "Wait—give me the coordinates of that beacon, we'll home on it, scan around it for them, and beam them—"

He remembered. *"Hell* and damn!" he reiterated. "We can't beam anybody on board because of that plague!"

"They're not carriers, Captain. The doctors tested Korsal very thoroughly, and his younger son Karl has been through every test our doctors could conceive of in the past two days. Klingons are definitely immune to the plague."

". . . Klingons? They *are* Klingons?"

"Yes—but Korsal is a scientist, and his sons grew up right here on Nisus. Never mind—if you can locate them and beam them to the *Enterprise,* you'll save their lives. *If* they're still alive."

"Perhaps we could hold them in stasis without materializing them on board," Kirk suggested, "and redirect them to the Nisus hospital."

"Captain—they're *not* contagious, but they will probably be very weak. A two-man hoverer doesn't carry much survival equipment, and if they crashed they may be injured. I know that what you suggest has been done, but I also know that being held in stasis while coordinates are changed causes temporary weakness in a perfectly healthy person."

"How would you know that?" Kirk asked.

"It's not classified; any member of Starfleet can look it up. I've never liked allowing my molecules to be scrambled, but since it is necessary, I found out everything I could about the procedure, including experimental techniques."

"You'll have to meet our Dr. McCoy," said Kirk.

"That's another reason to beam Korsal and Kevin to your ship: the hospital here is impossibly over-crowded, and all personnel and facilities are working against the plague. Kevin and his father will get much better treatment in your sickbay. Now, Captain —could we please dispense with further argument and rescue those two men? They could be dying while we're talking."

"You're right, of course. Hold on." Kirk punched

the engineering switch on his intraship console. "Scotty, I need you to do some fancy transporter work."

"Aye, Captain."

Tersely, he explained the situation.

"Klingons?" his chief engineer protested. "We're under strict orders not to beam so much as a scientific journal up from Nisus—and you want to beam *Klingons* aboard?"

"That's an order, Scotty."

Only a moment's pause. Then, "Aye, Captain. I'll calibrate my scanners."

Kirk turned back to the viewscreen, giving Commander Smythe a confident smile. "Once Scotty goes to work on it, consider it done."

"Thank you, Captain. I just hope you're in time."

"We'll know in a few minutes," Kirk told her. "If you'd like to stay on-line—"

"Definitely!" she replied.

"While we're waiting, would you satisfy my curiosity? The records show that you're an ethnographer. What are you doing on Nisus, instead of off studying new civilizations? Typical Starfleet assignment foul-up?"

"No, indeed!" she replied. "I've been studying the culture here on Nisus, which is unique in our galaxy —there's even more ethnic diversity than in nineteenth- and twentieth-century America, with far more interdependence. I *asked* for this assignment. I thought I had finished my study and was about to request reassignment when the plague began. Now, suddenly, I have an entire new study: the reaction of Nisus' unique society to crisis."

She sighed. "I will probably get a book and a promotion out of it. To tell the truth, Captain, I'd have been far happier with just the original mono-graph!"

"I understand," he said. "Another question: how did you come to recommend a Klingon for admission to Starfleet Academy?"

"Kevin's mother is Commodore Catherine Patemchek. But I'd recommend Kevin solely on his own merits. He's brilliant, clever—"

"How about loyal?" Kirk asked. "What happens if he comes up against Klingons in battle?"

"Captain, I recommended Kevin because I believe the Academy will give him the best education possible —and he has a mind deserving of such education. Yes, he will eventually face taking the oath of loyalty to the Federation if he continues to graduation and a commission. I hope he will choose the Federation. As I understand it, the Klingon Empire will force a choice on him anyway in the next couple of years; if he does not enter *their* required military training, they'll disown him."

"I see," said Kirk. "You view him as a prize worth fighting for, then."

Even through the viewscreen, Kirk saw Smythe struggle to curb annoyance. "Kevin is not a piece of equipment. He is a young man who is going to contribute technological advances to someone—and I prefer that the someone be the Federation. Kevin's no more the career military type than his father is. The whole family are thinkers and dreamers. Kevin will *design* starships, not command them."

"They don't sound like any Klingons I've ever met."

"Of course not—because in Starfleet we only meet the soldiers. And whom do the Klingons meet? *Our* soldiers. Captain Kirk, we always say that starship crews represent the best the Federation has to offer. But surely you would not say that you and your crew are average Federation citizens?"

"No."

"There you are," she said. "I hope you'll have a chance to get to know Kevin and Korsal. Except for their scientific brilliance, they are average citizens of the Klingon Empire. Or at least Korsal is; Kevin has never been there. Anyway, you'll find them quite different from the warriors we're accustomed to confronting."

"Captain!" Scotty's voice intruded on their conversation.

"Are you ready to beam our guests aboard?" Kirk asked.

"Not yet—but we've located the beacon. We're scanning. But Captain, I just discovered something in the transporter room. The controls have been reset."

"What do you mean?"

"I left them not half an hour since, set to Nisus Transporter Central. When I came back, they were set to beam down—but to a point somewhere out on the ocean. As if someone had changed them at random, perhaps to cover an unauthorized beaming."

"Check last transporter use!" said Kirk. It wouldn't tell them much except which direction it had gone. Had something really been beamed down into the ocean?

There was silence for a few moments. Then Scotty's voice again. "Captain . . . I canna tell where it came from, but the last transporter function was *to* the *Enterprise.* In spite of your orders, someone or something has been beamed aboard from Nisus."

Chapter Eighteen

KORSAL HELD HIS son in his arms and watched the last of the wood Kevin had gathered go up in flames. When it sputtered and went out, the little warmth the fire had given disappeared as if it had never been.

Twice more since they had crashed, Kevin had foraged for wood during brief breaks in the blizzard. The second time he had had to dig for it, and returned with frostbitten hands and a pitiful supply of twigs.

His son had fought well. If the storm had lasted only the night, they would have survived to be rescued. But now it was well into its second day. Their situation was hopeless.

The snow continued until it was shoulder high, covering their shelter, providing insulation as long as they could maintain a fire. But they had no shovel, no snowshoes, and even if they had, and both had been uninjured, the storm showed no sign of abating.

The mountains cut off transmissions between here and the city; people would have to search for them with hoverers or other craft, rising above the cliffs and canyons before they could home in on the emergency beacon of the crashed hoverer. If it was transmitting.

And of course they would search the hoverer first, before they discovered that there were no bodies in it. If they were dead and frozen, infrared scanners would not reveal their location. They wouldn't be found until the next thaw.

They still lay huddled together to conserve body heat, but now there was little to conserve. Korsal could not feel his hands or his feet, but at least his broken ribs had stopped hurting. When Kevin fell asleep, his father didn't try to wake him. Let him go peacefully; Korsal would not be long in following.

"Kai Katasai," he whispered defiantly to the approaching darkness . . . and watched it swirl and disintegrate dizzyingly before his weary eyes.

Korsal blinked.

Of all his senses, only sight was working. He felt nothing. He was lying on the floor of a small gray room. Before him was some kind of console, and behind that a Human male in a red uniform. Beside the console stood a man and a woman in red, with phasers trained on Kevin and Korsal.

Humans in the Black Fleet? Korsal's mind questioned crazily. Then other Humans in blue pushed past the security guards, hurrying toward him with blankets and medscanners, prying Kevin gently from his arms.

"They're both alive, Mr. Scott," said a young woman in blue.

"Ya hear that, Captain?" the man at the console said, and a disembodied voice replied, "Good work, Scotty!"

"Where . . . ?" Korsal tried to ask.

"Lie still!" said a short, brisk woman with graying hair and kind eyes. "Mr. Scott, inform the captain that these men need immediate emergency treatment. Frostbite, hypothermia, broken ribs, exhaustion, shock—"

"Take them to sickbay," came the order. "If they're

carrying the disease, you've all been exposed anyway. Stay there, in isolation, until we're certain Dr. Smythe is right."

Korsal realized that he and Kevin had been beamed aboard a starship. "This is . . . *Enterprise?*" he whispered as he was lifted onto a gurney. He was still numb; he felt no pain.

"Yes," said the woman. "I'm Dr. Gardens, temporary CMO. You'll be all right if we get you into treatment before there's any tissue loss. Mr. Scott, please clear the halls between here and sickbay—just in case the captain's information was wrong."

"Aye, lass," Scott replied. Korsal could hear the announcement echoing from speakers in the halls ahead.

The passage was swift. In sickbay Korsal and Kevin were placed on diagnostic beds, which promptly began to sound alarms. "Arthur!" shouted Dr. Gardens. "I told you to recalibrate these units for Klingons!"

"I'm lookin' it up, ma'am," came a voice from the next room. Then a thin young man with curly auburn hair came in with a computer printout sheet. "Sorry, Doctor—never set them for Klingons before, have I?"

Reading from the printout, he quickly made adjustments to the controls, and Korsal's unit stopped bleeping. Dr. Gardens turned to Kevin with a frown. "My son," Korsal told her. "He's half Human. Higher iron and hemoglobin; heart rate normal at eighty per minute, body temperature—" He told them all he knew of his son's normal vital signs, while the technician made the adjustments. Finally the alarm stopped.

"So far as I can tell," said Dr. Gardens, "your son is suffering from exhaustion more than anything else.

Both of you have severe frostbite, but his hands are worse than yours. Arthur, regeneration units, stat."

Then she turned to Korsal. "The nurses are going to help you undress, and then we'll repair those broken ribs. The scanners show that you had some internal bleeding, but it stopped of its own accord. That's why you're still alive."

"Kevin did all the work," Korsal replied. "That's why he's exhausted—he wouldn't let me move."

"Good thing," said the doctor as one male and one female nurse efficiently stripped him. "Otherwise you probably would have bled to death."

Korsal gave an involuntary moan as the nurses slid his shirt out from under him.

"Pain?" Dr. Gardens asked quickly.

"Good pain," Korsal replied. "It means I'm still alive."

She smiled. "Well, let's see if we can keep you alive but take the pain away."

Korsal was accustomed to Federation medical techniques, and so was not surprised when Gardens and Arthur positioned a surgical unit over his right side and the dull ache disappeared. He could not see what they were doing, or feel that area of his body, but when Gardens picked up a bone-knitter, he grinned. "Did you know that's a Klingon design?" he asked.

She held it up. "This? The principle goes back to twentieth-century Earth."

"Perhaps, but *that* design, miniaturized and concentrated, was one of the first trade-offs when the Klingon scientific mission came to Nisus. Believe me, we got plenty in return."

"Good horse traders, eh?" asked Arthur.

"You know what they say," Korsal replied, "sharper traders than Vulcans bargaining over the price of *kevas* and *trillium!*"

In the midst of Korsal's surgery, Kevin woke up. "Father?" he cried out, sitting up and looking around blindly.

Korsal could not move, but he said, "It's all right, Kevin. We're both safe. Lie still."

"Where are we?"

Two nurses were already at Kevin's side. "Aboard the *Enterprise,*" one of them told him. "You need immediate attention, but you're going to be fine, and so is your father."

When the surgery was finished, Korsal's hands and feet were encased in regeneration units, as were Kevin's. By that time, they were both recovered enough to be hungry, and the nurses fed them juice and soup and then left them to sleep. Both were still weak; sleep came quickly.

They were wakened at times, to be poked and prodded, examined, fed, and otherwise cared for, but most of the time they slept. Korsal could not have said how long this procedure went on, except that he sensed that it was more than a day, ship's time —possibly two or three. In his drug-numbed state, he could not calculate how long that was in Nisus time.

Then, suddenly, Korsal was brought wide awake and fully alert by an alarm. It didn't sound in the patient-care areas of sickbay, of course, but it was still loud enough to waken anyone asleep rather than unconscious.

The siren sounded alone for a few seconds, and then a voice joined in the clamor.

"Red alert! Red alert! Security to engineering! All hands, red alert! Intruders in engineering! Red alert!"

Korsal sat up, realizing that during his most recent sleep he had been freed of restraints. He flexed his hands, finding that they looked and felt normal. When he stretched, there was no more pain in his side.

In the next bed, Kevin was also awake, but his hands were still encased in the regeneration units. "What's going on?" he asked, and Korsal could hear from the slur in his voice that he was still on medication.

"Nothing that concerns us," Korsal told him. "Just lie still—you're still healing."

From the outer room he heard cursing, in a voice he recognized as that of Mr. Scott—the man who had operated the transporter. Then, obviously shouting into the intercom, "What's goin' on doon there? Who's muckin' about with my engines?"

Chapter Nineteen

ON THE DAY their unexpected Klingon guests were beamed aboard and isolated in sickbay, Spock left the bridge at the end of his watch in search of his parents. As usual, they were not in their quarters. He found them in one of the recreation rooms, where some off-duty crewmembers were putting on an impromptu performance. "Get your harp and join us, Mr. Spock," said Lieutenant Uhura when she saw him in the doorway.

"Yes, Spock," said Amanda, "please do."

It would have created more of a scene to refuse than to agree, so Spock went to his quarters for the instrument and returned to the rec room.

Uhura was singing, accompanied by Ensign Paschall on the violin. It was a sad love ballad, leaving all the Humans in the room teary-eyed.

When it was over, Paschall began to play his instrument like a "fiddle," breaking into a lively dance tune. Several people jumped up to dance, while everyone else clapped hands in time to the music—except, of course, Spock and Sarek.

Spock caught his father watching him and knew Sarek was wondering why they were still in orbit around Nisus. Fortunately, the music and laughter drowned conversation.

When it ended the dancers sat down, flushed and panting. Uhura urged, "Play something Vulcan, Mr. Spock."

"I bow to my father's talent," Spock replied quickly, and handed the lytherette to Sarek.

But the ploy did not gain him more than half an hour. Sarek graciously played several selections suited to Human aesthetics and auditory range. But then, despite the protests of a genuinely appreciative audience, Sarek said, "I'm afraid there is something I must discuss with my son. Amanda, please stay and enjoy the performance."

Spock saw his mother's blue eyes flash—she seldom responded positively when Sarek took an authoritarian tone—but then she put on her most gracious air and replied, "Certainly, my husband. I will meet you in our quarters, later."

And Spock knew that ten minutes thereafter she would have out of Sarek everything Spock was about to tell him. It was useless to try to shield Amanda anyway, although both her husband and her son instinctively desired to do so.

However, as they walked down the corridor toward Spock's cabin, Sarek opened the conversation by asking, "Why was the corridor outside the transporter sealed off this afternoon?"

"What were you doing there?" Spock asked.

"We had research from the Academy to beam down, and your mother wanted to bid farewell to our friends. Everyone who beamed down today is risking death."

"I know," Spock replied. "However, it was thirty-one-point-three-seven minutes after the last beamdown that the corridor was sealed."

They had reached Spock's cabin. As they entered, Sarek said, "How can you live among Humans and not know their idiosyncrasies? After the beamdown, people remaining aboard lingered outside the transporter room, talking, expressing concern for those who had left. There is a conference room nearby, and everyone without pressing duties went in—except Sendet, who undoubtedly perceived that he was not welcome."

"Sendet? What was he doing there?" asked Spock.

"Did you not observe the interest he took during the voyage in the woman T'Pina? And have you not noticed the imbalance between men and women among the Followers of T'Vet? In Sendet's generation there are three males for every two females . . . and Sendet is unbonded."

Spock swallowed convulsively. The unbonded males among the Followers of T'Vet were also risking death; in fact, given the imbalance Sarek had just mentioned, one in three was under sentence of death. At this point, they simply did not know which ones.

As the males reached *pon farr,* they would have to mate . . . or die. All the available women would soon be bonded, leaving a third of the men without mates, battling for their lives. There were no other communities on Vulcan Colony Nine from which women could be enticed or stolen; the Challenge would become a way of life from the first day an unbonded male entered *pon farr.*

"So," Spock said, "Sendet tried to the very last moment to persuade T'Pina to bond with him and join him in exile."

"That is correct," said Sarek.

"But she refused."

"Also correct. She is an intelligent young woman. It is unfortunate that you did not have the opportunity to gain closer acquaintance with her, Spock."

Deliberately, Spock refused to feel annoyance. He knew Sarek was expressing only concern. "I have time, Father."

"And I will never again try to force a choice upon you, Spock. But you still have not told me why the corridor was cleared."

"Most of the crew do not know, Father. By the time it is necessary to tell them, we will be certain that there is truly no danger."

"Then you *did* beam something aboard."

Sarek's mind was too quick to fool. When Spock hesitated, he added, "Amanda and I were among the last to leave the conference room. We had to share the turbolift with Sendet after the others had gone ahead. While we were waiting for a car to arrive, we heard the order to clear the corridor. Since we were leaving the area, it was no inconvenience."

"Yes," Spock told him. "In fact, we beamed two people aboard—but according to the best information Nisus can supply, they are not carriers of the Nisus plague." He explained the nature of their unexpected hospitality.

"Klingon scientists," said Sarek. "Intriguing. I should like to meet them."

"We know that the incubation period of the plague is between sixteen and forty-eight hours; we cannot leave orbit now for two days. Everyone who came in contact with the Klingons is isolated in sickbay. If no one becomes ill in that time, it is correct that Klingons neither contract nor carry the plague, and it will be safe for you to visit them." Spock frowned.

"You said Sendet did not go into the conference room with you."

"He did not. He must have remained in the transporter room or the corridor, for he was there when we left."

"Then," said Spock, "Sendet is our most likely suspect."

"Suspect?" asked Sarek.

"Mr. Scott discovered that something was beamed up from Nisus—before he beamed up the Klingons. I wonder . . . what could be so important for Sendet to get from Nisus that he would risk illegal use of the transporter?"

"And exposure to the plague," added Sarek.

"Unlikely. The epidemiologists have ascertained that, although deadly, the virus is short-lived outside its host. That was in the last report we received, less than two hours before entering orbit.

"The plague does not appear to be transmitted on objects or clothing, unless they are touched within minutes of contact with a contagious person. Airborne, it dies in the same time unless it finds a suitable host. Contagion, unfortunately, occurs well before the carrier exhibits symptoms. So there is a slight chance that if whoever handled what was beamed to Sendet was unknowingly contagious, and he touched it immediately before it was beamed . . . it could have been contaminated."

Spock reported what his father had told him to Captain Kirk, who immediately called Sendet to the briefing room.

"What did you beam up from Nisus?" Kirk demanded.

"Nothing," Sendet replied. "What would I want from there?"

"That's what we want to know," Kirk told him. "You endangered this whole ship—"

"If I had, which I deny, would it be any more than you have done by beaming Nisus residents aboard?"

"Spock—I thought you had corrected that security leak!"

"Affirmative, Captain. However, I might point out that sickbay is crowded with people who are not ill, and are annoyed at being confined. They are not under arrest, and so are not denied access to the intercom system—"

Kirk glared at the ceiling for a moment. The news was undoubtedly all over the ship by now.

"If you know that," Kirk said to Sendet, "then you know that the people we beamed aboard are not carriers. That does not change the fact that *you* beamed something up."

"I did not," Sendet said flatly.

Kirk glanced at Spock with a frown. Spock had to agree: the man did not appear to be lying.

"Would you care to search my cabin?" Sendet offered. "Perhaps you can locate this mysterious object you think I beamed aboard."

"That will not be necessary," said Kirk. "Whatever it was, it's obviously not in your cabin. You may go."

When Sendet had left, though, he looked at Spock. "I am very tired," he said. "I got the feeling that I just couldn't think of the right question to ask. *Something* happened in the transporter room; Scotty doesn't misremember how he left the controls, and Sarek wouldn't be wrong about finding Sendet skulking about the corridor after everyone had beamed down. Damn! If I stick *him* in sickbay now, I have to put myself in, too, and you, your parents, anyone who's been near Sendet since the mysterious beam-up."

Spock shook his head slowly. "It is not feasible, Captain, and it is too late even if it were. We have nowhere to confine so many—and we cannot filter and decontaminate the air for the entire ship as we do for sickbay. If Sendet brought the virus aboard, and it found a host, it is in the ventilation system by now. We seem to have no choice except to wait out the next forty-eight hours."

Chapter Twenty

IT WAS ONLY twenty hours later that the first case of the Nisus plague appeared aboard the *Enterprise.*

Spock had the con, maintaining synchronous orbit over the science colony on Nisus, when the turbolift doors opened to admit Amanda.

"Mother? What can I do for you?" he asked in surprise. Passengers were allowed on the bridge by invitation only.

She stared as if she were confused to see him there. "Spock? What are you doing in that uniform? Oh, Spock, what have you done? Your father—"

Spock pulled his lips between his teeth with the effort not to show emotion. Amanda's eyes were glazed, her words an echo of that long-ago day when he had told his parents of his decision to make a career in Starfleet . . . after which Sarek had refused to talk to him for eighteen years.

"It's all right, Mother," he said calmly. "Nothing is wrong." He had to get her to sickbay, for either this was the first symptom of the plague, or his mother was suffering a stroke. In either case, he had to keep her calm.

"What do you mean, nothing's wrong?" she demanded. "Sarek wants you to follow in his footsteps at the Vulcan Academy!"

Everyone on the bridge turned to look at mother

and son, and Spock could feel their sympathy, a palpable wave encompassing him. They didn't know Amanda's babbling could be a plague symptom, didn't understand the danger to themselves.

"Please, Mother," said Spock, "let's go some place where we can discuss it. Mr. Sulu, you have the con."

Spock got up, trying gently to guide Amanda toward the turbolift—just as the doors opened and Sarek stepped out. "Amanda!" he exclaimed. "Why did you—?"

Suddenly Spock's normally gentle, restrained mother became a fury, leaping at her husband with a shriek, raking her nails down his cheek.

Caught completely off guard, Sarek gasped "Amanda!"—his face showing every nuance of horrified realization.

But Amanda was shouting, "How can you *do* that to him? He's your son! You can't disown your own flesh and blood!"

This time Sarek caught the flailing fists as his wife sought to strike him. Spock came out of his momentary shock and grasped Amanda's shoulder for the nerve pinch.

Sarek swept her into his arms as she collapsed, and strode into the turbolift, Spock following. "Sickbay," Spock instructed, and then punched the intercom. "Dr. Gardens, the plague is aboard. Segregate everyone already there. We'll come in through Entrance C—straight into the isolation unit."

When the doors opened, Sarek carried Amanda out. Spock lingered in the turbolift only long enough to instruct the computerized system to take that carriage off-line until it had been sterilized.

A futile effort, he thought, seeing people in the halls, the warning to clear them blaring now, too late.

And everyone on the bridge had been exposed. He had to call the captain, have the bridge crew isolated, send in a decontamination crew before another shift could take over—

And it was all useless; if the virus had not been in the ventilation system before—if Amanda had caught it by contact with Sendet—it was certainly in the ship's air supply now.

Wearing protective gear, Dr. Gardens met them, helped Sarek arrange Amanda on one of the beds, and turned on the life-signs indicator. It began wailing, for her fever was at the danger level, her heartbeat rapid and irregular.

The doctor started the bed cooling and quickly shot two different medications into Amanda. "Please help me get her undressed," she said to Sarek. "No one we've had isolated has become ill so far. I'd rather not expose my nurses yet if I don't have to. I fear our whole staff is going to be desperately needed before this thing runs its course."

While Amanda was being settled, Spock called Kirk. There was a moment's silence from the captain's quarters after Spock relayed the news. Then, "God, Spock, I am so sorry. Don't worry, I'll take care of it from here on."

Don't worry. How typically Human. Spock did not bother to claim Vulcans don't worry—he admitted to himself that he was indeed worried, and knew that Sarek was as well. He turned from the intercom, going back to where his mother lay, pale and unconscious, now clad in a green sickbay coverall.

"She's stabilized for the moment," said Dr. Gardens. "Now there's nothing to do but wait, and treat symptoms as they occur. Stay with her if you like. You can't be more exposed than you've already been."

Sarek pulled up a chair beside the bed. Spock started to do the same, when he suddenly realized—

"Doctor, I must be isolated. You saw the reports from Nisus. I have both Vulcan and Human blood: even now, my body may be spawning some even deadlier form of the disease, one that could kill both my father and my mother."

Chapter Twenty-one

DR. LEONARD McCOY was already tired when he beamed down to Nisus. Within a day, he was exhausted. Every able-bodied physician was on call, for the hospital was flooded with plague victims. When he was not treating patients, he was in the computer room with Nisus medical staff and whoever of the experts they had brought along was also free at that moment.

He saw why more than half the doctors and nurses here had died; in the perpetual exhaustion caused by caring for such huge numbers of patients, they had no resistance.

Exposure was inevitable; no one could spend his life in mask, gloves, and protective clothing. Even in the contagion wards, stress brought mistakes. All it took, for example, was wiping one's own bare forehead with the same gloved hand that had just touched the patient's arm while administering a hypo. In his long career, McCoy had seen it many times before. Most would never even remember the slip that introduced the virus into their systems, nor would they ever know whether it was an error while on duty, or other exposure while off.

So far, the only hopeful discovery was the fact that the virus lived for less than an hour outside a living organism; any environment unoccupied for at least an hour was plague-free. But people could not stop interacting altogether. Families could not separate. Victims had to be cared for, and every day more succumbed than recovered.

Finally, after eighteen straight hours of physical labor interspersed with concentrated mental effort, McCoy fell asleep in his chair. When someone tried to lift him, he woke only enough to cooperate in transferring himself to a couch.

But he had slept hardly enough to take the edge off when someone shook him. "Sorry, Doctor— emergency priority from the *Enterprise*."

He was led to a communications console. "Yeah," he said groggily. "McCoy here."

"Bones." The gravity in Jim's voice brought him wide awake.

"What's happened?"

"We've got it aboard. Amanda. Spock and Sarek have both been exposed."

"Beam me up," was McCoy's first thought.

"Wish I could—but you're needed where you are."

"Jim, it's a shambles here! I'm working like a damn intern, and so are all the other doctors. We're not getting anywhere on research because of patient crises. Half their doctors and nurses have died of this thing, and the rest are walking wounded with stress and exhaustion."

"All the more reason to stay," Kirk told him. "Your staff can handle sickbay. At least there's one good thing."

"What's that?"

"We can't go off and leave you now. The *Enterprise* is stuck here until you figure out a cure. So when we *do* leave, you can come with us."

"Thanks," McCoy said cynically. Then something

the captain had said penetrated. "Jim! Remember the mutation pattern! If Spock's been exposed—"

"He knows. He isolated himself immediately," Kirk replied. "So I'm stuck without either of you. But then, I don't have anything to do except stay in orbit." McCoy heard the frustration in his captain's voice; a virus was not the kind of enemy a man of action knew how to fight.

Do I? McCoy wondered as he broke contact.

After that bad news, McCoy could not go back to sleep, so he went over to the bank of computers. Sorel and Corrigan were conferring over schematic diagrams of the virus in its varied forms. "Computer," said Corrigan, "schematic of strain C-four, interacting with the blood sample from Karl Katasai."

McCoy watched as the impersonal patterns on the screen shifted and changed. "There it is again!" said Sorel. McCoy thought he detected actual excitement in the Vulcan healer's voice. "Daniel, it appears we have identified the factor that prevents this virus from growing in Klingons."

"What is it?" asked McCoy.

"Here." Corrigan pointed to a location on the screen where the now-familiar schematic of the virus had attached itself to an unfamiliar organic molecular structure. "This blood factor binds with the virus and prevents it from multiplying. It just shrivels up and dies!"

"I've seen a structure like that somewhere before," McCoy said, "but I can't think where. Wasn't exactly the same but—" He frowned. "I dunno. I've analyzed Klingon blood before. That must be where I saw it, but didn't know what it was for."

"It's a hemoglobin factor," said Sorel. "It is similar to something I have seen before too—but not identical. If we can isolate that factor, we may be able to produce a vaccine for iron-based blood."

"What about a cure for someone who already has the disease?" McCoy asked.

"It should work," said Corrigan. "We'll certainly try it."

"Let me transmit this to the *Enterprise*," said McCoy. "Spock can work on it there—maybe we can develop a serum in time to help Amanda."

Suddenly both the healer and the doctor were staring at him. "Amanda?" asked Corrigan. "The plague is aboard ship?"

McCoy told them about his message from Kirk. "So it won't hurt to beam some serum aboard now, if we can make it."

"We should beam up and work on it in the *Enterprise* laboratory," said Sorel. "You've got two of the three available suppliers of the blood we need aboard."

"Huh?" Weariness was catching up with McCoy again.

"The other two Klingons," Corrigan explained. "Karl's father and brother—they're in the *Enterprise* sickbay."

"Klingons in my sickbay?" McCoy roared.

"Leonard," Daniel said reasonably, "Captain Kirk would not have beamed them aboard if they were a danger to the *Enterprise*. As it turns out, if we are correct about being able to make a serum from Klingon blood, our only problem will be supply. It simply will not be possible to make *enough*."

Chapter Twenty-two

CAPTAIN JAMES T. KIRK walked the corridors of his ship, silently cursing the virus attacking his crew and his friends. The closed system that ordinarily protected them was now providing a perfect environment for the virus to spread. Short of redesigning the ship, there was not a thing to do about it.

He longed for an enemy he could face man-to-man, outfight, or outwit. How was a starship captain supposed to combat the unseen menace of a virus?

"Captain Kirk," came Uhura's voice.

Kirk walked over to a wall unit and punched the button savagely. "Kirk here."

"Message from Dr. McCoy."

"Put him through."

"Jim, we think we've found—" McCoy began.

The red-alert claxon drowned out whatever the doctor was going to say. "Bones, we've got an emergency. Contact you later. Kirk out."

He punched intraship. "What the hell's going on?"

"Intruders in engineering!" came a voice he didn't recognize. "Captain, they're—" A yelp, a muffled thud.

Kirk punched the button. "Engineering! Status!"

There was no answer.

"Computer! Give me engineering status!" he demanded.

"All systems operational," the calm mechanical voice informed him. "Alarm manually operated. Access to engineering closed."

"Get those doors open!" Kirk demanded, starting to turn away and head for the turbolift.

"Access to engineering locked and both computer and manual override disengaged," the computer informed him.

"Damn!" He punched the intercom again. "Scotty—"

But his chief engineer was isolated in sickbay.

So was Spock.

The captain of the *Enterprise* remembered to turn off the intercom before he swore vehemently, then turned and ran to the turbolift. "Engineering deck!"

The doors opened into a locked room. In all three directions, the emergency doors were closed across the corridors. Kirk could not go farther than ten meters from the turbolift in any direction.

Two men and a woman from security were slumped on the floor. Kirk quickly checked that all were breathing.

The engineering intercom came to life, Scotty's voice demanding, "What's goin' on doon there? Who's muckin' about with my engines?"

"I don't know yet, Scotty," Kirk told him. "Whoever it is has secured the emergency doors. Stay put. I'll let you know what we find out."

The turbolift doors opened. Lieutenant Nelson and three more security personnel hurried out, armed with phasers.

"They're all alive," Kirk quickly assured them as they glimpsed their fallen comrades. "Must've been stunned."

"No," said Nelson, pulling open one man's shirt to

show the bruises. "Nerve-pinched. It's those Vulcan rebels. Shoulda carried 'em in the brig from the start."

"That's where they'll make the rest of the trip!" Kirk vowed. "Get them out of there!"

"Aye, Captain," Nelson said calmly. "Olag, schematics for these doors. Corcoran, find all engineering personnel not trapped in there and put them to work on—"

Just then one of the emergency doors slid open.

They all turned—to see the limp bodies of the engineering crew lying in the corridor, and behind them the next emergency door, securely shut.

All of these people were also alive, also unconscious.

Kirk left Nelson there and went to the bridge.

Soon the rebels were ready to communicate.

Sendet appeared on the screen. "Captain Kirk, we have control of your engineering section. As you know, the entire ship can be operated from here. We will leave orbit in two hours. Have crew and passengers beam down to Nisus before that time. When we leave orbit, we will expose all areas of the ship outside engineering to lethal doses of radiation."

"Why would you do that?" Kirk asked.

"You have brought aboard the *Enterprise* two people contaminated with the IDIC plague, and it has spread to one of your passengers. The radiation will kill the virus, but it will also kill anyone on board outside the area we have secured. The Followers of T'Vet intended to go peacefully into exile. But you have acted irresponsibly and failed to provide safe conduct. Your ship stands forfeit. We have the right to preserve our lives, and the *Enterprise*—"

"Wrong, Sendet," Kirk interrupted. He could see Satat out of focus behind Sendet and was sure the older Vulcan did not know the true story. *"You* brought the plague aboard. *You* were the only person in contact with the Lady Amanda who—" It suddenly dawned on him why Sendet had not appeared to be lying when he claimed he had beamed nothing up from Nisus.

"You didn't beam some*thing* up!" Kirk exclaimed. "You beamed yourself down to the planet—and then back up again! How many people did you contact? What did you touch? The transporter controls at Nisus Central, certainly! And you breathed the air; you brought it back here in your own lungs, and breathed it on Sarek and Amanda."

Rebel Sendet might be, but he had been raised in the normal Vulcan culture, which made him a poor liar. As Kirk deduced what had happened, Sendet's face froze with the effort to control.

Satat came forward, took one look at Sendet, and demanded, "Why? Why would you do something so illogical?"

"I had to try once more to persuade T'Pina," Sendet admitted. "Satat, you know we need females. I thought there was no danger of exposure to the disease in the small area where I meant to go."

Sendet's voice became perfectly flat, the way Spock's did when he spoke of something that would have had a Human racked with emotion. "I beamed down outside the terminal. Inside, I would certainly have faced the transporter operator; outside I risked being seen materializing, but I succeeded as I intended in beaming into the freight storage area.

"I walked out into the street and found everything

deserted. In the distance, the group from the *Enterprise* were walking toward the hospital. They were the only people moving on the streets.

"I realized then that I would not be able to get to T'Pina as I had hoped. I had thought she would go home first, and that I would follow and speak to her alone. Instead, she went with the others directly to the hospital.

"As I was considering my course of action, a Human male came out of one of the buildings, screaming. An Andorian ran after him, but he turned and began to attack the one trying to help him. Two Vulcans came out, subdued the Human, and began to carry him toward the hospital. I heard one say to the other, 'There are no more beds. They are treating patients in the corridors and sending home anyone recovered enough to be moved.' The Andorian followed them, saying, 'Few recover. We can only hope these new doctors can help.'

"I heard something inside the transporter terminal —I thought it was something else being beamed down from the *Enterprise,* so I went in, thinking to hide until all the transporter operations were finished and then beam back aboard. But only one platform was in operation, with no one to run it. I found the operator behind the console . . . dead. It appeared that the sound I had heard—she . . . had turned a phaser on herself. I had no desire to see more. I set the controls and beamed back up to the *Enterprise.*"

"Oh, my God," Kirk whispered. "You touched those controls that the dead woman had just been handling—"

"She was a suicide, not a plague victim!" said Sendet.

Kirk winced. "Violence is the first symptom of the

worst strain; that's what you saw on the street. That woman was alone when it struck her, and she turned the violence on herself. Sendet, you exposed yourself, and then you beamed back and gave the disease to Lady Amanda. Probably to Sarek too—the incubation period appears to be longer in Vulcans than in Humans."

Satat stepped forward. "Isolate him," he directed the other Vulcans, who came into monitor range. "Don't touch him. Snil, rig a filter for the room you put him in—"

"You're too late," said Kirk. "You're all exposed."

"Not necessarily," Satat replied. "Sendet, you had the sense to disinfect yourself as soon as you returned to the *Enterprise,* didn't you?"

"Of course," Sendet replied.

"So, unless you have become contagious already, we may not have been exposed."

"Satat, you're dreaming," said Kirk. "Sendet has seen to it that we need do nothing about getting you out of engineering. The *Enterprise* cannot go anywhere until a cure for the plague is found. Except to make certain you cannot leave orbit, we can just leave you in engineering until you open those doors of your own accord, to ask for medical help."

Chapter Twenty-three

T'PINA WAS WORKING in the isolation ward where all Nisus citizens of mixed heritage were housed, away from the rest of the population. As many of them were ill as was true among the population in general. While her mother had been assigned nursing duty among those who were stricken, T'Pina's job was to try to keep the many healthy children occupied.

It was not easy. They had been isolated for more than three days now, occupying the entire medical residence and attached minimal-care facility. Even so, they had three to four people in each room intended for two. In the daytime, the adults tried to entertain the children in the game and viewing rooms, the solarium, or the cafeteria area where T'Pina was assigned today.

All the children were restless; most were frightened. A number had become ill during their confinement and been taken away, and the older children inevitably talked about their friends dying, frightening the younger children even further.

There were, of course, adults of mixed heritage in the isolation ward as well, but they were so outnumbered by the children that even with help from volunteers like T'Pina they were constantly occupied, teaching lessons, organizing games, and explaining over and over why the children could not go home, or even outside, and why their parents could not come to see them.

It was equally difficult to explain why T'Pina and the other volunteers wore protective clothing, masks, and gloves.

"Why are you hiding from me?" demanded Ziona, a tiny, usually charming girl who was half Rigellian, half Hemanite. Today, though, she was close to hysterics, for she missed her family and was too young to understand what was happening.

"Why can't I see your face?" Ziona demanded fitfully of T'Pina, making a grab for her mask that the young Vulcan woman was only narrowly able to evade.

"Why, if this lady of the lovely eyes showed 'er entire face, you might not be the prettiest girl here anymore," answered a male voice, speaking English with an accent that reminded T'Pina slightly of Dr. Corrigan's, but yet was not the same.

"Then how could you be my best girl?" the voice continued. T'Pina turned as Ziona shot past her to jump into the arms of a man who appeared to be Human, but . . .

He was not quite a head taller than T'Pina, somewhere around average for a Human male. His hair was black, close-cropped, but thick and fine—as if, were she to touch it, it would feel like fur. His face was rather ordinary, except for his eyes, which were the darkest, most vivid blue she had ever seen, and fringed with thick black lashes.

It was his skin that suggested he was not fully Human; he was clearly not ill, and yet his skin was pale, utterly unblemished, almost translucent, with just the slightest hint of green.

Then he smiled, and his face was no longer ordinary at all, but mobile and charming. "Beau Deaver," he introduced himself, "and unlike you, I'm in here because I have to be." At her raised eyebrow, he laughed. "Half Human, half Orion, and how me mum 'n dad arranged the technology for that's such a well-kept secret even *I* don't know. But here I am. There's them as say I'm the worst of both worlds, especially when it comes to a weakness for beautiful women."

"I am T'Pina," she replied, uncertain how to respond to his strange introduction, "and I am Vulcan, although I have lived most of my life on Nisus. How is it I have not met you before?" she asked, certain she would not have forgotten such a unique individual.

"Only been here two years," he replied, sitting down at one of the tables, Ziona on his lap. "Bumped all over the Federation as a boy. Me dad was a free trader."

T'Pina understood that common euphemism: smuggler. "But you are a scientist," she said, taking the opportunity to sit for a moment. Why else would he be on Nisus?

"Mathematician—inherited me dad's ability to juggle numbers, it seems. Woulda followed in his footsteps, 'cept that when I was fourteen or so we had an unexpectedly protracted stay on the planet Sofia. You know Sofia? You wouldn't *want* to know Sofia," he continued, not giving her a chance to reply.

As Ziona was now sitting happily on Deaver's lap, listening to him in fascination, T'Pina did not attempt to interrupt his monologue. It was the first time the child had stopped crying all morning.

"Me mum got work as a dancer," Deaver continued, making T'Pina realize that "protracted stay" meant his father had been incarcerated, "but the truant officers rounded me up and made me go to school—first time in me life, an' a grand time I had of it too! Not that my teachers had such a good time, mind you. But me mum and dad had only taught me to read an' count an' inveigle whatever I wanted out of a computer. On Sofia I found great stuff to learn —'specially numbers."

As he spoke, Deaver bounced Ziona on his knee, making her giggle. Other children were watching now as he told her, "That's right—found out numbers are fun. Want me to show you?"

"Yes!" said the little girl, nodding her head vigorously.

Deaver held up his hands. "How many fingers do I have, Ziona?"

"Ten," she responded, "same as me!"

"No," he said, "I have eleven fingers."

"Do not!" Ziona protested.

"Yes I do."

"Do *not!*" Ziona insisted. "I c'n count that good!"

"I can prove it. Shall I show you?"

"Yeah!"

First Deaver counted all his fingers, starting with his right-hand thumb and ending with his left-hand smallest finger. "—eight, nine, ten. You see ten fingers, right?"

"Right!" Ziona nodded eager agreement. By this time there was an audience of boys and girls gathered around them. T'Pina realized that Deaver was well known and popular with all the children.

Now he held up his right hand. "How many fingers on this one?"

"Five!" Ziona said triumphantly.

"All right. Now, we just counted the ones on the other hand—but let's make sure." This time he began with the small finger. "Ten . . . nine . . . eight . . . seven . . . six"—which brought him back to his thumb—"and five on this one." He held up his right hand again. "How much is six and five?"

Ziona's eyes widened in utter bewilderment. "Eleven!"

"What did I tell you?" Deaver asked.

"How did you *do* that?" Ziona demanded, her bewilderment turning to delight. She grasped his hands, examining them as if she truly expected to find an eleventh finger lurking somewhere.

"Here," Deaver replied, "I'll teach you on your hands, and then when you go home you can tell your mum and dad that while you were in hospital you grew an extra finger."

It took Ziona three tries before she got the trick right, but when she did she burst into a fit of giggles. "I gotta show Dominic!" she said, sliding off Deaver's lap and running off to find her friend. The other children who had been watching also hurried away, and T'Pina knew the trick would be played on every child there before evening.

When the children had scattered, T'Pina asked, "Is that what you learned on Sofia—children's games with numbers?"

"Nah, that was one of me dad's old tricks. On Sofia I discovered mathematics—the inside of everything in the universe. By the time I got into calculus and quantum mechanics, I didn't have time for pickin' locks or booby-trappin' the principal's desk chair anymore. We was stuck there for two years—nor nobody was as surprised as me when I won the quadrant maths prize! Got me a full scholarship to any university in the Federation; they was fightin' over me!" He laughed. "You coulda knocked me dad over with a feather. He always said I'd amount to nothin', that I was just something to keep me mum occupied."

"What university did you choose?" T'Pina asked.

"Always wanted t'see Earth—me dad had enemies in that neck of the Federation—so I tried MIT first. Spent two years there, one term at Oxford, where the tutors kep' raisin' objections to the way I talk, an' then I went off to Corona, to the Royal Academy, where I finished my degree—to me own surprise as much as the faculty's!"

T'Pina was impressed: if there was any institution in the Federation to rival the Vulcan Academy in the areas of science and mathematics, it was the Royal Academy of Corona.

But Deaver was saying, "Beware of mathematics, Lady T'Pina. 'Tis an addiction gets in yer blood and don't let go. I find a corollary to T'Prol's Functions —just playin' around for me own amusement, you understand—and next thing I know I've got a teaching fellowship at the Vulcan Academy!"

"You've taught at the Vulcan Academy?" T'Pina suddenly wondered if he was lying—perhaps everything he had said was a lie, or a trick of language such as he had shown Ziona.

But Deaver answered her question. "For a year. Kinda fun bein' on the other side of the desk."

"I have been at the Vulcan Academy for the past three years," said T'Pina. "I just graduated."

"It was before your time, then—seven Federation Standard Years ago. I liked the people there—you Vulcans keep a man on his toes, and there were folks from all over the galaxy, just like here. Tell me something," he added, looking her up and down as if he could tell all about her appearance, swathed as she was in protective gear, "does the Vulcan Academy have a beauty requirement for the women it admits?"

"What?"

"Listen, all the time I was there, I never saw a woman who wouldn't win best of breed. Even the Tellarite females were, um, not ugly, anyway. And every last one of 'em's got a brain—thinkin' man's paradise! If I could've took the heat and the gravity, I'd be there yet."

"Indeed," T'Pina said flatly. She did not approve of the turn the conversation had taken. "If you will excuse me, Mr. Deaver—"

"Beau," he said. "And please, sit back down, Lady T'Pina. Some kid'll be screamin' for attention soon enough."

"The children who scream are not always the ones requiring attention," she said, walking over to the soft-sided pens near the windows, where toddlers played in the sunshine. She laid a thermometer patch on each child's forehead, checking his tag to determine his normal temperature, for each of these children was unique. "And if you spent a year on Vulcan, you should know that it is not proper to address me as 'lady,'" she added as Deaver followed and knelt beside her.

"Ah . . . not yet. You are younger than I thought, then," he said, touching the cheek of a sleeping child with the back of his hand. "That means you are even braver than I thought. Why have you volunteered to work in here, among us pariahs?" Automatically, he collected toys the children had thrown out and dropped them back into the pens.

"The work needs to be done," T'Pina explained. "I do not have the experience to be useful in the laboratories under these emergency conditions. Therefore—"

"Therefore you doubly risk your life?"

"I am protected."

"Ziona almost pulled your mask off today." A little boy who looked to be mostly Tellarite held out his arms and pleaded with soft cries. Deaver picked him up, bounced him a little, laid his cheek against the child's, then tickled him into helpless giggles before he put him back down in the pen.

"A thermometer is a much more accurate way to check for fever than touching a child," T'Pina told him.

"Not to *my* mum. Three different temperatures, her, me dad, an' me—an' she could always tell when t'start cookin' up chicken soup. Plomeek soup to you, ma'am."

"I am familiar with the Human dish," T'Pina told him. "Like plomeek soup, folk wisdom traditionally endowed it with great curative powers—and modern medicine has shown that it is similarly antibiotic and symptom specific. However—"

"T'Pina!"

Leyne Sweet, called "Sugar" by her Human friends, was hurrying across the cafeteria, her posture and the fact that she ignored the children who tried to attract her attention telling T'Pina that she brought important news. Like T'Pina, Sugar was a volunteer here because she didn't yet have the experience to do the other work of value in trying to stop the plague. And, like T'Pina, she was willing to do anything she could to preserve her home.

A lock of dark hair had escaped from beneath Sugar's protective cap and was falling into her eyes.

Just as she reached them, her hand rose automatically to tuck the hair back. Both Beau Deaver and T'Pina exclaimed, "No!" and reached to capture the errant hand just before it touched her bare forehead.

Deaver's hand closed over T'Pina's on Sugar's wrist. Even through the protective glove, she felt his alien coolness—and with it an almost electric shock.

They stared at each other for one moment.

Sugar didn't notice. "Oh, my God," she whispered, staring at her hand, spreading her fingers as T'Pina and Deaver let their hands drop away. "Thank you," she said. Then she looked at T'Pina, whom she had known all her life. They had grown up neighbors. "T'Pina, it's your mother. She collapsed at her work —they think it's the first or second strain, not the third. She has a good chance of recovery, but—"

"I will go to her," said T'Pina, every other thought gone instantly out of her mind.

The disease was now attacking T'Kar—the only family T'Pina had left.

Chapter Twenty-four

SOREL RAN HIS medscanner over T'Kar. She had a soaring fever, but otherwise her readings were normal. "Do you have pain?" he asked.

"I can control," she replied.

"We will administer a broad-spectrum antiviral agent, and then I will help you achieve healing trance."

T'Kar nodded weakly. She was a nurse; she understood the dangers of the trance under these conditions.

There were no diagnostic beds available; they were all in use by patients currently in critical condition. If it turned out T'Kar had contracted Strain B, she would not be in any danger for three more days, and her strength would be enhanced if she spent those days in healing trance.

Without the diagnostic bed, however, there would be no warning if she went into systemic failure before the time it was to be expected. All patients in this wing would be routinely scanned every hour; there were not enough nurses or technicians to do it more often.

If her heart or lungs failed, though, T'Kar would die in minutes, for no Vulcan could come out of healing trance by himself. For that reason, healers always put patients in healing trance into automatic diagnostic units.

And . . . what if T'Kar's illness were not Strain A or B as it appeared? She had been working for days among the Nisus residents of mixed heritage—what if this were some new strain, masking itself in the early symptoms of less dangerous ones? The pathology laboratory was hopelessly backlogged; it would be hours before any report came on T'Kar's culture.

Sorel found that logic did not govern his reaction to T'Kar's illness. He had come to know her better on the journey here, found her interesting and intelligent, seen her handle her daughter's newfound maturity with wisdom and sensitivity. He liked the daughter, too: well controlled for one so young, yet neither cold nor distant.

Sorel's own youth was long past—but as time healed the wound of T'Zan's death, he rediscovered feelings he had once known with his wife. They focused on T'Kar. She was not an ordinary patient to him; he was as concerned as if she were a member of his family.

If T'Kar had lived on Vulcan, and if these had been ordinary times rather than the middle of an epidemic, it would have been entirely logical for Sorel to pursue his acquaintance with T'Kar. A healer, a nurse; a widower, a widow; both from Ancient Families; both with their children grown and educated. It was an entirely suitable match. In ordinary times, if both had been residents of Vulcan, their friends and families would have been arranging every possible means of bringing them together.

But the times were not ordinary.

More important, T'Kar would stay here where her

work was, where her daughter was, on Nisus. Eventually, Sorel would return to Vulcan.

And . . . he had other patients, and other duties beyond patient care. He stood, saying, "I will be back as soon as all your tests have been completed."

But before he could leave, T'Pina entered, swathed as Sorel was in protective garb. But so had T'Kar been.

If it were Strain A or B, chances were she had caught it while off-duty, indicating that their precautions within the hospital were sufficient. But if it were not—

"Healer," T'Pina politely acknowledged Sorel, but her attention was on T'Kar. "I am here, Mother."

"I am pleased thou hast come, child. I am comforted by thy presence," T'Kar said.

Sorel had been about to leave them to their privacy, but at T'Kar's tone and language he turned. The formal phrasing indicated that T'Kar gave great importance to the simple words—as if they might be her last. Something was wrong.

Long years of medical experience told Sorel. Filial affection told T'Pina; he saw it in her eyes as she looked at him, then back to her mother.

The younger woman put her gloved hand on her mother's arm. "Healer!" she exclaimed. "Scan her!"

He was already halfway across the room, scanner out.

T'Kar's temperature was four degrees below Vulcan normal and dropping! Her eyes had lost their fever brightness, and their blue seemed to drain away to gray even as he watched.

"Mother!" T'Pina gasped.

The scanner showed her heart laboring, faltering.

They could see her gasping for breath, growing weaker—

Sorel hit the Code Blue button on the wall, then turned to his patient, pushing her onto her side so he could gain compression, as he had not so much as a portable stimulator. CPR was much more difficult on a Vulcan than a Human, for the heart did not lie conveniently beneath the sternum.

The green flush had died out of T'Kar's face; it paled to waxen yellow. She passed out and stopped breathing.

"No!" T'Pina cried. "Mother! Mother, don't die!"

With the hospital so overcrowded and equipment limited, patients like T'Kar, who appeared noncritical, were placed in rooms with minimal equipment. Sorel had routinely taken inventory of the room's supplies when he had entered; he already knew there was no breathing mask. T'Pina wasted no time searching elsewhere: she tore off her protective mask and put her mouth to her mother's, forcing air into her lungs even as Sorel exclaimed, "T'Pina—no!"

Between breaths, T'Pina raised her head and said, "I won't let her die!"

It was too late. T'Pina had exposed herself to this new strain of the plague. Sorel continued to pump T'Kar's heart while T'Pina breathed for her.

The resuscitation team arrived. A Human, a Vulcan, and a Tellarite, they grasped T'Kar with the ease of long practice, laid her in the unit, and while the Human and the Tellarite attached the controls, the Vulcan calibrated the instrumentation to Vulcan norms.

T'Kar lay still, the machine now breathing for her and forcing her heart to beat. But was she alive?

There was only one way for a healer to know, and for that he had to touch his bare hand to her face.

But her daughter would know. Sorel looked to T'Pina, whose whole face he could now see. She looked serene, content. "T'Pina . . . ?"

"No, Healer. My mother's *katra* did not pass to me. She lives."

Indeed, within half an hour T'Kar's own system began to struggle against the life-support system. They moved her to a diagnostic bed that became available when another patient died, and within an hour she regained consciousness.

"Where is T'Pina?"

"Unfortunately, in saving your life she was exposed to your illness," Sorel explained. "She is being examined—and once the symptoms start she will immediately be placed on life support. We won't be caught off guard again."

But where do we get the equipment? he asked himself. *This disease is outrunning our ability to cope with it, simply in terms of equipment and personnel.*

When Sorel returned to the computer lab after finishing his rounds, he found T'Mir and Daniel already studying the schematic of the new strain of the virus. "We're about to find out if Klingon blood eats this one for breakfast as well," said Daniel.

Sure enough, when it was introduced to Klingon blood cells, it acted like the other strains, shriveling up and dying. Daniel grinned. "We've got it! Now all we have to do is test it on somebody!"

"We have a list of volunteers," said T'Mir. "All critical and unstable."

"Let's hope none of 'em are allergic to Klingons," said Daniel. "Start with three?"

Sorel nodded. "A Human, a Tellarite, and a Lemnorian—all with iron-based blood."

"Right," said Daniel, looking from his partner to his wife, his hopeful smile fading. But he said only, "Let's go. At least if we can protect personnel with iron-based blood, we can put together a medical staff to care for everyone else."

They administered the serum, and T'Mir returned to the laboratory while Sorel and Daniel went back to their patients. There were three more cases of the new strain already, two of whom had died before being diagnosed as such. By the time they had examined and treated a dozen more patients, hearing on every side complaints about lack of equipment, lack of personnel, Sorel could see the tension and fatigue in his Human partner.

He knew Daniel's dedication, knew that he would force himself beyond endurance to save lives. But when they had finished in the hospital proper and Daniel said, "We'd better go over to the mixed-heritage section, check for this new strain—" Sorel interrupted him.

"Not until you have eaten a meal and slept for at least two hours. That is a prescription, Daniel. You have forgotten again that you are not physically Vulcan."

The Human smiled, but there was no humor in it. "I'm not hungry, either."

"Shall I insist that you have your blood sugar levels analyzed?"

"You'd get the report back in about three days! Okay, okay—let's see if the cafeteria has anything palatable."

It was late afternoon, but no one was keeping a normal schedule these days. Only computerized food was available. They dialed up their choices, then waited their turn to go through decontamination and into a small room where it was safe to eat without masks and gloves.

Or was it? What if one of them was carrying the plague right now?

It was on Daniel's mind too. "Sorel," he said, "have you noticed a growing fear of interaction, even in the short time we've been here?"

"It is normal, Daniel . . . and healthy, given the current circumstances. Even our best precautions are not preventing the spread of the disease—but if people are overly cautious, at least that may slow it."

"That's not what I meant. Earlier today, T'Mir and I were talking outside the computer lab. We were speaking Vulcan—and a Rigellian came up, stared at me, and demanded to know why I wasn't over in the medical residence with the rest of the . . . *'ergoflin'* was his word. I suppose that means 'person of mixed heritage' in Rigellian, but I got the impression that it was not the polite term for it."

Sorel did not speak Rigellian, either. Here on Nisus, the standard languages were English and Vulcan; there were not the universal translators everywhere, as there were aboard a starship, and he and Daniel were not carrying translators, since they were fluent in both languages.

Daniel was still puzzling over the incident. "Even under decontamination gear, you'd think anyone could see I'm Human."

"You look Human, but to a Rigellian, your Vulcan probably sounds accentless," said Sorel. "Only a native speaker would know that you are not one."

"Thanks, but that's not really the point. The man was insulting and aggressive. When I identified myself, his focus of anger turned away from me, but in another direction. He began to rant against allowing people of different races to have children together. Said this plague is nature's way of showing us how wrong it is. He didn't know T'Mir was my wife, of course—but Sorel, if she had not exerted calm on me through our bonding, I would probably have slugged him."

"I do not think so," said Sorel. "It is my experience that civilized Humans frequently defuse negative emotions by thinking about aggressive acts, but then they 'think twice,' and do not perform them."

"Yeah? How many 'civilized Humans' do you know?"

"You, for one. And you are under severe stress, Daniel, as we all are . . . including that offensive Rigellian."

"I know. We walked away from him. But haven't you heard the same thing, usually put more politely, at least ten times a day since we've been here? God, Sorel, what if they're right? I don't mean the prejudice. I mean—sometimes the best intentions bring about the worst results. Take Earth's Eugenics Wars, for example. We meant to improve the species, prevent genetic defects, delay aging. Instead, we created supermen who tried to take over the world, and let loose new diseases, new defects."

Daniel's dejection was palpable as he continued. "What if you and I, intending only to help good people like Sarek and Amanda have children, have helped start that process all over again—this time on a galactic scale? What if this plague, which mutates through such children, is only the beginning?"

His eyes fixed on Sorel's, devastation in their depths. "You approved my marriage to your daughter.

I married T'Mir because I love her. Suppose we do find a cure for this particular disease. T'Mir and I are still left with a terrible decision: either we must deny ourselves children, or live with the fear that at any time a plague like the one we are fighting, or something worse, could come again."

Chapter Twenty-five

WHEN THE CHIEF medical officer of the USS *Enterprise* beamed aboard and released everyone from sickbay except those in the isolation unit, Korsal expected that he and Kevin would immediately be sent back to Nisus. Instead, Dr. McCoy came to stand between their beds, looking from father to son.

The Human doctor rocked back and forth on his toes, his face a portrait of mixed emotions. Finally he said, "My staff has taken a great deal of blood from you two."

"We've noticed," Korsal replied.

"Do you know why?" the doctor pursued.

"I assume you're searching for the reason we're immune to the Nisus plague."

"Have you found it?" Kevin asked eagerly. "Can you use our blood to protect other people?"

McCoy frowned at the boy. "Is that what you want?"

"Of course! Doctor, all my friends are in danger." Korsal saw his son's realization. "You don't trust us!"

"I've been told that I can," said McCoy. Then he smiled. "Your reaction says I've been told the truth. Yes, we've got a serum, and if you're willing to help us, we can make more."

"How can we help?" Korsal asked.

"I know you want to go home," McCoy explained,

"but I'd like you to stay here. You'll need medical supervision, and the hospital on Nisus is a madhouse."

"What do you want us to do?" asked Korsal.

"Take some drugs that will stimulate production of blood cells, and let us have as much of your blood as possible."

"Certainly," said Korsal. "Kevin?"

"Of course. Uh, do you have to put us to sleep again?" This was the first day the boy had been off medication.

"No," McCoy assured him. "But you can't run around. We can offer all the entertainment tapes you want and—"

"We'd prefer a computer link," said Korsal. "Kevin has studies to catch up on, and I have work to do."

"You'll have to ask Captain Kirk about that. He's coming to see you today. Now, about your younger son—"

"Karl? Is he all right?" Korsal asked.

"Oh, yes, he's fine. Once he was sure he was immune, he volunteered to work in the high-risk ward, caring for the mixed-heritage children we isolated after we got your report. He's only a child himself but—"

"Don't you say that to Karl!" warned Kevin. "He's passed Kahs-wan, you know."

"Kahs-wan? Isn't that a Vulcan ritual?"

"No ritual," Korsal replied. "A life-or-death survival test, completely comparable to the Klingon Survival every boy must pass. When Karl was at the appropriate age, not enough Klingons remained on Nisus to supervise Survival for him, but I obtained permission for him to substitute Kahs-wan, and the Vulcans accepted him for the trial. So you must ask

Karl himself, Doctor. He has the right to make the decision."

The doctor's weary face broke into a grin. "I love it—a Klingon passing Kahs-wan! You folks really do live IDIC on Nisus, don't you?"

"I suppose we do," Korsal replied. "I had not thought of it in those terms. Doctor, are you going back to Nisus soon?"

"Within the hour, probably. Why?"

"Would you do me the kindness to carry a message tape for my wife? I'm sure she has been told that Kevin and I are well, but I have been unable to talk to her directly because ship's channels are all on priority status."

"Of course," said McCoy.

Korsal added, "I was not even allowed to send the warning about the dam directly, but I am sure your ship's communications officer delivered it."

"The dam?" McCoy asked.

"The safety sluice—the reason we were up on the mountain when we were caught in the storm," Korsal explained. "If that safety isn't repaired, more slabs of ice could get through to hit the turbines, and the power plant could be knocked out."

"Why don't you folks use solar or fusion power, like most planets?" McCoy asked.

"Nisus is a watery planet, like your Earth," Korsal explained. "It was much simpler and cheaper to build the hydroelectric plant than a fusion plant, since the dam was needed anyway. And the atmosphere blocks too much sunlight for solar power to be efficient. Nisus is warm more from a greenhouse effect than from direct solar radiation."

"Well, I'm a doctor, not an engineer." McCoy

smiled. "I'll ask Lieutenant Uhura to make sure your message got through. If there's anything I hate, it's to have the power go out on me—it always seems to happen in the middle of surgery!"

McCoy's efficient sickbay staff soon had Korsal and Kevin hooked up to equipment that monitored their tolerance and administered the flow of blood stimulant. Soon Arthur came in to draw a unit of blood from each of them, and then the captain of the *Enterprise* paid them a visit.

Korsal had heard of James T. Kirk. From the legends, he had expected a more imposing figure of a man than this average-height, average-build Human with light brown hair and eyes and the same air of nervous fatigue that gripped everyone here and on Nisus.

But he soon experienced the power of Kirk's personality as the man smiled and said, "I want to thank both of you. With your cooperation, we've now got a vaccine for everyone with iron-based blood."

"Only people with iron-based blood?" Kevin asked. "But that means—"

"It means," said Korsal, "that approximately half the residents of Nisus can be protected. Captain, we were not told this fact. I am sorry."

"Sorry?"

"We have Vulcan, Rigellian, Orion friends too. There is still no vaccine for them, then." *No protection for Seela.*

"Father," said Kevin, "we couldn't possibly give enough blood for the whole planet."

"Your son is right," said Kirk. "But inoculating medical personnel will mean proper care for those who *do* fall ill. Inoculating those of mixed heritage with iron-based blood will eliminate at least *those* opportunities for mutation. You've given us a place to start, and we are grateful."

Korsal smiled, carefully keeping his teeth covered. "You thank us for something we have no control over, a factor in our blood."

"No, for your willingness to aid others. Now, is there anything I can do to make your stay more comfortable?"

"Your staff is treating us like the emperor himself," Korsal replied.

"Well, then, at least I can bring you a piece of good news." He turned to Kevin. "Kevin Katasai, I have the honor and the pleasure of informing you that you have been granted early admission into Starfleet Academy. As I understand it, you will complete your schooling on Nisus by stardate 4100."

"That is correct," said Kevin, his certainty telling his father the boy had calculated the stardate well before today.

"The next class after that begins on stardate 4168," said Kirk. "If you accept the appointment, you will report to Starfleet Academy on that date."

Korsal saw his son's eyes sparkle with delight as he shook hands with Captain Kirk. "I am honored, sir," he said. "Even more so that you should be the one to tell me. I've read and heard so much about you—"

"That you just had to start breaking my records, eh?" said Kirk with a smile.

"No one will ever break them all, sir," replied Kevin. "Besides, I don't plan to go into the command program. I want to be an engineer, like my father. In Starfleet, I can design ships that can go even farther and faster than the *Enterprise,* bridge the distances

170

between the farthest planets in only days. Or—maybe not need ships at all. Imagine a transporter that would reach from Nisus to Earth!"

The boy fell silent, realizing: "I'm sorry, sir—it's just that I'm excited. I was not sure I would be accepted."

"You have every right to be excited," Kirk told him, then turned to Korsal. "Are you . . . comfortable with your son's decision?"

"He has the right," Korsal replied. "I know he will be well educated. And it will be good for Kevin to learn something of the Federation outside Nisus. He has been sheltered in many ways." His smile this time was forced; he knew quite well that Kevin would come up against blatant prejudice at Starfleet Academy.

Yet . . . Starfleet Command had overcome its prejudices to allow a half-Klingon cadet to enter the Academy. He knew his son had the courage to succeed. "I am proud of my son's achievements," he said, then added, "Captain, would it be possible to have a couple of computer terminals? Kevin needs to catch up on schoolwork he's missed the past few days."

"I thought the schools were closed," said Kirk.

"They are, but the students have assignments in those subjects which can be conducted by computer."

"Yes," said Kevin. "I'm way ahead in math and physics. When the schools reopen, we'll probably spend all our time on discussion subjects—like literature and poetry."

Those subjects had not had a large place at the schools Korsal had attended, and he had been surprised to find them such a major part of the curriculum in Federation schools. Kevin's tone of voice clearly indicated that he considered them a waste of his time.

Kirk did not miss the boy's attitude. "You don't like literature and poetry?"

"I prefer what's real," said Kevin. "That stuff is all imaginary."

Kirk laughed. "And where would engineers be without imagination? Kevin, starships had to be imagined before they could be designed and built. Besides, literature deals with *people*—and if you think about it, all your life you're going to be dealing with people. You can't experience all possibilities, but over the centuries writers have described every one of them. Let me see—have you ever read *The Canterbury Tales,* by Geoffrey Chaucer?"

"No, but it's on our reading list."

"Our first officer, Mr. Spock, has been reading it while he's been in isolation; said his father made a reference to it, and he wanted to refresh his memory. So I know it's in our library computer. Why don't you read that while you're sitting around here with nothing to do but save the world?"

"Half the world," Kevin said. Then he added, more brightly, "I'd rather study the schematics of your warp engines."

Kirk laughed again. "Tell you what—I'll set you a course of *The Canterbury Tales,* and some Earth history of medieval Europe for background. Then I'll come back and discuss it with you, and you can explain to me what the Canterbury pilgrims and their world have in common with the world you live in on Nisus. In return I'll get my chief engineer to *show* you the warp engines. Deal?"

"Deal," Kevin replied.

Korsal could see where Kirk had gotten his reputation for diplomacy. He asked for a terminal for himself and access to his own plague data. If he projected it forward in time, assuming inoculations of the half of the population his and his sons' blood could protect, perhaps he could find the most efficient order in which to use the vaccine.

"Certainly," Kirk agreed. He walked over to the intercom on the wall, but before he could punch the button, it came on.

"Captain Kirk," said an urgent female voice.

"Kirk here," replied the captain.

"Uhura here. Captain, when communications cleared, I took us off priority status and started sending through the personal messages to Nisus. But there's one from the Klingon engineer Korsal to the engineering staff at the dam—"

"Khest!" exclaimed Korsal. "It wasn't sent? They don't know that that safety sluice is out!"

"Shall I send it? Security suggested it could be some kind of code, Captain."

"Send it!" Kirk shouted. Then, more calmly, "We don't know who all are sick or dead. That message means exactly what it says. Send it, emergency priority, to its original destination and to every Nisus official and every engineer—both home and office."

He turned to Korsal. "I'm sorry. If I'd known . . . how bad is it?"

"Obviously there has not yet been another accident like the one that caused Kevin and me to fly up there in the first place. But the moment there is a thaw, Captain—if that safety has not been repaired, ice will get through and damage the turbines. We never got high enough to check more than the nearest safety sluice, either. As soon as the weather breaks, all of them need to be checked out, and repaired if necessary. Otherwise, Nisus is virtually certain to lose electrical power just when they are still trying to fight the epidemic."

Chapter Twenty-six

WHEN JAMES T. KIRK left the two Klingons, he found Dr. McCoy leaving the decontamination lock from the isolation units. "How's Amanda?"

"Weak. Hanging on, though. I gave her the serum; now there's nothing to do but wait."

"Been to visit Spock and Sarek?"

"Yes. Jim, have you talked to either of them?"

"Spock, of course. Why?"

"Doesn't anything strike you as odd here?" asked McCoy.

"Bones, I've been concentrating on some way of getting those Vulcan rebels out of engineering, short of explosives."

"Oh—yeah. I forgot about that problem. Making any progress?"

"Not yet. Now that Scotty's out of sickbay, though, I'm sure he'll get those doors open. Now, what's this about Spock and Sarek?"

"The *time*. You know that damn Vulcan time sense. Sarek has had nothing to do for the past three days but worry about his wife. Some of what he said to me the translator wouldn't handle, but what he was really mad about is that he's been cooped up in there for three days. *Three* days, Jim."

"What? You mean neither Spock nor Sarek—?"

"That's right, and I just don't get it. Spock—well, who can predict how his system will react to anything? But Sarek is full Vulcan, and he's been exposed twice now. First at the same time Amanda was, and then again *by* Amanda. My God, she made a gash on his face, put the virus straight into his blood, and he's *not sick.*"

"Could it be that weird blood type that they both have?" Kirk demanded.

"T-negative? It's rare, but I can't believe no Vulcan on Nisus has that type," said McCoy.

"What about Vulcans on Nisus who haven't caught the plague? Bones . . . !"

"I'm on it, Jim." He went to the intercom. "Uhura, put me through to Sorel and Corrigan—emergency priority."

There was a short wait, then a cultured voice said, "M'Benga here, Dr. McCoy. Sorel and Dr. Corrigan are attending patients."

"You can check this for me, Geoff. I want to know if any Vulcans with blood type T-negative have had any strain of the plague."

"Just a moment. They'll be in a separate computer file . . . yes, here are the records. Six in all Nisus' Vulcan population. One moment while I check their names against the disease records. T'Ara . . . Strain A, recovered. Skitra . . . Strain B, deceased. Suter . . . Strain B, recovered. T'Gra . . . Strain C, critical—"

McCoy sighed. "Thanks, Geoff. I thought we might have had an answer, but obviously T-negative's not it."

"So why is Sarek immune?" asked Kirk.

"Let's get some of his blood and see," said McCoy.
A few minutes later, Kirk was in the lab with McCoy, both swathed in protective gear against con-

tamination. McCoy showed him on the magnification screen how the Klingon blood samples destroyed the various strains of the virus. But Sarek's blood didn't; the very first specimen McCoy introduced to it began to multiply like wildfire.

"He's *not* immune," said Kirk.

"But he's definitely not sick," McCoy responded. "Oh, hell—we might as well let Spock and Sarek both out. They're not going to infect anyone when they're not sick themselves, and I don't think either one wants to sit in isolation forever just to avoid the possibility of catching this thing."

When they were released, both Spock and Sarek insisted on seeing Amanda, but McCoy would not allow them into her room. They had to look in through an observation port, to see her lying pale and still, only the flashing of the heartbeat indicator showing she was still alive.

Spock was already speculating as to why neither he nor Sarek had caught Amanda's illness. "I want to see those studies Korsal did," he said. "The graphs that identified the mutation pattern."

McCoy explained that Korsal was still in sickbay. After passing through all the decontamination procedures in leaving isolation, they went to where the Klingon engineer was. As Kirk had ordered, the computer terminals had been set up, and Korsal was working. Fields of multicolored dots flashed across his screen as he watched, frowning.

Korsal looked up as the group entered his room. "Captain Kirk, have you started beaming materials and personnel up from Nisus?"

Kirk shrugged. "Once we had the plague aboard, it didn't matter any longer. No one beamed up right away, though."

"Not till yesterday," McCoy affirmed.

"You, Dr. McCoy," said Korsal. "Who else?"

"Sorel and Corrigan. M'Benga. Some of our nurses went back and forth too, and several lab technicians."

"Then . . . both kinds of the virus may be aboard by now," said Korsal.

"There are four strains now," said McCoy.

"No—not the strains, the . . . substrains, I suppose is the term. When you told me that our iron-based blood could not provide immunity to those with copper-based blood, I revised the chart, using only red for iron, green for copper, and white for silicon-based blood. People with silicon-based blood have had only Strain A."

"How many such people are there on Nisus?" asked McCoy.

"Forty-seven," Korsal replied, "and *no one* of mixed heritage combining silicon with either copper or iron. Look at the spread pattern, then: white to white, red to red, green to green. But just as the mutations to more deadly strains of the virus have occurred in people of mixed ancestry, so have the substrains developed. Watch. Here is Strain B."

With only the three colors, instead of the original host of varying shades, they could see the mutation spread, red to red to red to red to red—until it reached someone whose dot was both red and green, someone whose ancestry combined iron-based and copper-based blood, as Spock's did. From that person three patterns spread: red to red to red, and green to green to green of Strain B, and Strain C, in this case going green to green to green.

Spock had moved forward to study the screen. Kirk saw him swallow, very hard. "Doctor," he said, his voice absolutely flat, "I think I must go back into isolation."

Kirk saw the doctor look at their Vulcan . . . their *half*-Vulcan friend, first startled, then sad. Then, "Yes," he said, "I'm afraid you're right, Spock. Let's just hope you're not contagious now."

Chapter Twenty-seven

SINCE SHE WAS already as exposed to the plague as it was possible to be, Sorel allowed T'Pina to nurse her mother. The younger woman had been working, like everyone else not sick or recovering, almost without rest. The healer expected her to show the first symptoms sooner than forty-eight hours from her exposure, but the first day brought no sign of the disease.

T'Kar continued to run a dangerously high fever and did not regain consciousness. Sorel ordered a cool bath, for there was plenty of water on Nisus. On Vulcan such cooling would be done with an environmental-control unit.

There were many, many other patients. Sorel had not slept since their arrival on Nisus—perfectly possible for a Vulcan, but he was beginning to reach his limits.

Now that they were able to produce a serum for those whose blood was iron-based, the time of the doctors and healers was divided even further: patient care, research into a cure or vaccine for people with other blood bases, and preparation and administration of the serum.

Their three Klingons could produce only a finite amount of blood. Sorel was especially concerned about the younger boy; his strength should be going into growth, not blood production stimulated by drugs. But they had no choice. Karl Katasai was sent up to the *Enterprise* and put on the same regimen as his father and his brother.

Priorities for the serum were critical patients, medical personnel, people of mixed ancestry with iron-based blood, anyone showing the first signs of the disease, and finally general population with iron-based blood, beginning with children and anyone else at high risk. However, their supply covered only the first two categories and part of the third.

At least Daniel is safe, Sorel thought as he administered the serum to his friend and colleague of so many years.

"But you're not, and neither is T'Mir," Daniel replied sadly to his unspoken thought.

Sorel started in shock—Daniel's ESP rating was virtually nil. The Human locked eyes with him, then stared at Sorel's hand, still gripping his arm. "You are *exhausted,*" he said. "I've never known your shields to slip like that before."

"You've never known it," Sorel replied. "Forgive me, Daniel."

"For what—proving again that we're family? You wouldn't ask T'Mir's forgiveness if you slipped with her."

"You must be retested when we return to Vulcan," said Sorel. "Your bonding with a Vulcan appears to have increased your ESP."

"Don't change the subject. If you can slip mentally, you can slip physically—and that possibility is as dangerous to the physician as to the patient. I've accepted your advice to nap every few hours, but you haven't slept at all. You're not going near any more patients until you've had at least six hours of sleep. Doctor's orders, Healer!"

Daniel was right. Sorel reluctantly accepted the prescription, used a meditation technique to fall asleep, and awoke feeling rested, although no less concerned. It was warranted: there were seven more cases of Strain D, all in people of copper-based blood. They had no cure for them, could only treat the symptoms.

T'Kar's fever raged despite cold-water lavage and an ice bath; she had gone into convulsions twice. T'Pina remained at her side, replacing the ice as fast as it melted, her concern and frustration showing in her eyes, even though she schooled her face into calm Vulcan lines. She was pale, but that was a symptom of weariness, not plague.

All T'Pina's vital signs remained astonishingly normal. Sorel did not understand how her system could resist the virus for so long. "The first moment you feel feverish, you must call for help," he cautioned her, and reminded the Human nurse who was checking T'Kar's progress every half hour to scan T'Pina each visit as well.

At least it was refreshing to see the medical personnel who had been vaccinated coming out from beneath the cumbersome protective gear. And to see Human, Lemnorian, Caitian, and Hemanite patients recovering.

But just as fast, the diagnostic beds filled with Vulcans, Orions, Rigellians—and emptied, as fully two-thirds of those with Strain D died within the first twelve hours.

In the computer room, McCoy showed Sorel Korsal's new findings. "And there we went, possibly contaminating the *Enterprise* with every strain and substrain, when Sendet had carried up only a strain which attacks iron-based blood—a strain for which we now have a cure!"

"We had no way of knowing, Leonard."

"No," the Human doctor agreed, "no way." He snorted derisively. "I was hoping to see Sendet hoisted on his own petard."

"You do not mean that," said Sorel. "You would never wish illness on anyone."

"No," McCoy agreed. "I've seen enough to last a lifetime."

The intercom beeped. McCoy punched the switch, considerably harder than he would have had to. "McCoy here."

"Gardens here, in the *Enterprise* sickbay, Doctor. I think you will want to beam aboard. Mr. Spock has gone into systemic failure."

Chapter Twenty-eight

PERFECTLY HEALTHY, not medical personnel, and not of mixed heritage, James T. Kirk was at the bottom of the list to be vaccinated against the plague. That meant he was stuck aboard the *Enterprise*. Everyone who had been near Amanda between her exposure by Sendet and her confinement to sickbay had been inoculated. It seemed to work: no one else had come down with the disease except Spock.

Not being on the priority list for the vaccine also meant that Kirk could not visit Spock, although McCoy reminded him that he was not a doctor, and could really not do the now-unconscious Vulcan any good. Somehow, though, he had the irrational feeling that Spock would know he wasn't there, and that if he could be, perhaps he could will a fight for survival into his friend.

Amanda was out of danger now, weak, greatly worried about Spock, but recovering. Sarek spent most of his time at her side, which McCoy said was probably safer for him than anywhere else on board. "All the medical staff's been vaccinated," explained his CMO, "not that Sarek could catch it from them anyway. Either he's already caught it from Spock, or he's safe unless the copper-based strain was brought aboard by our carelessness."

"The way Sendet brought aboard the iron-based strain," Kirk said angrily.

"We'll know soon enough," said McCoy. "We're filtering the air through the entire sickbay, not just the isolation units. Sorel and the other Vulcans are staying planetside for now—they've added to their tasks trying to develop a quick test for the disease before the symptoms start to show." The doctor rubbed weary eyes. "Things are *better* now that we've got the vaccine. So why are we busier and tireder than ever?"

"We only have part of the answer," Kirk replied, "and we can't implement it because we can't make vaccine fast enough."

"I can't keep Korsal and his sons on those drugs much longer, either," said McCoy. "They're not as dangerous as that drug I used on Spock the time I needed so much blood for Sarek's heart surgery—but on the other hand, they increase production by only twenty-five percent, not two hundred percent like that Rigellian serum."

"But the Rigellian serum—" Kirk began.

McCoy chorused with him, "—only works on people with copper-based blood."

Kirk shook his head. "Bones, did you ever think there'd be a time when we'd *wish* we were hip-deep in Klingons?" Suddenly he realized, "Wait a minute! Maybe we can be!"

"Huh?" said McCoy, that brilliant repartee evidence of how tired and overstressed the CMO was.

Kirk left McCoy's office and went into the area where Korsal was with his two sons. One look at the younger boy, and he called, "Bones! Come here!"

Karl was asleep. When he didn't wake at Kirk's shout, though, both his father and his older brother were immediately at his side. "What's wrong with him?" Korsal demanded as McCoy hurried in.

Kirk saw McCoy study the life-sign indicators over the bed, but they meant nothing to him as he had no idea what the vital signs of a half-Klingon, half-Human boy ought to be.

The doctor peeled back one of Karl's eyelids, shined a light in—and the boy woke, feebly pushing McCoy away and turning onto his side, sliding immediately back into sleep.

"He's all right," said McCoy. "He's just exhausted. I'm taking him off the drugs, effective immediately. He's just too young to take the stress."

Korsal looked from his son to the doctor, and Kirk saw the emotions flicker over his face. "You are sure he has not been harmed already?"

"Look at the indicators," said McCoy. "The warning is set to go off well above the danger levels, and it didn't. Would have in another few minutes, though. Korsal, there's no telling how many lives you're saving; do you think we're going to repay you by allowing your son to come to harm?"

"No. I have observed your precautions. But now your production of vaccine will be cut by one third."

"It doesn't have to be," said Kirk.

Korsal stared at him, frowning. "What do you mean?"

"Korsal, I can't believe that the Klingon Empire would maroon you here, on a Federation planet, with no means of calling for help if you need it."

"I report regularly to the empire," Korsal replied, "but my mission is to acquire and transmit scientific data."

"But you can contact the empire?"

"Yes. Why?"

"You *know* why! Even Klingons respond to a medical distress signal! The moment you found out we could make a vaccine from Klingon blood, why didn't you send out a call for volunteers? Surely you've lived among us long enough to know we wouldn't take the opportunity to lay a trap and kill them!"

Korsal was staring at him impassively, Kevin in horror. Then the boy looked to his father, equally horrified. "I didn't know you could call directly to the empire. Why didn't you, Father?"

Korsal walked heavily back to his bed and sat down. "I can send a message that will reach an empire outpost in approximately two days. No, I have not sent such a message. Captain, have you thought about what you are asking?"

"Help. From Klingons. Are you saying, then, that Human prejudice is justified: that if a Klingon saw a man bleeding to death by the side of the road, not only would he not help him, but he would rob him before he left him to die?"

"Jim!" McCoy protested.

Korsal looked up, wearing a smile that just barely showed the points of his teeth—a warning. Kirk had seen that Klingon expression many times in a long career, but never before from Korsal.

Then the Klingon said, "You are a soldier, Captain, among your people that sets you apart. Among my people, the fact that I am *not* a soldier sets me apart. Despite that, I know something of military thinking."

He continued, "If I sent a medical distress signal, the empire would send help. But consider: those who came to the aid of Nisus would take back a full report. Captain Kirk, have Humans never engaged in biological warfare?"

The Eugenics Wars. Kirk's stomach clenched. "We

consider it the most heinous crime imaginable," he replied.

"And to consider it so means that at some time in your history your people have experienced it. Among Klingons, it is considered equally reprehensible, dishonorable, forbidden. However, every military man knows that once a weapon exists—"

"—it will be used," Kirk completed the statement. "A Klingon saying too, I take it."

"An observation from life," Korsal replied. "Now do you understand, Captain? This virus has mutated into strains that are deadly, and rapidly so. It is effective against every race in the Federation . . . but Klingons are immune. It is a weapon that you cannot turn back upon us.

"James Kirk, you cannot be so naive as to think that for all Klingon belief in the honor of direct confrontation, there are not those—and it takes only a few, even just one—who, if they knew about this virus, would use it. Once loosed upon the Federation at large—"

"—no cure," said McCoy, "for the vast numbers of Federation citizens whose blood is based on copper. And for Humans and others with iron-based blood—"

"—the only cure," Kirk took it up, "has to be made from the blood of Klingons. To save their lives, and the lives of their families, what bargains might any planetary government be willing to make?" He suppressed a shudder.

"And," added Korsal, "it could have the effect of turning your race into . . . vampires, I believe, is the legendary term . . . preying upon my race."

"Oh, God," said McCoy. "He's right; we'd attack

their ships to get blood to make vaccine, and rationalize it by saying they started it."

By this time, Kirk was feeling thoroughly sick. "I didn't realize there were Klingons who didn't want war."

"Not *that* kind of war," Korsal told him. "Not any sane Klingon. However, just as among Humans there are those—"

"You don't have to say any more," said Kirk. "Korsal, I am sorry. Thank God you thought it through."

"A scientist's job, extrapolation," said Korsal.

Then Kevin spoke up. "Father, now I understand why my admission to Starfleet Academy did not disturb you."

Korsal looked over at his son, but said nothing, so the boy continued, "I expected it to, if it came, because when Karl and I are grown you would have had a choice of whether to return to the empire or remain in the Federation. If I had graduated from Starfleet Academy and you had returned to the empire, there was the remote possibility that we might meet as enemies one day. But before my acceptance came, the plague began—and we were immune. You knew that you would not impart that information to the empire. And that means . . . you can never go home again."

Chapter Twenty-nine

DR. LEONARD McCOY beamed reluctantly down to Nisus, leaving Spock in the hands of his staff. He sought out Sorel and told him, "I need a Vulcan healer. I've seen Spock through all kinds of illnesses and injuries, but this one has me stumped. His temperature and his blood pressure are shooting up and down like a yo-yo. He's had a nosebleed. When he comes to he starts vomiting—and there's nothing left in him. He can't even hold water down. This last time he vomited blood. I'm giving him a transfusion from his father right now, and he's unconscious again."

The healer was swathed in protective gear, grim reminder that they still had no protection for Vulcans from the plague. "Leonard," he said, "we agreed that no one with copper-based blood would beam aboard the *Enterprise*. You have not had any cases there yet among Vulcans, other than Spock?"

"No."

"Then take Dr. M'Benga. There is no need for a mental touch in treating this plague, Leonard; Geoffrey can treat Spock as well as I can."

Reluctantly, McCoy sought the black Human doctor. He was sleeping, and his eyes were bloodshot and weary when he forced them open, but he jumped up when McCoy described Spock's symptoms. "That's Vulcan undulant syndrome," he said. "He'll be bleeding from all mucus membranes in a few hours if we don't get it stopped—and once that happens, transfusions can't keep him from bleeding to death."

"How do we stop it?" McCoy demanded.

"Anticoagulants and pressure points. I'll show you."

"*Anti*coagulants?" McCoy asked, suddenly afraid that M'Benga was so fatigued that he might make a fatal mistake.

"Coagulation in the capillaries forces blood through the membranes. Vulcans aren't Humans, Leonard."

"Spock's *half* Human," McCoy reminded him.

"Not physiologically. There are few Human factors to his anatomical structure. Spock is the first Vulcan/Human hybrid—he is *the* specific case we studied in my classes. I'm glad for the opportunity to examine him in real life—except that I would prefer less grim circumstances."

It seemed to take forever to go through all the decontamination necessary before they could beam up, but at least now the two Humans knew they were not carrying the disease in their own blood.

McCoy was impressed with M'Benga's knowledge. M'Benga checked Spock's vitals, ordered medication, adjusted the temperature of the room a few degrees higher, and said, "Now, we must place pressure on his main arteries in sequence, to drive the blood through the capillaries so it doesn't pool and clot. Vulcan blood pressure is normally so low that it becomes a problem in a disease like this one; the bouts of heightened blood pressure are Spock's body's own attempts to accomplish cleansing of the capillaries."

M'Benga showed McCoy where to apply pressure, then release it so that the blood surged through with extra strength, like water released from behind a dam. They went systematically over his body, applying and releasing pressure until their fingers went numb, and then went on anyway, working to save his life.

Finally M'Benga stopped and drew a blood sample, and they examined it in the laboratory. "It's okay," said M'Benga. "His blood is back to normal consistency. If his heart stays strong, this particular crisis is over."

But Spock was still unconscious, pale, breathing raggedly. McCoy knew the disease had not yet run its course.

Chapter Thirty

WHEN SOREL LEFT McCOY, he went on to T'Kar's room. The Vulcan woman was also in undulant syndrome; her daughter and a Human nurse were working on her as he entered.

This latest twist of the disease might spell death for the Vulcans on Nisus: there were simply not enough personnel to treat them. It took two people and nearly an hour's work for each such bout with the syndrome. At least one of the two people had to be trained, to be able to direct the other as the nurse was doing with T'Pina.

Sorel saw that for all their efforts, death had outmaneuvered them. There were plenty of willing Human, Lemnorian, Caitian hands—but they were *untrained* hands. These latest strains of the disease had everyone who knew Vulcan anatomy on standby . . . and there were just too few.

The critical portion of the plague was also getting longer with each new strain. T'Kar had been sick for over three days now, and—

Three days!

He stood back from checking T'Kar's vital signs and stared at T'Pina. The younger woman's face was pinched and drawn with concern and the effort to control; her eyes were sunk into olive-green circles from lack of sleep.

But she was not ill.

T'Pina might be on the edge of exhaustion, but she definitely did not have the plague.

"How long?" he asked the nurse.

"Forty-nine minutes."

"Let me draw a blood sample," said Sorel. All the doctors and healers now carried tricorders to do this one simple blood test immediately, without sending it to the overworked laboratory. "All right," he said, "she's through this crisis." *But how many more can she survive?*

"T'Pina," he said, "lie down now, and try to sleep. And I want a blood sample from you."

The girl frowned. "Why? I do not feel ill."

"That is *why* I want the sample," he replied. "Child, you should have been as sick as your mother after two days—less, because you have been over-working so that you have little resistance. Yet your body resists the plague. Let us see if we can find out how."

She did not protest further.

Sorel returned to the computer laboratory, where his daughter T'Mir was working. "Put this through the same tests you did on the Klingon samples," he told her.

She stared at the vial of green fluid, then back at her father as if she feared for his sanity. "Humor me, child," he said, and only then remembered that he had addressed T'Pina in the same way, as if she, too, were his daughter.

What was it Daniel called such things? A Freudian slip? Was his subconscious mind already making T'Kar and T'Pina a part of his family?

He sat down and rested his head on his hands while T'Mir set up the tests. Healers and doctors learned early in their careers to snatch any moment of rest in times of crisis. Deliberately, he turned his mind from the plague, let it blank, then allowed whatever thought might wish to enter.

He saw T'Kar as she had been aboard the *Enterprise,* dignified, stately, beautiful. Her blue eyes looked into his, so unlike the usual dark Vulcan eyes, so easy to read. In them he read—

"Father! Father, look. You've found it!"

He looked up, to see his daughter staring at the computer screen.

T'Mir had introduced the most virulent strain of the virus into the sample of blood he had brought her—T'Pina's blood. Just as in the Klingon blood, there was an analogous hemoglobin factor that bonded with the virus and would not let it grow. Before the eyes of father and daughter, the deadly infection shriveled up and died.

Chapter Thirty-one

T'PINA LAY ON the cot that had been placed in her mother's room for her, but she could not sleep. Why hadn't she caught the plague when her mother was so dreadfully ill?

For all her Vulcan training, T'Pina was afraid. T'Kar was dying. She was badly dehydrated, could not take even water by mouth, and went into undulant syndrome every time they tried to put blood, plasma, or even just hydration solution into her veins.

T'Pina was not ready to lose her mother—not so soon after her father had died! She had been through the healing process; the healers had said she was recovered. Yet the memory came back time after time, of the feeling, the knowledge, hours before the message came from T'Kar. Sevel was dead. Gone. She had sensed his *katra* again when T'Kar came to Vulcan to return it to his ancestors, but she would never again have her father to advise her, his strength to lean on, his wisdom to guide her.

But T'Kar had still been there, wise and strong.

Illogically, T'Pina got up and went to stand by T'Kar's bed. "Mother," she whispered, although she knew T'Kar could not hear, "please don't die. Please, Mother—"

"She's not going to die, T'Pina—thanks to you."

It was the healer, Sorel. He pressed a hypodermic against T'Kar's thin shoulder.

T'Pina looked at the healer, afraid to feel hope. "You are trying some new medication?"

"Watch her vitals," Sorel instructed.

They remained critical . . . until the faltering heartbeat suddenly strengthened, speeded, raced, and then settled back to Vulcan norm! T'Pina looked at the other indicators. T'Kar's temperature, which had been at one of its low points, was climbing upward —but instead of soaring on to fever pitch, as it had been doing, it settled at normal.

T'Pina stared at Sorel. "You've found a cure!"

He nodded, unreadable black eyes still on the life signs. "We have hope—and T'Kar is confirming it. There!"

Blood pressure stabilized. The crisis was over.

T'Kar stirred and opened hollow eyes. "T'Pina?" she whispered.

"I'm here, Mother," T'Pina assured her, taking her clawlike hand in both of hers. "You are going to be well."

"Yes," T'Kar managed. ". . . thirsty."

Hastily, T'Pina helped her to a sip of water. She was so weak that her head fell back on the pillow afterward, but Sorel said, "Go to sleep, T'Kar. Rest, and you will be well."

He turned to T'Pina. "Come with me, child. You have saved your mother's life, but many more need your blood."

"My blood?"

"We don't know how, but you carry something like that factor we found in the blood of the Klingons—a factor which destroys this disease. We can make a serum from your blood that will immunize the rest of us."

T'Pina did not react. Outwardly, it might appear to be perfect Vulcan control, but in truth she was simply dazed as the healer led her toward the laboratory, stopping twice to enter other rooms and administer the other doses of serum in the hypo to critical patients.

One of them she recognized, although it took a few moments, he was so changed: Beau Deaver, unconscious, dehydrated, several days' growth of beard making him look all the worse. At first he looked dead, the skin around his eyes wrinkled and shrunken inward like that of a corpse.

But as had happened with her mother, this man's vital signs also responded, heart strengthening, breathing regulating. Sorel did not wait for him to wake up, but left a nurse with him and hurried T'Pina to the laboratory.

There they drew more blood from her arms and began to prepare more serum. "How much blood can I give?" she asked.

"No more right now," Dr. Corrigan told her, "but this will make serum to save ten more people."

"But—but there are hundreds of people very ill," she protested.

"We're waiting to hear from the *Enterprise,*" said Sorel.

He had hardly spoken before the communication came through—Dr. McCoy, face lit with a huge Human grin. "It worked! By God, you found it! Spock's coming out of it, feisty as ever. What *was* that stuff?"

"A serum from T'Pina's blood," Sorel told him. "She appeared to be immune, so we tested and found a similar hemoglobin factor to the one in the Klingons' blood. Here it is," he added, pressing a switch to play a computer analysis.

T'Pina watched the screen as the virus, which she had seen schematized before, tried to attack something that she assumed was her own blood structure. Instead of thriving, the virus collapsed and died.

"I *knew* I had seen something like that Klingon blood factor before," said McCoy, "but I couldn't remember where."

"I was remiss," said Sorel. "I also recalled something similar. I should have remembered—I have never seen that factor anywhere in Vulcan blood, except T'Pina's."

"There's a good reason you haven't," said the *Enterprise* chief medical officer. "That's not Vulcan blood you've got there, Sorel. That's Romulan."

Chapter Thirty-two

FOR THE NEXT several hours, Sorel was too busy to wonder how T'Pina could be Romulan. First priority was to use her blood serum to save their most critical patients. That was quick work, but preparing her to give more blood was not.

Fortunately, Leonard McCoy had an answer: a Rigellian drug that would cause the girl's body to produce blood cells at a highly accelerated rate. Because the Starfleet surgeon had had experience with it, they did not have to search the computer records for it and then adapt it for Vulcan use.

There was a supply of the drug at the Nisus hospital, for use by Rigellians, but Leonard beamed down to help them adapt the drug for T'Pina.

"I had to use it on Spock once," he explained. "He's not fully Vulcan, but the drug wasn't affected by the Human factors in his blood. Let's hope that Romulan factor doesn't negate its effectiveness on T'Pina or give her any serious side effects."

"Leonard," Sorel asked as they worked, "how did you recognize that blood factor as Romulan?"

"It must have been about a year ago," Leonard replied, "the *Enterprise* had a run-in with a Romulan vessel. No one in the Federation had ever seen Romulans before, so we wanted to find out all we could. Despite their booby traps, we got one body on

200

board, along with what we could find of the others after their ship was destroyed. I ran autopsies. Except for that factor in their blood, they could have been Vulcans."

"That one factor is all that separates Vulcans from Romulans?" Sorel mused.

"Seems to be—and that factor could be an artificially created one. Spock thinks they're an offshoot of the Vulcans," McCoy said. "Same people, different philosophy—like the Followers of T'Vet, perhaps."

Sorel nodded. "Please tell that to T'Pina. She is controlling her emotions outwardly. However, her shields are up so strongly that I cannot reach her thoughts without a meld, and she will not permit that. She insists she can meditate on her own, and that it is more important that I spend my time with critical patients. Do you . . . ?"

"I understand," the Human doctor replied. "I can't ever reach Spock's thoughts, of course, but I can tell when he's overcontrolling. I'll talk to T'Pina, but it's her mother who can do her the most good. Uh . . . I take it the girl is adopted? Or could her father have been . . . ?"

"No, Sevel could not have been Romulan," Sorel told him, amused at the absurdity of the idea. "And yes, T'Pina is adopted, her ancestry unknown." He told Leonard everything he knew about T'Pina.

"So T'Pina was the only child not identified?"

"That is correct."

"And you have never heard of any other Vulcan with this blood factor?"

"When T'Pina became my patient, I searched all records," Sorel replied. "In fact, since I first examined her as an infant, my medical computer has had a notation to call to my attention any instance of that blood factor. It was originally intended to locate any relatives she might have. There has never been a reason to remove that notation. Leonard, your report should have triggered it."

Leonard smiled. "You haven't dealt much with Starfleet, have you? Oh, they'll get around to releasing the information eventually, but they tend to classify anything about Klingons or Romulans in case it might be strategic. But if the Romulans were planting cuckoos in the Vulcan population, that blood factor would have turned up through civilian channels and your computer would have picked it up."

"Planting cuckoos?" Sorel asked. Daniel would have automatically interpreted, but he was making rounds again.

"Birds on Earth that lay their eggs in other birds' nests," the Human explained. "But it doesn't make sense for intelligent beings. Blood factor be damned, T'Pina *is* Vulcan—so what good would that do the Romulans? Leaving an infant to be raised as one of the enemy is not the same thing as planting adult spies."

"You are correct that T'Pina is Vulcan," replied Sorel. "And if there were more like her, or if there were adult spies among us, I cannot believe that none of them would ever have had a blood analysis. So T'Pina's origin remains a mystery."

McCoy looked at him sharply, reading him as easily as Daniel ever did. "And if there is anything a Vulcan cannot stand, it's a mystery. This one appears insoluble, though. Insufficient data."

The adaptation of the drug for T'Pina was not insoluble, however, and soon they went to look for the young woman. Not surprisingly, they found her at her mother's bedside.

T'Kar was sleeping, her vital signs normal, her color pale but otherwise natural.

"Come, T'Pina," said Sorel. "We must administer the drug."

"Mother hasn't awakened," T'Pina protested. "I have not been able to tell her—"

"—that you're Romulan?" asked Leonard McCoy. "T'Pina, surely you know it won't make any difference to her. Sorel tells me you're adopted—so you already know that what makes T'Kar and you mother and daughter comes from ties far stronger than those of blood. Nothing will change just because you now know what that mysterious factor in your blood means."

T'Pina nodded. "It would be illogical to assume it makes a difference," she said flatly.

"Never mind logic!" said the Human. "You may not like the term 'love' to describe what you and your mother feel, so how about 'loyalty,' or 'family'? Those are revered Vulcan concepts."

"Indeed," T'Pina replied, but Sorel could see that she had not yet truly assimilated the news of her ancestry.

"T'Pina," the healer said, "you must lie down now so that we may administer the blood stimulant. Perhaps you will be able to meditate for a time."

"For a time?" she asked.

"The side effects don't start right away," Leonard explained. "After a few hours it produces a physical weakness that affects the mind. You may feel dizzy, and we will keep someone at your bedside because you may try to act irrationally. That's nothing to worry about; the effects will go away as soon as the drug is out of your system."

"Yes, Doctor," T'Pina said with one last glance at

her mother. Then she squared her shoulders. "People are dying, and my blood can save them. I am ready."

But just as they were about to leave the room, the wall intercom gave a loud squawk, followed by a voice announcing, "Paging T'Pina—all channels emergency—T'Pina to any communicator." Sorel could hear the announcement reverberating from other speakers down the corridor.

Leonard McCoy charged up to the wall unit and pounded the switch with his fist. "T'Pina's here with us," he growled. "What's the damned emergency that you have to disturb critical patients?"

It should not have been possible, in fact, for whoever was calling to override the safeguards and broadcast into the patients' rooms. Sorel had never seen it happen in any hospital before.

"I must talk to T'Pina," the voice insisted.

There was a blast of static, through which they could hear James Kirk's voice saying, ". . . cut off that—"

But he was the one cut off.

McCoy said, *"Enterprise?* What's going on? Jim?"

"We are controlling communications," said the original voice. "T'Pina, are you there?"

"It is Sendet," T'Pina said, stepping to the intercom. "I do not wish to speak with you, Sendet," she said calmly into the speaker.

"T'Pina, I need you!" The young Vulcan's voice was suddenly hoarse. Then, more calmly, as if he had grasped control, "It is my time, T'Pina. You are one of us, young and strong, from good family stock. You must beam aboard and bond with me. It is my life, T'Pina."

It was the final blow to T'Pina's control. Sorel saw her cheeks flush green, and then—she laughed!

The laugh was harsh, bitter, edged with tears. Sorel moved toward her, but T'Pina raised a hand and straightened, forcing herself to tenuous control.

She breathed deeply, twice, and then said into the wall unit, "Other lives than yours depend on me, Sendet, and you have other choices. Make one. And when the madness passes, consider this: you think yourself a judge over other Vulcans. You judge by such things as strength and ancestry—but T'Kar and Sevel are my *adopted* parents. Until today I did not know my ancestry, but, unlike you, my parents did not care. They judged me for what I am, not whose blood flows in my veins."

"As I will, T'Pina," Sendet pleaded. "It doesn't matter—you are strong and intelligent and pure Vulcan—"

"Fool!" the girl exclaimed. "If I were pure Vulcan, there would be no way to stop this plague! Meditate upon the irony, Sendet: I carry the cure for Vulcans in my blood . . . because I am Romulan!"

There was silence from the wall unit. Then, in the background a voice said, "Sendet, what are you—?"

There was the sound of a chair overturning, an animal growl, and the noise of a struggle.

Those sounds cut off, and Uhura's voice said, "Dr. McCoy?"

"McCoy here, Uhura. What's going on up there?"

"The rebels—perhaps just Sendet—overrode communications from engineering, and blasted through all the safeguards on Nisus. Everyone who was anywhere near a communications console must have heard all that."

Kirk's voice cut in. "We've got it under control now. Scotty got the doors open, and security's escorting the rebels to the brig."

"That's a relief," said McCoy. "Uh, about Sendet—"

"I know what's wrong with him, Bones. Or what he thinks is wrong. I'll have him taken to sickbay. You want to come up and examine him?"

"Is M'Benga aboard? He can handle it. We're about to administer the blood stimulant to T'Pina, and I want to monitor her personally until I'm sure it's going right."

"Good work," said the captain. "T'Pina?"

"Yes, Captain Kirk?" the girl managed to say calmly.

"On behalf of all those whose lives you have already saved, and those you are about to—thank you."

T'Pina's upbringing among the diverse cultures of Nisus showed in her automatic, "You are welcome."

As Kirk signed off, though, a weary voice spoke from behind them. "T'Pina?"

"Mother!" The girl hurried to T'Kar's side.

Weakly, T'Kar raised her hands, crossed at the wrists. T'Pina echoed the gesture, touching palms with her mother in Vulcan greeting, parent to child. Then, "You heard?" T'Pina asked warily.

"It was . . . very loud," T'Kar said. "It is true? You are—?"

"Romulan."

T'Kar frowned. "How can that be?"

T'Pina straightened. "I do not know," she said flatly. "I must go now, Mother."

"T'Pina, no—we must talk," T'Kar pleaded.

"Others have need of my blood," T'Pina said stiffly. "Healer, Doctor—"

Sorel said, "Please take her and start the process, Leonard. T'Pina is right: we cannot delay further. There are lives at stake."

As the Starfleet surgeon escorted T'Pina out, Sorel turned to T'Kar, who was trying feebly to sit up. He pressed her back against the pillows, saying, "Rest. T'Pina is safe with Dr. McCoy. He has performed this procedure before."

T'Kar lay for a moment with her eyes closed. Then she opened them and said, "I failed her. I could not tell her she is my daughter, no matter what blood flows in her veins."

"You'll tell her tomorrow," Sorel assured her. "T'Pina has experienced a great shock and not had time to meditate and come to terms with it. Nor have you, T'Kar. These are the times we must use the techniques we learn as children."

"I must talk with her."

Sorel looked into the guileless blue eyes. "You will. After you have rested. I recommend that you try a meditation trance, T'Kar. I will help you if you wish."

"No, Healer," she replied as coldly as her daughter, "I remember the technique." And she composed herself and closed her eyes.

Sorel straightened, rebuffed. T'Kar had been calling him by name for days now. He had thought—

I also need to meditate, he told himself. T'Kar had been critically ill, and awakened to discover that her cherished daughter was a Romulan. There was no wonder that at this moment she should not have a thought for anything or anyone other than T'Pina.

Chapter Thirty-three

KORSAL WOKE FROM restless sleep to find Arthur, the mop-headed med tech, removing the tube through which his blood had flowed into waiting containers. The apparatus that fed the blood stimulant into his arm was already gone. "What are you doing?" he asked.

"Doc Gardens says ya gotta recover fer a coupla days," the young Human replied. "Can't keep you goin' forever on that stuff. We took you off it last night; most of it's out of you by now, but you'll be knackered for a bit."

"Surely you don't have enough serum!" Korsal protested.

"An' if you go and die on us we'll be in a pretty fix, won't we?"

The Klingon knew the *Enterprise* medical staff were correct. As a matter of fact, he felt miserable: mouth dry and foul-tasting, muscles stiff, head in a delicate balance with the rest of his body, threatening to float away if he lay still, but punishing him with dull, pounding pain if he moved.

"Drink this," Arthur told him, handing him some blue liquid in the bottom of a plastic sickbay tumbler.

Korsal sniffed it. "What is it?"

"Cure fer what ails ya. Ol' blue eyes' private stock, so taste it on the way down!"

It was, indeed, a very fine brandy. "Ol' blue-eyes," Korsal surmised, was Chief Medical Officer McCoy. He did not ask how Arthur had gained access to his private stock.

The brandy helped, but still wisps of a headache blurred the edges of his perception. He saw that Kevin's bed was empty, but it wasn't long before his son returned, greeted his father, and turned on his computer terminal.

Korsal didn't feel like talking, either. People were dying because he and Kevin and Karl simply could not give enough blood. Karl was in the third bed in the room, still on the drug because he had gone on it later than his father and his older brother. Kevin had not been able to stay on it as long as Korsal, and it was clear of his system now. He was studying the assignment Captain Kirk had given him.

It wasn't long before the captain appeared to check his student's progress. Korsal was still too weary to think about his own work, so he sat and listened as his son drew an analogy between fourteenth-century Englishmen and the population of Nisus.

"So the Canterbury Pilgrims come from all different classes except the ruling class, and all different occupations. Some of them are pretty despicable characters too. But although they quarrel among themselves, they are together for a common purpose: to travel to Canterbury and back safely. If they were to meet bandits, they'd band together to fight them off—only they didn't meet any," Kevin said in disappointment.

"Chaucer died before he finished the work," said Captain Kirk. "I've always thought that if he'd finished it, there would have been bandits. And probably a sixth husband for the Wife of Bath. Go on."

"They're like us because they have a common purpose, and they can only achieve it by working together, no matter how different they are in their views and values."

Kirk grinned and looked over at Korsal. "Bright boy you've got here."

"He does me honor," Korsal replied. But he could not confide his deep concerns about his son, both his sons. Lying here with nothing to do, not yet strong enough to concentrate on the plans he was drawing up for better safeties above the dam on Nisus, the thought preyed on his mind: now that Korsal was exiled, what would happen to his sons?

Soon after Kirk left, Arthur came around the partition to ask, "You feelin' up t' visitors?"

"That depends on who they are," he replied.

"Yer wife an' her uncle, they say."

Then it was true: he had half wakened from his drug-fogged state to sounds of happy excitement in sickbay, and half understood that there was now a way to protect people with copper-based blood from the plague. If Seela and Borth were allowed aboard ship, it must be true.

Korsal closed his eyes. "Because I wish to see my wife, I suppose I shall have to suffer Borth's company."

Seela came to hug Korsal, nothing more. When she went to greet Kevin, Korsal looked up at the unwelcome visitor she had brought with her. "What are you doing here? And how did you get aboard?"

"We've been inoculated—all Orions on Nisus have," Borth replied. "Diplomatic courtesy to non-Federation citizens."

And you would use that leverage, wouldn't you,

210

Korsal thought viciously, *while Vulcans and Rigellians die because there's not enough serum to go around!* But he didn't voice his anger. Borth was here for a reason.

The Orion drew a chair close and leaned forward to say, "You think you've won, don't you, Korsal?"

"I was not aware there was a contest, Borth."

The yellow eyes held a feral gleam. "The game goes on, whether you are player or merely pawn. This plague will set the Federation and the Klingon and Romulan empires at one another's throats—and the winners will be the Orions."

"You are wrong, Borth," said Korsal. "You underestimate our intelligence."

"Whose? The Klingons?" the man hissed. "Surely you cannot mean the Federation! Have you applied for citizenship in that pitiful mix of slave-born races, Korsal?"

"I am a Klingon," Korsal replied, refusing to admit that the thought had crossed his mind often since he had realized he could never go home. Where was home? Nisus was the only place he had ever felt truly welcome.

"You're no Klingon," Borth told him. "You're weak as any Federate—you belong with them. When I sell this plague to the Klingons and the Roms, though, how will your fine friends treat you?"

Sell it to the Romulans? Then it *was* a Romulan on Nisus whose blood carried the immunity factor. He had thought he dreamed that part of what he had overheard. There weren't supposed to be any Romulans in the Federation.

Borth continued with his threats. "Oh, the Federation will keep you alive, you and your half-breed sons.

They may even breed you, for your precious blood. You'll be a laboratory animal to them—along with other Klingons they'll capture for their blood."

Anger gave Korsal the strength to grasp Borth's shoulder in a bruising grip; had they been alone, he might have strangled him. "Do you think I will allow you to tell them, Borth? I will kill you first."

"Then you'd better do it now," Borth replied coldly. "I will be leaving Nisus soon—along with everyone else."

"What?"

"Fool! This intermingling of races weakens both the Federation and the Klingon Empire. We Orions sell our excess women to both, diluting your bloodlines. When the Federation Council gets the report on the Nisus plague, they'll recognize its source and disband the colony here. Then where will you go, Korsal? Whatever happens, you have lost. Unless—"

"Unless?"

Borth glanced over to where Seela now stood by Karl's bed, stroking her sleeping stepson's forehead. "When I let you marry Seela—"

But that was not how it had happened. Korsal had purchased his wife from Borth to prevent the man from sending Seela back to the Orion system when she had reached an age to be valuable. Her beauty and her dancing skills would probably have meant her purchase as an expensive pleasure slave. Korsal had set her free before marrying her.

"Leave Seela out of this!" Korsal told him. "You *sold* her, just another transaction. You don't care about her."

"Ah, but you do," said Borth. "She is amazingly loyal to you, Korsal. Since you married her, I haven't gotten a single piece of useful information out of her."

Hearing her name, Seela returned to Korsal, sitting on the edge of his bed. Her presence could have clouded his senses, but it did not. Instead, he felt her support, as if she lent him strength. All his friends had warned him against marrying an Orion, then become silent on the subject after he had done so. But he had been right: Seela did not manipulate him . . . except when he wanted her to.

"I know why you wanted me to marry Seela, Borth," he said, taking his wife's hand. "You badly underestimated her. She knows exactly what you are."

"She is merely a woman. A commodity. You are a fool to treat her otherwise. However," the Orion continued, "you can salvage her, make a place for your sons, escape before you become prisoners of the Federation. Come with me to Klinzhai. Report the plague to your people, Korsal. Be a hero, giving them a new weapon against their enemies. Your enemies."

"No," said Korsal. To his astonishment, Seela spoke the word in unison with him.

Then, "No, Uncle," Seela said. "Whatever happens, we will not be party to starting interplanetary war."

"You had your chance," said Borth, extricating himself from Korsal's grip and rising. "Now I will do what must be done for the good of Orion."

When Borth had gone, Korsal said, "He does not know the codes for contacting the Klingon Empire. He will have to go there—and I must prevent him."

"You are right, my husband," said Seela.

Korsal stared at her and remembered several times recently when she had asked favors of him—always by communicator, so that her pheromones could not affect him. The third or fourth time it had happened, he had realized how much she wanted his trust. How she struggled to overcome her upbringing, her dependence on men to tell her what to do, her instinctive and practiced use of sensuality to obtain favor.

"You were supposed to persuade me to agree to what Borth wanted," said Korsal.

"That is what he instructed me to do. And also get the codes from you. I do not take instructions from Borth," she replied. "Korsal, I had never known a man could be so strong and honorable until I came to live with you. Whatever happens, I will stay with you."

"Father," Kevin said from the next bed, "what *is* going to happen?"

Korsal sighed. "The last thing Borth expects, or we would not be alive right now. I must tell Captain Kirk about Borth's plans. There is no other way. Borth must be stopped, and short of killing him, I have no other way to do so."

But after Seela had gone, when he tried to contact Kirk, the communications officer informed him that the captain was busy and would return his call. "Then the second in command, please," Korsal said.

"Mr. Spock is not on the bridge. I will page him for you."

While he was waiting, another visitor appeared, this one unannounced: the Human male who had operated the transporter the day he and Kevin had been beamed aboard.

"I'm Montgomery Scott, chief engineer," said the Human. "We've met, though ye may not recall, bein' you were near froze t' death." Korsal saw wariness in the man's eyes, though he was trying to cover it. Whatever Korsal might do, Mr. Scott saw only "Klingon."

"My son and I have you to thank for saving our lives," Korsal replied.

"An' ye've returned the favor manyfold," Mr. Scott replied, if somewhat stiffly. "Captain Kirk tells me he has promised your son Kevin a tour of engineering."

"Oh—yes!" Kevin said. "But, Father—"

"I'll take care of it, Kevin. You go along with Mr. Scott."

Kevin swung his terminal aside and got off the bed, searching for his slippers. Scott studied him. "The captain tells me you've been accepted to Starfleet Academy," he said with faint skepticism.

"Yes, I want to study engineering too. Like my father," Kevin said. "Maybe I can adapt the antimatter generators you have aboard ship for planets like Nisus."

"It requires the absolute zero of deep space as a cooling system," said Korsal. "Only starships can safely make use of it."

"Aye," said Mr. Scott. "Come on along, lad, and I'll show you why."

"Emergency communication for Korsal," a female voice suddenly said from both the wall unit and the terminal that Korsal had left turned on.

"Korsal here."

His screen came to life with the image of Emily Torrence. "Korsal, are you in any condition to work? Ask your doctor—"

"I'm fine," he said impatiently. "What's wrong?"

"Spring thaw," she replied significantly.

"Ice?"

"A new problem. The river has slowed to a trickle, and investigators report an ice dam in the pass above the safety sluice where you crashed. The spring runoff is building behind it—"

"And if it lets go, the dam and sluices can't handle it!" exclaimed Korsal.

"We're sending every engineer we have up there —and it's not enough. This plague has killed seven of our best people."

"Dinna fret, lass," Mr. Scott said from behind Korsal's shoulder. "I'll gather my crew an' be down there as fast as the transporter can operate. Have ye made sonar scans of the ice dam? We'll hae t' phaser runoff tunnels, let the pressure ease slowly. It'll be delicate work t' keep it from all breakin' loose at once." He glanced at Kevin. "Sorry, boy—that tour will have to wait."

"Of course!" said Kevin. "We're coming along to help—aren't we, Father?"

But as Korsal and his son followed Mr. Scott out of sickbay, they ran straight into Dr. Gardens. "Where do you think you're going?" she demanded.

"Planetside," Korsal explained. "We've got to prevent a flood!"

Dr. Gardens spared a glance at Mr. Scott's retreating back. "Scotty's going down to fix it?"

"Yes."

"Then you're not needed. Back to bed, both of you. Kevin, you look flushed—too much excitement already today."

"Doctor," said Korsal, "we are not prisoners on board this ship!"

"No, but you are our only source of iron-based serum against the Nisus plague. Not only dare you not endanger your lives, you can't afford as much as a cold. If you stay here, in another twenty hours we can administer the blood-stimulant drugs again and save more plague victims. If you beam down, you risk illness or injury. You will certainly exhaust yourselves, and delay the time we can start drawing blood. More people *will die* than would have had to."

Korsal knew she read in his face that she had won. He made no further protest. The doctor softened. "Korsal, Montgomery Scott is one of the best engineers in the Federation. Under emergency conditions and with a tight deadline, he is probably *the* best. If anyone can prevent that dam from bursting, it's our Mr. Scott."

Chapter Thirty-four

Spock was still in sickbay when Sendet was brought in, fighting and raving. From his rantings, he recognized that the man thought he was in *pon farr*, the time when a Vulcan male must mate or die, but the diagnostic indicators quickly showed that what he had was the Nisus plague.

Not surprisingly, the blood tests showed that the young man had Strain C. The initial paranoia symptomatic of that strain had triggered Sendet's greatest concern: his unbonded state, combined with exile to a world where males outnumbered females.

Spock's mother, also still in sickbay, did not need Vulcan hearing to notice the commotion. Amanda was nearly recovered. When the noise level indicated that Sendet had lapsed into unconsciousness, she came to sit beside Spock's bed.

"Spock—" Although she hesitated, he knew what was on her mind.

"Yes, Sendet reminds me that I am unbonded and adult. But there is no use discussing it. By the time I need fear *pon farr* again, I promise that I will do something about it."

She smiled sadly. "I had hoped that while you were home, you would meet an appropriate woman."

"I met several appropriate women. However, the

long separations that weakened my first bonding will continue as long as I remain in Starfleet. I have time, Mother. You married out of free choice. Allow me to do the same."

His mother's smile became warmer. "If that is your attitude, Spock, then I need not be so concerned. I take it the Followers of T'Vet have been removed from engineering?"

"Yes. Mr. Scott got the doors open, and then the Nisus plague gave impetus to their desire to leave rather than fight. I suppose we may expect several more of them to require beds in sickbay soon. Dr. McCoy informs me that I may resume light duty tomorrow."

"And I will be released later today," said Amanda. "Did I hear correctly that your life was saved with serum from *Romulan* blood?"

"Yes. T'Pina's. I searched her records, but there is nothing to indicate how a Romulan infant could have been on that Vulcan colony planet where she was found."

"Does it matter?" Amanda asked. "Spock . . . perhaps Sendet and Satat were right to call this disease the IDIC Epidemic, for look what is happening. The disease may spread where infinite diversity is combined, but that combination is the cure, as well! Our rescuers are Klingons and Romulans—"

"Mother," Spock interrupted, "neither empire has flocked to our rescue. Korsal is the only Klingon on Nisus, his sons are half Human, and T'Pina is Vulcan to all intents and purposes. You have enough diplomatic experience to know that what we have here is no hope for future cooperation, but a deadly secret that must be kept from both the Klingons and the

Romulans. Otherwise, this plague to which they have natural immunity could become a weapon against the Federation."

As promised, the following day Spock resumed his duties. Captain Kirk welcomed him back, but no one had any great cheer to impart. Despite restricting the serum for iron-based blood to only critical patients now that all medical personnel had been inoculated, there was still not enough to go around. Dr. McCoy was fuming that the Orion contingent on Nisus had used diplomatic pressure to obtain the scarce copper-based serum for people who were not ill. And their Klingon guests had developed side effects and been taken temporarily off the blood stimulants.

Nor could it be hoped that one solitary young woman could produce enough blood, even with the help of the Rigellian drug, to inoculate everyone with copper-based blood.

Their great discovery was too little, too late—and the only possible sources of help were enemies who could not be allowed to find out what was happening.

Soon Spock was back on his normal schedule, but since they were doing nothing but orbiting Nisus, that left him with little to do and too much time to think. Thus when he heard that Mr. Scott was going down to Nisus to prevent a flood, he volunteered to join the landing party.

"Ye're always welcome when there's technical work to be done," Mr. Scott informed him.

They beamed down to the lip of a canyon in the mountains above Nisus' science colony. It was a sunny spring day, warm enough even for Spock to compensate for temperature without resorting to cumbersome clothing.

But the very warmth was their enemy.

Mr. Scott took one look at the ice jam in the canyon, the wall of water built up behind it, and whispered, "Good God!"

Two Tellarite engineers brought them the readings they had already taken. "Why weren't we sent up here yesterday? It could go at any minute," one of them said angrily. "There are three weak spots. Melt any area—"

"Aye," said Scott. "Anything we do is going to break it. We're too late!"

He flipped open his communicator. "Captain! That ice jam's about t' give. I'll stay here and make a stab at evening the pressure, but send out an evacuation order for the city—an' I suggest ye beam Mr. Spock and the others aboard. There's naught they can do here but wish me luck."

"Captain," Spock added into his own communicator, "beam me down to the city and prepare our emergency teams to combat flood conditions."

"Right," said Kirk, and Spock heard him saying, "Uhura, send that evacuation warning."

Then Spock prepared to beam, stepping away from Mr. Scott, who was setting up the phaser equipment for a futile try at precision melting of the ice jam.

Just before the beam took him, before Mr. Scott had even finished setting up his equipment, Spock saw the ice break.

The center gave first, and water rushed through like a rocket thrust!

Then the sides crumbled, and with a roar the wall of water surged forward, carrying everything in its path—dissolving into sparkles as Spock was beamed aboard the *Enterprise*.

Chapter Thirty-five

AFTER A FEW hours on the blood stimulant, T'Pina drifted in and out of consciousness. When she was awake the world was oddly skewed; at times she was not certain what was real, what was imagination. At other times she felt normal, until she found herself saying or thinking things alien to her.

There was always someone at her side, but she did not recognize most of them. Her mother was there once, she thought—but at a distance, somewhere beyond some long tunnel stretching between them. T'Kar's voice echoed hollowly as she told T'Pina, "You are my daughter, Blood never mattered before—why should it now? T'Pina?"

T'Pina wanted to answer, but words would not come. She didn't know what they were. She only knew that she had displeased her mother and could not correct the error. It was in her blood . . . in her blood . . . her blood.

T'Pina woke when someone took her hand. The hand on hers was cool, perhaps one of the Human medical personnel—

But it was not a nurse or doctor's touch, nor did it either move or let go. Somebody was offering comfort, she recognized, in the manner of Humans and several other species. She did not pull her hand away, but merely let her eyes open.

There was a man seated beside her bed, wearing pajamas and a robe—a patient. She recognized Beau Deaver and vaguely remembered seeing him, critical and close to death, that day they had found the immunity factor in her blood.

He was obviously alive now, although he still looked haggard. He had shaved, but it must have been some hours ago, for his beard again shadowed his cheeks. His black hair had grown just enough longer than on the day they had met that it looked shaggy, giving it more than ever the appearance of fur.

He smiled at her, his dark blue eyes warm and encouraging. "You were dreaming," he said.

"Why . . . are you here?" she asked.

"Saved me life, you did," he replied. "Least I c'n do is see that with that drug, you don't do yourself an injury. Takes no medical skill—yer friends're takin' it in turn. Now don't go Vulcan," he added, closing his hand over hers as she belatedly attempted to withdraw. "Yer healer says you can't be logical with that stuff, so just don't bother to try."

"I am not Vulcan," T'Pina said, closing her eyes. She believed it at last. "Why should I be logical?"

"In that case," Deaver replied, "lemme take advantage of yer condition to ask you to go out with me. As soon's the epidemic's over an' we're outta this place —the minute they reopen the restaurants."

T'Pina opened her eyes again, having trouble following, not so much what he was saying as any logical purpose in it. So she asked, "What do you want of me?"

"Your company for a nice dinner, maybe a concert or a play, and after that . . . who knows?"

She frowned, honestly puzzled. "But why?"

"Because you are beautiful," he said, "you are brave . . . and it just might help you t' talk to someone with a lifetime's experience at bein' a betwixt-an'-between."

"A what?"

"Someone not what they appear. I look Human at first glance—but prick me, I bleed green." He chuckled. "Won me a few fights that way over the years —some blokes are so startled to bloody me nose an' get pea soup that they let me land the next coupla blows gratis."

"Do you often engage in fistfights?" she asked, her mind able to focus only on parts of what he was saying.

"Not now, but in me misspent youth there was hardly a week I didn't black somebody's eye." He shrugged. "'Twas that or let 'im black mine. Hardest thing when I started goin' t' proper schools was learnin' most people don't solve arguments by dukin' it out. Where I come from, most did."

T'Pina could not imagine such an upbringing. Deaver gave her a sardonic smile. "Oh, yes, there are plenty of places in the galaxy where you get by on yer wits an' yer fists—and some skill with a knife don't hurt none."

T'Pina turned her gaze away, saying, "Please forgive me; I did not mean to exhibit surprise."

"Thought you'd abandoned logic for the duration," he teased, causing her to look back at him, finding again the warm, friendly smile on his face. "Hey," he added, "told you: yer fulla drugs. Even that walkin' statue Sorel says nothin' you do or say can be held against you, okay?"

Since she was still feeling very far from normal,

T'Pina nodded and agreed, echoing the Human term, "Okay."

"Of course if you'd like t' hold—" Deaver began, but then, inexplicably, broke off what he was about to say.

She saw something in those dark blue eyes that disturbed her already precarious equilibrium; but at her glance the eyes suddenly were shadowed. He hid his feelings as effectively as any Vulcan. "Almost went too far, didn't I? Me worst habit. Always have to push the limits."

Even more confused by the apology she didn't understand, T'Pina took the opportunity to withdraw her hand from Deaver's. He didn't move his hand, leaving it on the edge of her bed. It made her feel inexplicably as if *she* now ought to apologize . . . but she didn't know for what.

Instead she took up what she did understand. "Pushing the limits makes great scientists. Or mathematicians," she added, remembering his profession. "If you confine it to your work—"

"I'll solve the Universal Equation, but get no fun outta life," he told her.

"I thought mathematics was 'fun' to you."

"You *were* listening!" he said, eyes shining in delight, a reaction T'Pina recognized even in her drugged state as inappropriately enthusiastic for its cause.

"Certainly," she replied. "I always listen."

"Ah, but you *remembered,*" he said, refusing the rebuff. "Now—"

He was interrupted by a voice over the intercom. *"This is an emergency alert. The hospital is being evacuated because of the possibility of a flash flood. Patients please remain in your rooms until hospital personnel come to help you. Personnel, this is Emergency Procedure Three, repeat, Emergency Procedure Three.*

"Ambulatory patients, follow hospital personnel to the designated areas of safety. Immobilized patients, do not attempt to disconnect equipment. Hospital personnel will move you."

The message began to repeat.

Deaver said, "A flash flood? There's been no rain to speak of."

T'Pina, who had lived on Nisus most of her life, remembered. "It's the spring melt-off. Sometimes the ice blocks the canyons up in the mountains, and if it lets go all at once, it can overflow the dam. Twice we were evacuated when I was in school here, but there was no serious flooding either time."

"That's a relief," said Deaver. "Still—"

A Rigellian technician entered the room, pushing a gurney. "Ah, Mr. Deaver," he said. "You're ambulatory. Take the corridor outside to the left. Follow the blue lines to—"

"I'll help you with T'Pina," said Deaver.

"You are a patient yourself—" the man began.

"Ya wanna fight about it?" Deaver suggested as if he wouldn't mind a bit. "Or ya wanna get this lady with the precious blood to safety?"

T'Pina tried to sit up, but dizziness swept over her. "Lie still!" Deaver ordered. "Come on, you can bloody well disconnect her faster'n that! 'Ere!" he gasped as bright green blood flowed when the tube was disconnected from the needle in T'Pina's arm. "You gonna let 'er bleed t' death?!"

"The blood stimulant is still in her system," the technician replied. "She is producing blood at a very rapid rate." Swiftly, he connected another tube, leading to a container on the gurney, to the needle left in T'Pina's arm.

He then changed the container of fluid leading to her other arm, saying, "This is just hydrating solution, no more drug in it. But T'Pina will become dehydrated if her fluid loss is not replaced."

Deaver moved into position as the Rigellian prepared to move T'Pina to the gurney, and she recognized that he had done this before. So did the technician; he stopped protesting and accepted the help in transferring her.

Being wheeled through the halls was dizzying. Then they were in a lift, and then more corridors. Finally they reached the emergency-room doors to the outside, where other patients on gurneys and in wheelchairs waited for ambulances.

Two ground vehicles departed with their loads, and a hoverer landed on the nearby pad. It was loaded quickly and took off, and T'Pina was moved forward in the line. More patients were being brought out behind her. T'Pina could hear an argument going on about the hopelessness of trying to segregate contagious plague victims from the other patients, but she couldn't see who was talking.

Another hoverer carried off two more patients, but then a ground vehicle pulled up and T'Pina was taken to it, along with a Vulcan male who appeared to be unconscious.

The attendants were two Human males, one tall and blond, the other short with curly black hair and eyes almost as blue as Beau Deaver's.

What a strange thought, T'Pina recognized. The tall one checked the ID bracelet on her wrist and said, "Gotta be extra careful with this one on board, Dave: she's the one whose blood can stop the plague."

"I'm always careful," replied the other man. "Why're you always criticizin' my driving?"

"'Cause it's nice to get the patients there in one piece!" his colleague replied as they lifted the Vulcan male into the ambulance and fastened him safely. He studied the patient and said seriously, "This one's supposed to be recovering, but he doesn't look good to me."

"Let's just get them to the medcamp and let the healers take him over," said the one called Dave.

They turned to lift T'Pina and found Beau Deaver ready to help. "Sorry, sir," said Dave, "these vehicles are for nonambulatory patients only. If you'll go around to the front of the hospital, there are buses—"

"I've got medic training," said Deaver. "Done ambulance duty before." He turned to the Rigellian technician. "I c'n take care of her."

There was only a moment's hesitation. Then the man said, "Switch blood containers as they fill and fluid containers as they empty. In about five hours her blood production will start tapering off, but maybe by then we'll have everyone back in the hospital." He smiled. "Thanks—there are other patients who really need me more, but you all know how important this one is." His glance included the attendants.

With everyone aboard and the doors shut, the ambulance started off, Dave driving, his blond colleague turned in his seat to watch the two patients. Deaver sat on a pull-out seat between them. He watched T'Pina until the ambulance surged sharply around a corner, fishtailing wildly.

"What the bleedin'—?" Deaver began furiously, but the moment he looked forward he paled. "Oh, my God!"

The ambulance lurched and turned, changing direction.

"It's coming down this street too!" exclaimed Dave, spinning and skidding the ambulance as if it were a racing vehicle. The siren began to wail.

"The dam's burst!" said the other attendant. "We can't outrun it! Hope we all know how to swim!"

Deaver turned and shook the Vulcan. "Wake up, dammit!" The man remained unconscious.

T'Pina eased up on her elbows as the ambulance sped back toward the hospital. She could just see out the back window.

A wall of water higher than she could see pursued them!

It was overtaking them!

The ambulance was lifted like a toy, spun and swirled, tossed high—

Deaver hung on, one hand on either gurney.

They were smashed against a wall.

The opposite side of the ambulance caved in toward T'Pina. The other patient was thrust against Deaver and the two men toppled onto her.

Water poured in through the burst roof.

They were sinking!

"I can't get loose!" T'Pina heard the blond ambulance attendant exclaim.

"Hold still!" Dave responded. "I'll cut through the belt!"

Then both attendants were trying to squirm into the crowded back of the ambulance.

The water was up to the level of T'Pina's bed and pouring over them as they fought to escape. She tugged at the fastenings holding her in place.

Trapped under the still-unconscious Vulcan, who

now hung from his safety straps, Beau Deaver tried to turn to her, but there was not enough room for his wide shoulders. "Wait!" he said, and began working the Vulcan man's straps loose. "Can you blokes take him?" he asked.

"If we can get out," the blond attendant replied. "Watch yourselves! It's jagged metal."

He took a deep breath of what little air was left, and struggled over them, leaning back in to grasp the Vulcan under the arms as Dave maneuvered him upright. The lurch as the ambulance hit bottom thrust the Vulcan and the two attendants out and away.

Deaver reached for T'Pina. He took a scalpel from the equipment on board and slashed through the straps holding her.

By this time the water had covered her. She broke free, gasping, and hung for a moment in the last bubble of air trapped under the roof.

"Can you swim?" Deaver asked.

"Yes," she replied.

"Then hang on to me, and kick—don't try to go on your own," said Deaver. "Take a deep breath—"

T'Pina drew air into her lungs. Deaver went first, pulling her out after him. She felt the needles pull from her arms. That did not bother her as much as the thought of losing hold of Deaver's hand as she emerged into swirling black water.

She couldn't see. She couldn't breathe. She couldn't tell up from down.

The only reality was the freezing water, tumbling her at will.

Remembering Deaver's instruction, she kicked, wondering if they were floating upward or caught in some current carrying them into an airless trap. It was cold—so cold.

Why was it so black?

Her limbs were numb. Something hit them—tree branches trying to drive them apart.

She tightened her grip, letting a little air out of her bursting lungs, fighting the urge to draw in when there was nothing but water all around her.

Suddenly she was caught in a whirlpool!

She was tossed to and fro. Not even her Vulcan strength could hold on to Deaver. They were hitting other objects now; she felt him lurch away.

Merciless current took her.

She couldn't see him, couldn't feel him, knew only burning lungs and numbing cold, endless water—

And then nothing.

Chapter Thirty-six

ONLY MINUTES AFTER the ice dam burst, Spock stood on the flat roof of the Nisus Trade Center, the tallest building in the city. The *Enterprise* was using it as a beamdown point. Directing the rescue effort, Spock watched the evacuation of the city below and saw that the facilities of the *Enterprise* could not possibly make a dent in evacuating those thousands of people. Nonetheless, they had to try.

By foot, on the slidewalks, and in every kind of vehicle, people were moving out of the city toward the nearest hills. But above them, the wall of water moved relentlessly down the mountain, roaring toward the swollen reservoir before any but those on the outskirts of town could reach safety.

No one knew how high the water would reach when it hit. Spock reported the oncoming tide, and emergency workers started directing people into the Trade Center and other tall buildings as it became obvious they could not make it out of town.

On the Trade Center roof, groups of people alternated with equipment in the transporter beam. Some were regular landing parties, accustomed to working together, like the medical crew setting up an emergency unit in one corner.

Spock watched Landing Party Seven arrive, six people drawn from engineering, computer sciences, medicine, economics, security, and ship's stores. Kirk sometimes referred to this team as "the IDIC party," because their talents were so diversified, but the designation was actually one of the captain's jokes, for to hear them squabble you would think they could not agree on so much as who would stand on which transporter pad.

Despite their disagreements, though, they were as efficient as any other team. They were directed by the engineer, Rogers, a portly man with curly brown hair. Running to the marine vehicle that landed just after them, they began to assemble it, the giant security officer holding the pieces together by sheer strength while the two women in the party bolted them into place.

Meanwhile, the third man assembled the onboard computer, working with almost Vulcan concentration, while the last member of the party, a small, nondescript sort of man, always had the right tools ready to hand to those who needed them.

Four separate arguments broke out in the process of assembly—and yet the vehicle was together and ready to go before the next landing party and set of equipment had coalesced on the beamdown point.

"Humans," a calm voice observed from behind Spock. "I sometimes wonder how they ever learned to cooperate well enough to achieve civilization."

Spock turned. "Father. What are you doing here?"

Sarek was not only present; he was dressed in a borrowed Starfleet uniform, ready for action.

"I understand that every available able-bodied person is needed," replied Spock's father. "When I pointed out to your captain that I am able-bodied and available, he succumbed to the logic of the situation."

"Logic? To send a Vulcan into a flood? Can you

swim, Father?" Spock asked, looking for an excuse to send Sarek back aboard.

"Of course I can swim," Sarek replied. "Your mother taught me when we first met on Earth."

Oh. Of course she would have. He wondered whether Amanda would appear with the next landing party.

As if reading his thought, Sarek said, "Amanda is with the staff waiting to care for flood victims beamed aboard the *Enterprise.*"

Spock was looking at Sarek, so he saw the sudden tightening of the jaw, the forced control as he looked out over the city. Spock turned. The wall of water had hit the reservoir and was traveling across it, at least thirty meters higher than the surface.

The water sailed straight over the top of the dam and crashed over it into the narrow valley, engulfing the buildings below. If everyone had obeyed instructions as it appeared, there were no people within a kilometer of the dam. But the water was not going to stay in that vicinity.

"All available air vehicles launch!" Spock instructed into his communicator. "Marine vehicle crews stand by!"

Helplessly, Spock and Sarek watched as the flood waters pooled and swirled for long moments at the foot of the dam, but as water poured across the top into the valley, the wall of water rebuilt itself and rushed inexorably toward the central city. As it roared into the populated areas, taller buildings created channels, speeding the rushing water and at the same time driving it to new heights in the narrow streets.

Hoverers and shuttles swooped down, snatching people out of harm's way—but there were simply not enough such vehicles! Spock and Sarek were too far away to see individual people, but they saw air vehicles dart away from the oncoming wave, saw it engulf the streets below. A hoverer remained down too long, trying to pick someone up. It was caught by the wall of water and smashed like a fragile insect.

Sarek turned and strode toward where the landing party he had beamed down with were assembling a small air car. Deftly, he began installing the communication and navigation computers. It was a two-man vehicle, fitted with two outside pods for evacuees. Two crewmembers sprang aboard and took off.

Sarek turned to pace the edge of the roof, scanning the rising waters for signs of survivors. Spock joined him.

Sarek turned. "Is there a way to tell people trapped in buildings that if they have air, they should stay where they are?" he asked.

"I'll have the *Enterprise* broadcast on all channels, although most intercoms are probably flooded out."

Spock sent the order, and Uhura acknowledged it.

Sarek watched his son, then looked back over the flooded city. All around them, *Enterprise* crew and Nisus citizens were taking people out of the water, off rooftops, and from upper windows. On a rooftop below, a Tellarite and an Andorian helped a Human woman out of the stairwell, then turned to bring out a Hemanite. A Lemnorian, who had obviously been lifting people from below, climbed out after them. Another *Enterprise* marine vehicle, in which Spock recognized Chekov and Sulu, took them all from the roof and headed off.

"IDIC in action," Sarek said, almost too softly for Spock to hear above all the other noise. But he caught his son's eyes on him and knew he had heard, for he continued, "It should never have surprised me that you chose Starfleet, Spock. It is the product of diversity as much as you are. You could equally have chosen Nisus."

"Or the Vulcan Academy," Spock admitted. "There is a Human saying: true happiness lies—"

"—in your own back garden," Sarek completed it. "I do not comprehend 'happiness,' Spock, but I am aware of the Human propensity for seeking it far from home, usually unsuccessfully. What I tend to forget is that you are half Human, and have the right to exercise that part of your heritage as much as your Vulcan half."

"You also forget," Spock reminded him, "that all my life I have had before me the example of my mother. Remember, Father, she truly *has* found happiness light-years from the world where she was born."

The slightest of smiles curved Sarek's lips. "And I found *her* light-years from *my* home. You are the son of both of us, Spock. I hope you never again hesitate to come home."

"I shall return to Vulcan, Father, when my time in Starfleet is over." Spock could not say when he had made that decision; he only knew that it was true.

"That will please your mother greatly," was all Sarek said, but Spock saw in his father's eyes that Sarek was pleased as well. Logic was irrelevant at that moment; the reunion that had begun on the perilous journey to Babel and continued when they had melded on Vulcan to save Amanda's life only a few weeks ago, was finally complete.

Father and son looked out together over the flooded city.

Chapter Thirty-seven

WHEN SHE CAME to, T'Pina saw Beau Deaver leaning over her. She was wet and very, very cold.

"Where are we?" she asked, turning her head. She lay on freezing metal, only a few centimeters from the surface of black water.

"We're in an air pocket. The current carried us into a building," Deaver said slowly. "Water pressure must've smashed the windows. I don't know which building, or how high the water is above us. But we're safe here for a while, till we run out of air."

T'Pina recognized that the dim lighting came from the building's battery-operated emergency system. She and Deaver lay on top of tall cabinets. The ceiling was less than a meter above them; there was not even enough space to sit up in, but it had trapped a layer of air and saved their lives.

"What should we do?" she asked.

"Depends," said Deaver. "The water should subside pretty rapidly. We might do best just to stay here—unless we're near ground level," he added. "The sewer system's probably already taken all it can. The rest of the water will have to run off over the ground, which could take a day or two. Don't know how long the lights will stay on, either. Let's just rest awhile and then see if we can find a stairwell. Even if it's filled with water, we could swim to the top."

At the thought of going back into the icy water, T'Pina shivered. "You're freezing!" said Deaver. On their tiny island of safety, he ensconced T'Pina in a cocoon of warmth, wrapping his arms about her. It helped, for a while. But soon she began shivering again, and a strange prickling sensation broke out on her skin.

"T'Pina? What's wrong?" asked Deaver.

"I . . . don't know," she replied. "I feel very strange. I'm so thirsty, but—"

"Don't drink the flood water!" Deaver said quickly. Then he added, "Well, I don't suppose it makes a difference if you do now; we both certainly swallowed some trying to swim."

"I'm thirsty," T'Pina repeated, "and yet I feel bloated, as if—"

Deaver grasped her left arm. The blood flow had stopped. The medtech had told him to keep letting the blood flow out, but also to put fluid back in her veins. He wished the Rigellian were here now.

"We have two choices," he said. "Do nothing, and hope the pressure doesn't build up to a stroke or other vascular damage, or let some of your blood out, and hope it doesn't weaken you too much."

T'Pina did not know any more than he did what to do. She only knew, "If you bleed me, that blood's wasted. It can't be used to make serum against the plague."

"But if you die, or become so ill you can't use the stimulant," said Deaver, "then there won't be any more serum, either."

T'Pina was feeling stranger by the minute. The stray thought crossed her mind that Deaver's grammar and enunciation improved dramatically when the situation was serious. "Perhaps you really could have taught at the Vulcan Academy," she whispered.

She felt his sharp intake of breath. "We must do something!"

Deaver felt in his shirt pockets. "Didn't lose it!" he said in relief, and produced the scalpel with which he had cut them loose from the sinking ambulance. "Pretty dull after what I used it for, though." He smiled weakly. "God, I hope we're doing the right thing!"

There was no way to sterilize the scalpel. He nicked the vein inside T'Pina's elbow, and the blood spurted, the pressure behind it completely abnormal for a Vulcan.

"Better?" Deaver asked. T'Pina saw him swallow hard at the amount of blood coming from the cut.

"Better . . ." T'Pina replied.

Deaver wrapped his arms tightly around her.

Chapter Thirty-eight

ON THE ROOFTOP of the Nisus Trade Center, the rescue operation was now in full swing. Spock's attention was divided between his work and the horrifying fascination of the still-rising flood waters. It was difficult to send other crewmembers to do the rescue work while he remained safely on the rooftop. Behind him, Miss Nordlund picked up a component for one of the air cars and gave a yelp as she straightened.

Spock jumped to catch the equipment, asking, "What's the matter?"

"My back, sir," Nordlund replied. "It goes out sometimes." It had obviously gone out now.

Nordlund was a sturdy woman whose long thick curls of nearly white hair were now pulled back off her face for efficiency. Spock knew she would go on despite her pain if he let her, so he said, "You cannot pull people out of flood waters in that condition."

"But I want to help, sir," Nordlund protested. Her pallor was receding; she did not appear to be in pain once she let go of the heavy article.

"Then take over my job," said Spock, handing Nordlund the communicator.

He joined Sarek in assembling the air car and took the pilot's seat.

By now the waters were swirling two stories high around the trade center. He saw no one except their own people watching from the upper windows, trying to decide when to launch their boats.

Spock banked and flew toward the hospital; there had been ground ambulances moving steadily back and forth between it and the medcamp hastily constructed on the mountainside.

The hospital was almost underwater. There were people on the roof, safe enough for the moment—the objects in the water were what concerned him.

They hit updrafts over rooftops that had been in sunshine all day, then downdrafts over the icy water. The clash of temperatures created treacherous eddies of wind.

Sensor scans gave back anomalous readings in the swirls of heat and cold; the water would have to settle more before they could rely on their sensors for life readings. In the meantime, they searched for survivors by eye.

In a low area where two main streets crossed, flood waters meeting from two directions created a whirlpool. "There!" said Sarek, pointing to what at first seemed to be one blue-and-green object tossed on the water. When they came closer it resolved into three figures, two in the blue of hospital personnel, one in a green patient's coverall. The men in blue held the other's head above water. Spock swung down, saying, "Can you hold the air car steady, Father?"

"I am not familiar with this vehicle," Sarek replied, fastening a safety harness about himself and attaching a line to it. "You fly, and I will go down to help those people."

The moment Sarek opened the door, the wind tried

to tear them out of the craft. Spock's father braced himself and climbed out onto the pod on his side.

The patient in the green coverall was Vulcan, and unconscious. Such icy water was enough to knock out a Vulcan even in good health. Spock fought the controls, taking the craft down to skim the top of the water.

The air car's motors whined in protest, and the wind howled. Spock could see that one of the men in blue was trying to tell Sarek something, but that his father could not understand as together they rolled the Vulcan into the passenger pod.

The moment all were in place, Spock shot straight up until they were above the whirling winds, then let Sarek hold the craft steady while he leaned out his side to fasten the straps around the exhausted Humans.

As soon as both were secure, Spock streaked back toward the Trade Center, for it was too far from here to the medcamp for the exhausted men in soaked clothing.

By this time the *Enterprise* medical unit was in full operation. Two of McCoy's medtechs, Arthur and Westplain, plucked the patients from the pods and wrapped them in blankets. The Vulcan was still unconscious. Spock saw Dr. Gardens run her medscanner over him and gesture to have him taken to the beaming area, for transport to the ship.

Meanwhile, Westplain, a tall, lanky Human with auburn hair and a face strangely weathered for a man who spent most of his time on a starship, was bending over the other two they had picked up. Suddenly one sat up, grasping the medtech's arms, and nothing Westplain could do would calm him until he had told him something that made his usually laconic attitude shift drastically.

Spock and Sarek were almost ready to take off when Westplain ran toward them, waving his arms. Spock opened his door, and Westplain shoved his head in. "Those men were ambulance attendants," he said. "They had three patients when they were caught by the flood—that Vulcan man you rescued, another Nisus scientist, and that girl with the Romulan blood —T'Pina!"

Chapter Thirty-nine

T'PINA LAY IN Beau Deaver's arms, still feeling strange. Letting some of the blood out of her body had relieved her bloated feeling, but she was still cold and thirsty, and her mind would not track.

She tried to focus in on their situation. "We should try to reach the surface now, Mr. Deaver."

"Not yet, " Deaver said. "Let's make sure that yer all right. Besides, I know that water's not cold enough to kill me, but I don't know about Vulcans."

"Romulans," she muttered.

"Same as makes no difference," he replied. "One little blood factor."

She felt his eyes upon her, struggled to maintain control. "You should go, then. Bring back help for me."

Deaver shook his head slowly. "Not just yet," he repeated. "We can't even be sure the flood waters have completely settled."

In response, T'Pina shivered violently.

"Here!" said Deaver, pulling her tightly against his broad chest, trying to stretch his wet robe over both of them. "No," he concluded, "that won't do. Turn over, T'Pina."

"Turn over?"

"On your side, back to me. There, that's it," as she moved obediently.

He circled her with his arms and drew his knees up behind hers. Suddenly, even through her soggy hospital coverall, she could feel his warmth. His body temperature was much cooler than hers ought to be. At the moment, though, he provided a welcome warmth.

"That's good—you've stopped shivering," he said, squeezing her. "Don't get too comfortable, though. I don't want you falling asleep."

"I won't," she promised even as her eyelids drooped.

But Deaver was alert. "T'Pina, keep talking. Hey—I told you all about me sordid past. Now it's your turn."

"I . . . don't know anything . . . about my sordid past," she replied.

"Amnesiac, are you?"

"Don't know . . . who I am."

"Sure you do," he said. "You're the little girl who saved Nisus."

"Not a child," she protested, and felt his arms tighten, the movement of his facial muscles against her neck as he smiled.

"No," he said, "I can tell you're not a child. But I'm puttin' on me best gentlemanly ways, an' not takin' advantage of the current situation, am I?"

"Taking . . . ?"

"Alone, a beautiful woman in me arms. Anyone finds out I did no more'n hold 'er, an' me reputation's ruint, innit?"

T'Pina had no answer for that. She connected his comment with common jokes and innuendos that never made sense, although she had heard them from non-Vulcans all her life. It was not that she did not comprehend the biology of reproduction; it was that she had never understood what it had to do with the kissing and other odd touching activities she read about or saw in entertainment tapes.

Yet . . . now that she had matured, she began to realize that there were connections. She recalled her embarrassing response to Sendet. But he was an unbonded male of her own species—or at least her own culture. Why would Beau Deaver expect her to respond to him?

The memory of Sendet, though, recalled the reception aboard the *Enterprise,* where she had seen Sarek and Amanda, Dr. Corrigan and T'Mir. It was possible, then. She remembered the day she had met Deaver, how he had helped her with the children, how pleasant it had been to be with him.

Undrugged and in her normal state of health, could she respond to a man who was so different from what she was?

Were they so different? What had he called them —betwixt-and-betweens?

At her long silence, Deaver said, "Stay awake, T'Pina. Tell me more about yourself. You're a medical technician."

"Yes," she replied. "I'm going to work at the Nisus hospital for a few years, until I decide what area to specialize in. Then I will seek further education at an appropriate institution."

"Appropriate," he said. "Have you ever done anything inappropriate in your life, T'Pina?"

"Yes," she replied.

"You have? What?"

"Somehow . . . I got born Romulan."

She felt his chuckle at that. Humans were strange, this Human/Orion hybrid even more so. She did not understand why he found her statement amusing.

Before she could say so, however, he was asking, "Doesn't that change your plans in any way?"

"What do you mean?"

"Aren't you curious? I thought curiosity was the only emotion Vulcans allowed themselves."

T'Pina realized that she was curious; she simply had not had time to think since receiving the startling news.

Now, perhaps because the drug was working its way out of her system, she began to wonder how she could be Romulan. "I don't know how to find out," she told Deaver. "The Romulans are enemies of the Federation."

"Ask Korsal," Deaver suggested.

"Korsal? The Klingon engineer? Why would he know anything about me?"

"I didn't mean that *he* would know how you got to that Vulcan colony planet. But the Klingons have dealings with the Roms. Korsal may know how to put your questions through Klingon channels and get some answers from the Romulans."

"Mr. Deaver," she asked, "how do you know that?"

"Don't you think that under the circumstances, you could call me Beau?"

"You are evading my question."

"Ah—logic returneth. Too bad. I liked you all sorta muzzy an' sweet."

"I asked you how you know that the Klingons are in contact with the Romulans."

"Well," he replied, "I could suggest that you ask the Orions, but I think you can trust the Klingons a whole lot further. At least when they're hostile, they're open about it."

"Oh," she said, embarrassed. Then, "You're saying the Orions also deal with the Romulans?"

"Orions deal with anyone they can make a profit offa," he replied. "They deal any*thing,* too: weapons, drugs, slaves. Almost sold me once, they did."

". . . what?"

"You know they sell their women."

"Yes, everybody knows that."

"Well, that's the only commodity there's enough market for on the fringes of the Federation to make it worth the risk. But on their home planets they sell men, women, children. I was just a kid, but I musta had some o' me heartbreakin' charm already. An Orion trader named Zefat thought I'd go fer a high price as an exotic toy fer some rich Orion or maybe Klingon family. Got me dad into a rigged game. Gamblin' was always me dad's fatal weakness."

He fell silent.

T'Pina could not believe what she was hearing. "You mean . . . your father gambled, with you as the stakes?"

"Not only gambled; he lost."

"Then how—?"

"Me mum," he replied. "Orion women aren't stupid, you know. Orion men keep 'em ignorant. But me dad let Mum do what she wanted, long as she kep' him happy. She learned to use the ship's computer to do more than keep the place clean. When she found out what me dad had done, she come after me, armed with all the Federation had on Zefat, that she got outa the computer, and info she got from other Orion women."

T'Pina felt his arms tighten around her as he remembered what was obviously a painful experience. "The hints she dropped got her onta Zefat's ship. He thought she was tryin' t' blackmail him, an' she let him think it. Got me outa the hold and into the same room with 'em.

"Zefat planned to kill me mum there an' then—get ridda her an' teach me a lesson. But he didn't know Mum. She'd found out who his enemies were—and with the Federation info and the slan from the other women she'd let them know, in exchange for my life, exactly how Zefat had cheated them. She had Zefat surrounded by three of his worst enemies."

"Your mother was very courageous," said T'Pina.

"Yeah," he replied. "Always. She's the one I think about when the Orions do something dastardly, an' I wish I could deny I'm one of 'em."

"But you're not—" she began, and then suddenly realized what he had just taught her. "You are not Orion any more than I am Romulan."

He smiled. "Me point exactly."

"I thought you were a mathematician, not a psychologist," she said.

"Jack of all trades, ma'am," Deaver said. She shifted uncomfortably in his arms. "What's the matter?" he asked.

"I don't know," T'Pina managed. "It is suddenly . . . quite difficult to catch my breath." She swallowed painfully. "Perhaps the serum is still acting to dehydrate my body."

"Or maybe," Deaver said, "the air in here is starting to run out."

Struggling, T'Pina turned herself over to face him. "We cannot wait any longer. We have to try to reach the surface."

"Yer right," Beau said. "Only . . ." His voice trailed off.

She looked up at him. "What's the matter?"

"Well," he began. "I can't—'ere, maybe it's easier if I just show you." He lifted his robe to reveal a long, angry gash along the length of his thigh. T'Pina gasped involuntarily, her own pain forgotten.

"I must've cut meself comin' in through one of them windows," he explained. "Hurts like bloody hell—and I don't think the leg'll be much good in the water."

"You should have told me," T'Pina said.

Deaver smiled. "Give you one more thing to worry about? And what then? Nah, I was hopin' someone'd find us so neither of us'd have t' brave the water. Ah, well—a fine pair we make." He rested his hand on T'Pina's shoulder. "Shall we?" he asked, nodding toward the water.

T'Pina took a deep breath and nodded.

Chapter Forty

SPOCK GUIDED THE air car toward where they had picked up the three flood victims. Below, the marine vehicle manned by Landing Party Seven moved out now that the water was calming.

He punched the communicator button. "Party Seven."

"Chevron here, Mr. Spock," came the prompt reply. That was the computer tech, second only to Spock among the *Enterprise* crew at putting a computer through its paces.

"We know where the ambulance carrying T'Pina was trapped," Chevron told them, giving the location.

"On our way."

The watercraft sped toward the intersection, bouncing over the rough water.

From their vantage point above, Spock and Sarek ran a scan for signs of life—and picked up strong readings in one of the buildings. "Survivors in the Federation Building, Mr. Chevron," Spock reported. "Please have your squad rendezvous with us there, on the rooftop."

They set a course for that building. The roof was broad enough to allow the air car to land. Spock and Sarek jumped out and ran to the stairwell, where two security men wearing wetsuits were already disappearing into the depths, trailing a safety line attached to a stanchion on the roof.

Chevron was at the door, carrying extra air bottles and breathing masks. He turned to the two Vulcans and said, "We've got enough heroes, I should think. Besides, Vulcans are not exactly designed as aquatic animals, are they? You can help to haul us out if we get into trouble."

With that, he clipped his own harness to the safety line, pulled his breathing mask into place, and followed his colleagues into the stairwell.

Sarek frowned. "Insubordination?"

"Eccentricity," Spock replied. "Captain Kirk allows a great deal of leeway as long as his crewmembers do their jobs well. Mr. Chevron simply takes advantage of it."

"That good at his job, is he?" asked Sarek.

"Indeed," Spock acknowledged, "extremely good."

There was nothing to do but wait. Michaels, the other man in the landing party, paced nervously on the roof, checking every few moments that the safety line was playing out properly. Spock said nothing. Humans were perfectly capable of exhibiting stress and at the same time performing adequately.

Besides, he understood how the man felt. He was none too sanguine about standing here, waiting, while other *Enterprise* crewmembers risked their lives in the icy water below.

Taking a deep breath, Deaver eased himself off the cabinet into the water. T'Pina heard him gasp, saw him go white with pain as the water struck his wound. But somehow he gained control, teeth gripping his lower lip.

"All right, now," he said to T'Pina, who lay on the

very edge of the metal cabinet behind him. He reached up to her. "Give me your hand, and just lower yourself in—"

She started suddenly. "Listen!" she said.

"What?"

It came again: someone was pounding on a metal surface, three spaced strokes.

Deaver heard it this time. He boosted himself back up next to T'Pina and pounded three times on the cabinet they lay on.

There was a response of four strokes, which he immediately echoed.

When there was no further pounding, he said, "They must have us pinpointed. We'll be out of here soon, now."

Sure enough, three people in aquatic gear emerged near them. Treading water, one man removed his mask, saying, "Are you hurt? Can you swim?"

"We'll make it," Deaver replied for both of them.

Another of the divers helped them into breathing masks and air bottles.

Reluctantly, T'Pina slid into the freezing water, where one of their rescuers snapped a line to her, then took her hand.

"Most of the way's not lighted," they were told. "Just follow the line, though, and we'll get you out." Then the man who had spoken replaced his breathing mask, and they all dived beneath the bitterly cold water.

Being able to breathe was a great help, but T'Pina felt her hands and feet go numb. Although her head was clearer than before, her muscles had less strength; her rescuers had to drag her along.

Finally they came out into a narrow tower of still water, with gray light filtering down on them. As they rose, there was more and more light, and T'Pina recognized that they were in a stairwell, with a rectangle of sky above them where the door to the roof was open.

They surfaced, and were swimming toward the stairs when suddenly the water swirled madly!

T'Pina was thrown against one of her rescuers, and he was caught between her and the stairs as she smashed helplessly into him.

Then she was tossed in the opposite direction, her air bottle bruising her as she was brutally hauled along.

The leader dropped his mask again to shout, "Don't lose the line!"

Everything was sliding sideways!

The stairs collapsed, and those treads above water tumbled down on them.

The open doorway above sank toward them, and T'Pina tried to follow the example of her rescuers, rapidly passing the safety rope hand over hand as it sank into the water.

And then the roof tumbled in, forcing them all to dive beneath the freezing water once more, to avoid being crushed by the collapsing building.

As one, Spock and Sarek sensed the roof beneath them move, one side rising, the other sinking. They saw the empty air car began to slide down toward the water and sprinted toward it, trying to grab hold and swing into it before it could sink.

Behind them Michaels cried out, "The whole building's collapsing!" He made a dash for the boat, tumbled into it, and pulled the moorings loose.

Sarek reached the air car first, and sensibly did not

wait to try to pull Spock aboard, but revved the motor to get the craft airborne.

Spock leaped for the passenger pod on the opposite side just as the roof gave way beneath his feet. He hung on to the lurching flyer until his father had it flying level, then he climbed up and into it, quickly strapping himself into the safety harness.

Below them, he saw Michaels in the bobbing marine vehicle, stretching to reach the end of the safety rope floating on the water. He almost overreached himself as his fingers barely closed over it, but the two women grabbed his legs and yanked him back into the boat.

Then the three of them hauled on the rope, meters of it coiling into the boat before—

A head broke the surface!

It was one of the rescue party, in a wetsuit, but with the help of the people in the boat he quickly hauled more line in until they were dragging a man in pajamas and robe into the boat, wrapping a blanket around him and taking him out of their way while they turned their attention to the others in the water.

A second head in aquatic gear broke surface, and then a third. Between them they supported a woman in a green coverall, her long dark hair trailing in the water.

Air bubbles released from the collapsed building tossed the boat as the rescue team fought to get the woman and themselves into it. When they were finally aboard, Rogers picked up a communicator. "Can you bring that craft down so we can load the patients, Mr. Spock?"

He did, then left Sarek to hold it steady as he climbed out to help.

Although she was pale, T'Pina was conscious. The other patient, the man, was out cold. "Beau!" T'Pina shouted at him, but there was no response.

In the lurching water, it took several tries to get both T'Pina and the man with her strapped into the pods. Fighting the air car to steadiness, Sarek reported the news that T'Pina had been found, alive and conscious. By the time Spock climbed into his seat, Sorel was on the communicator. "Please bring T'Pina directly to the medcamp." They banked off toward the hills, carefully making their way through the flock of air cars and hoverers still busy rescuing survivors.

There were boats of all descriptions on the water now, plucking up survivors. Spock saw a green Orion woman take a Caitian woman and her cub from a treetop into a dinghy. A team of Tellarites glided over the water in a longboat, maneuvering the narrow streets between buildings to take people from windows. The waters were slowly receding, high-water marks on the sides of buildings a good two meters above the current level.

The worst was over. Now came the discovery of who was alive, the recovery of the bodies of the dead. And then the difficult job of cleaning and rebuilding.

Spock looked out over the drowned landscape and wondered how long it would take before Nisus rose again.

Chapter Forty-one

AT THE MEDCAMP, Sorel permitted himself relief at T'Pina's survival. He went in search of T'Kar, who was back at nursing despite being hardly recovered herself.

"Thank you, Sorel," she told him, her eyes warm with relief. "I will come with you."

They met the air car and helped Spock and Sarek unload the patients. There was too much rescue work still to be done for father and son to linger; they swung quickly back into their craft and went in search of further victims.

T'Kar bent over her daughter. "T'Pina—"

"I am well, Mother," the younger woman insisted, trying to climb to her feet. "Beau—he saved my life. How badly is he hurt?"

His medscanner quickly confirmed that T'Pina had suffered few ill effects, so Sorel turned to her companion, remembering the Human/Orion hybrid. Like T'Kar, he had been saved from death by the serum from T'Pina's blood, and was barely recovered.

"He is merely unconscious," Sorel assured T'Pina. "Exhaustion, not his wound. Let him sleep. He will recover in a day or two. Meanwhile, we must put you back on the Rigellian drug, T'Pina."

Her only emotional response was to blink. Then, looking around her, she nodded. "Of course, Healer."

For the flood had destroyed every attempt at quarantine. Drowning people did not hesitate to touch their rescuers, nor did rescuers consider exposure as they saved lives.

By the time the flood-related cases of the plague began, the Nisus hospital was back in operation. The crew of the *Enterprise* lent their efforts to cleaning out the mud and finding and repairing furniture and equipment.

The first task was locating and identifying the dead. The very plague that had turned everyone's attention from the safety of the dam, and thereby contributed to the flood, had kept all but minimal personnel out of the main area of the city. As a result, there were fewer than fifty fatalities.

The community mourned, pulling together in their tragedy as they had pulled apart in fear of the plague.

They took hope from the vaccines. Indeed, those of copper-based blood need not fear dying if they got medical attention immediately. Although T'Pina could not produce enough blood for serum to inoculate everyone, they could cure each new case of the plague as the victim was identified. For Vulcans, Orions, Rigellians, and the other races with copper-based blood, the crisis was over.

But not for the other half of Nisus' population.

Leonard McCoy had put Korsal and his older son back on blood stimulants, but Karl, the nine-year-old, could not continue them. There was nothing like the Rigellian stimulant for Klingons; as a result, there was simply not enough serum.

Everyone on Nisus asked why Korsal did not call for more Klingons to aid them, but the answer spread rapidly. Not only were the Klingons immune, but their blood carried the cure with which they could hold the Federation ransom. The plague was a weapon that could not be allowed to fall into their hands.

Fortunately for their peace of mind, they did not know it already had.

James T. Kirk had no such peace of mind. The captain of the *Enterprise* came in person to tell Korsal, "The Nisus Starfleet liaison officer, Commander Smythe, has taken Borth into custody. He refuses to say whether he sent a message to the Klingon Empire, but our computer recorded something in a code we cannot identify, sent just before the flood broke."

"May I see the message, Captain Kirk?"

When Kirk played it, he said, "It is not Klingon code. I refused to give him that. This is Orion; Borth routed the message through his own people, but that will merely delay its delivery and risk someone in the Orion system decoding it."

"But it will get through," Kirk pressed.

"I wish I could doubt it, Captain."

"I will forward your opinion to Starfleet Command. What happens next is up to them. Certainly Borth will be prosecuted. You may have to testify against him, Korsal."

"I know. Captain Kirk, I don't want interplanetary war any more than you do."

"But the Orions do; they tried to break up the Babel Conference, weaken the Federation. They see war as an opportunity to plunder all sides. Strange . . . only dedicated scientists come to Nisus. You're not a typical Klingon. Why did the Orions have to send a typical Orion?"

Korsal ignored the implied insult to Klingons in

general, knowing Kirk did not intend it, and said, "I do not think there is any other kind of Orion."

"There's your wife," said Kirk. "Quite a lady."

"Orion women," said Korsal, "are not educated, but neither are they indoctrinated. Seela grew up on Nisus, and despite Borth's efforts seems to have absorbed the . . . what the Vulcans call IDIC, rather than Orion self-absorption."

"You're right," said Kirk. "In fact, among the pictures our rescue craft took automatically, there are some you'll want to see of Seela rescuing people."

"You mean . . . she went into the flood?"

"In a little boat," Kirk told him. "Looked home-built."

"I built it with my sons," said Korsal. "Seela hates to go out in the boat; she's terrified of drowning."

"Well, she was apparently more afraid for other people in the flood," said Kirk. He smiled, and glanced at the two empty beds in the room. Korsal's sons were finally having their long-awaited tour of engineering. "I'd say you've got a whole family of heroes, Korsal."

Chapter Forty-two

THE HOSPITAL WAS overcrowded. So, as fewer Vulcans and others of copper-based blood fell ill, Sorel took T'Pina off the blood stimulant and put her to work in the laboratory.

At least everyone of mixed heritage had been vaccinated; there was no new strain of the plague, no more need to isolate children. The head of the laboratory had time to teach T'Pina his methodology, and soon there were glowing reports of the young woman's progress.

The biochemists began trying to synthesize the immunity factors in Romulan or Klingon blood, but that project would take months, possibly even years.

Meanwhile, Humans, Caitians, Lemnorians, and others with iron-based blood filled the hospital beds. The medical staff worked overtime while volunteers took over unskilled or semiskilled labor.

Beau Deaver volunteered. Somewhere in his checkered past he had had paramedic training; he filled in as ambulance driver and orderly, but finally insisted on demonstrating that he could find and pop a good vein on virtually anyone, of any race, and Sorel pressured Dr. Sertog, the head of medical services, to set him to drawing blood—even though the healer knew that Deaver's primary motive was to see T'Pina when he delivered the samples to the laboratory.

Perhaps Sorel felt a kinship with Deaver's attraction to T'Pina because of his own attraction to T'Pina's mother.

At the Vulcan Academy Hospital, Sorel worked with any number of nurses, all efficient, all skilled. With T'Kar, however, he found the same rapport that he knew with his partner, Daniel Corrigan. Words were not always necessary; teamwork was raised to the level of choreography.

Along with the plague, the usual injuries and illnesses in a city the size of this one continued. It was almost refreshing to join Daniel in surgery on a Vulcan who had sustained injuries in the flood.

In the OR, Sorel was in light rapport with the entranced patient, assisting Daniel in the physical surgery while T'Kar performed as nurse. Was it imagination—something Sorel had never credited himself with having—or was it the smoothest three-way teamwork Sorel had ever experienced?

Leaving T'Kar to install the patient in recovery, Sorel and Daniel walked back toward the plague-ridden world outside surgery. Before they went through the doors into that unpleasant reality, though, Daniel stopped. "Well?" he asked.

"Is that a question?" Sorel responded.

"Come on, my friend," said his Human partner. "What are you going to do about T'Kar?"

"Do about her?"

Daniel put his hands on his hips, blue eyes laughing up at Sorel. "If you don't ask her to marry you, I'm going to ask her for you."

"Daniel!"

"I have the right," Daniel pointed out. "I'm your son-in-law, remember? T'Mir agrees with me. If you don't approach T'Kar, we will. Sorel, she's perfect for you . . . and besides, I want her in *my* surgery!"

"T'Kar lives here, on Nisus," Sorel pointed out.

"She was born on Vulcan, grew up there," Daniel said. "Her daughter can choose to stay here or return to Vulcan as she pleases—and it looks to me as if T'Pina will choose a bondmate of her own soon. You have no reason to delay, Sorel. In fact, if you do, you may lose your chance. Don't you think there are other men who realize what a catch T'Kar is?"

"A catch? Is that not a hidden trap?" Sorel asked, familiar with the English expression "What's the catch?"

"Different meaning," said Daniel. "In this sense it means a fine choice, but one that is a challenge to obtain."

"Illogical Human languages," Sorel commented.

"And you're being logical? Standing here arguing with me when you should be sweeping T'Kar off her feet?"

"That is not the Vulcan method of proposing marriage."

"Oh?" Daniel said, eyes twinkling. "Tell that to your daughter. She certainly swept me off mine!"

It was useless to argue further. Sorel knew his partner only too well: if he did not propose marriage to T'Kar himself, Daniel would carry out his threat.

Feeling not quite himself, Sorel went in search of T'Kar. He found her just leaving their patient in recovery. Stopping to draw two cups of fruit juice from a hallway dispenser, Sorel offered one to T'Kar by way of greeting. "You performed admirably in surgery," he said.

"It is a pleasure to work with you and Daniel," she

replied. "I know now why you are the best medical team on Vulcan."

"After today"—Sorel seized the opening—"if you are not with us, we will feel that our team is missing a member."

Her eyes went to his. "Sorel . . ."

"T'Kar—come out with me into the garden."

The hospital was designed with small courtyards here and there, to give patients and personnel easy access to fresh air. All that had been done for this garden since the flood was to hose the mud off the pavement and benches. Where plants had been there was now only drying mud.

But there was warm spring sunshine, and when Sorel looked into T'Kar's blue eyes, he had no need of flowers to make the world a pleasant place to be.

They sat side by side on the bench, not touching, and Sorel drank his juice while he searched for words. The empty place in his mind yearned to be filled by a bond with T'Kar, but he did not know how to say so.

T'Kar was shielding her thoughts carefully; without touching her, even Sorel's strong ESP could not read through her barriers. He was forced to rely on words.

"T'Kar," he said softly, "if it seems as logical to you as it does to me, I would bond with thee."

Her eyes smiled, although otherwise she remained composed. "Sorel, it is not logical, but . . . no," she added swiftly when he would have interrupted to explain the logic, "do not say more. You pose a great difficulty for me. My home is here, and yours is on Vulcan. Your children are grown and married, but my daughter is unbonded and in tumult over the recent discovery concerning her ancestry."

"T'Pina has exceptional control for one so young,"

Sorel pointed out. "No Vulcan could be less than honored to have her as a member of his family."

"Nevertheless, she needs my counsel as she decides what to do. Here on Nisus, there will never be a question about her worth. On Vulcan—"

"Vulcan has exiled those who refuse to accept the concept of IDIC," Sorel pointed out. "T'Pina need fear no lack of acceptance, especially in ShiKahr. My partner and son-in-law, Daniel Corrigan, is accepted as Vulcan, even by T'Pau herself."

T'Kar shook her head. "Sorel, why must you argue? It is not a matter of logic."

"I . . . do not understand," he said flatly, comprehending only that she appeared to be refusing him.

"It is not logical," she repeated. "My daughter should be my greatest concern until she has assimilated this new knowledge about herself. I should not be thinking of myself, and yet you have come into my life now, and not at a more appropriate time. I cannot delay; you must have a wife."

"It is not an emergency," he assured her.

"But eventually, if I refuse, you must take another. I do not wish you to take another, Sorel. That is why I say it is not logical. I . . . will bond with thee."

It was so sudden, so unexpected that for a moment he did not realize that she had granted him his wish.

Then, not daring to say another clumsy word, he raised his hand, two fingers extended. T'Kar touched her fingers to his, and he felt her caring, warm with promise.

"When?" he asked.

"Soon," she replied. "As soon as the emergency abates so that we can plan a time when you and I, T'Pina, T'Mir, and Daniel, can all be together without fear of interruption."

"Yes," he replied. "And, T'Kar—there is no need for me to rush back to Vulcan on the next available transport. We will stay on Nisus until you are satisfied that your daughter no longer needs your counsel." He smiled, seeing her echoing smile set free, for him alone.

The cause was indeed sufficient.

Chapter Forty-three

KORSAL WAS STUDYING the writings of the human
—Chaucer, he was called—when Captain Kirk appeared at the door. "There are some people here who
would like to see you, if you're feeling up to it," Kirk
said.

"I may as well," he replied. "Please, ask them to
come in."

He recognized T'Pina, although they had never
formally met, and he was acquainted with Beau
Deaver, a mathematical genius who frustrated the
engineer by not giving a care whether there was any
practical application for his brilliant discoveries.
They were the last people he expected.

T'Pina approached Korsal hesitantly. "Thought
Master Korsal. I ask a favor."

"Anything within my power, T'Pina," he replied. "I
know what you've been going through. And please,
don't be so formal. No titles here. What can I do for
you?"

She looked toward Deaver, and said, "Beau—Mr.
Deaver—said you might know how I can find out . . .
how I can be Romulan. That Klingons have diplomatic relations with the Romulans, so—".

Captain Kirk turned sharply at that. "That's classified information, Deaver. The Klingons aren't supposed to know we know they've got an alliance with the Romulans. How do *you* come to know it?"

"From the Orions," Deaver replied, "when I was a kid driftin' around on the edges of the Federation. Ever'body knew it in the circles me family run in."

"Do not be concerned, Captain," said Korsal. "I am in no position to inform on you. T'Pina," he added, "I'm afraid all channels to Klingon High Command are closed to me. However, I can tell you what Romulan custom could lead to an infant being abandoned on an enemy planet."

"Please tell me." The girl's eyes widened, pleading, although otherwise she maintained Vulcan control.

"Both Klingons and Romulans care greatly about family lines," Korsal told her, "but the Romulans have a tradition of avenging themselves in feuds between families by stealing an infant—an important infant, the heir to a great dynasty, or a child whose marriage could one day cement an alliance between powerful families. The crude method is to kill the child and send the body to the parents. But the child may be abandoned among criminals. If it grows up an outlaw, eventually it is identified to the family, to cause them shame.

"The least practiced but most devastating form of this practice is for your enemy to steal your child and place him somehow with an even greater and stronger enemy—where you cannot possibly steal him back again, but must watch him grow up among people you hate, being taught to hate you.

"T'Pina," Korsal continued, "I believe you are a victim of that practice. We've heard all about your origins for the past few days, how you were discovered after the destruction of Vulcan Colony Five. That planet is well away from the Neutral Zone; the raid would not have been a warning to the Federation to stay out of disputed territory.

"I can only speculate, but that was a small colony. The raid could have been by members of a Romulan dynasty who had stolen you from their enemies. By killing all but the children, they guaranteed that those surviving children would all be taken to Vulcan, far inside the Federation. Knowing that Vulcans would adopt you, they thus placed you where your real parents would have no chance of getting you back. If they ever knew what happened to you."

T'Pina sat in silence, as if trying to assimilate what he had told her. "Then I can never find out who my biological parents were."

"I'm afraid not," said Korsal. "This is not something the Klingons can investigate for you, even if they were willing. And to my knowledge the Federation has no dealings at all with the Romulans."

Kirk was staring at him. "But the Klingons have had for a very long time, haven't they? It's not a new alliance."

"New? Oh, no—Klingons met up with Romulans not long after they first perfected star travel!"

"Captain Kirk!" Korsal had come to recognize Communications Officer Uhura's voice on the intercom.

"Kirk here," the captain replied, punching up a view of the bridge on Kevin's terminal. Uhura looked quite distressed.

"Captain, we are being hailed by Klingon imperial cruiser *Star Blaster.*"

"Put them through," Kirk instructed, his own anxiety showing.

The screen wavered, and the bridge scene was replaced with a head-and-shoulders shot of a Klingon captain. "Kirk," he said, "I am Kef, commander of the *Star Blaster*. We come seeking—" Suddenly the dark eyes on the screen looked past Kirk, to Korsal. "Ah—Korsal. It is you we seek. Are you ill? Why have we had no reports from you in so long?" Kef leaned closer. "Why must we learn of events on Nisus from the Orions?"

Chapter Forty-four

JAMES T. KIRK stared at the Klingon captain on the viewscreen.

"I . . . am not ill," Korsal was saying to Kef.

"Then why are you in the sickbay of a Federation starship?"

Korsal remained silent.

Kef asked, "Why do you refuse to speak, Korsal?"

"I cannot," Korsal replied.

The Klingon captain frowned. His eyes went to Kirk, then back to Korsal. "Speak. I command you."

"I cannot," Korsal repeated. He squared his shoulders. "To do so might embroil the Federation and the Klingon Empire in a war of such dishonor and desperation that when our children's children meet us in the Black Fleet, they will not fight our enemies but seek revenge on *us*."

Kef searched Korsal's face. When it was obvious Korsal was not going to talk, Kef exclaimed, "You fool! You and that *khesting* Orion think you have some new, unknown disease on Nisus. We know what it is, and that we are immune to it."

"Do you also know," Korsal asked flatly, "that Klingon blood can be used to immunize members of other races?"

Kef studied him. "You were . . . protecting us? Is that it, Korsal?"

271

"Yes. We have controlled the epidemic on Nisus. No one who has been exposed will leave Nisus without being immunized. There will not be a Federation-wide epidemic. There will be no . . . demand for Klingon blood."

Kirk cut in, "Kef, how do you know so much about the plague? If Borth wanted to sell it to you, he would not have given you enough information to locate his source."

The Klingon smiled, showing just the tips of his teeth. "That is why I wanted Korsal to tell me. Now you know we have broken Starfleet's latest code, and since you will report the fact to Starfleet Command, we will have the nuisance of breaking a new one."

Kirk had to smile in response. "Point counterpoint." Then he sobered. "Since you know about this disease, may we ask for your help? As Korsal said, the epidemic is controlled. It is not over. We can treat only critical cases with the supply of serum we have. And before anyone can leave Nisus, they must be immunized."

To Kirk's surprise, Kef replied at once, "Yes, my crew will donate the blood you need."

"Why?" asked Kirk, suspicious of too easy a victory.

"Perhaps we would rather give our blood than have you take it," Kef replied.

"We wouldn't—"

"Captain," said Kef, "to save Federation lives? If our situation were reversed, if you would not help us, would you not expect me to *take* your blood to save Klingon lives? You would volunteer, would you not?"

"I hope," Kirk replied, "that my reasons would be less cynical. I believe, Captain, that yours are, as well."

"The donations are already being taken," Kef said, ignoring Kirk's attempt at amity. "We also have the formula for synthesizing the immunity factor, but the process takes twenty days. In the meantime you can stop the plague with serum. The first blood is ready to transport."

Kirk let Uhura transfer the communications link to McCoy while Kef put his chief medical officer on to the Federation doctor.

While that was going on, Kirk turned to Korsal. "What do you think?"

Korsal smiled, no teeth showing. "I think perhaps Klingons and Humans are not so different."

"Then why were you afraid to report the disease?"

"Because we are not so different. Among both our peoples are those who would use even this disease as a weapon. If I had known that my people already had the means to defuse it, I would have sent for help immediately."

But Kirk was still unsatisfied. When Kef came back on screen, he asked, "Did you come to Nisus now because of the message Borth sent you?"

"No. If we had known about the plague, we would have come sooner, and brought a supply of synthetic serum. We are here because Korsal's transmissions stopped abruptly thirty days ago. The technological advances made on Nisus, even though nonmilitary, have been invaluable to the Klingon Empire. We do not want scientific cooperation between the Federation and the empire to cease.

"When the empire could not raise Korsal, we were sent to find out why. On the way, we received Borth's communication—but when we came in subspace radio range we decoded your transmissions and discovered that your plague was what we suspected."

"And you just happened to have in your computer the formula for synthesizing the serum?" Kirk asked.

"Our chief medical officer knew it, of course."

"Of course?" asked Kirk. "Why of course? Kef, you are *immune* to this thing! Why would your CMO know the formula for the cure?"

"Captain—" Korsal protested.

Kef was grinning. "You deserve your reputation, Kirk. You're right; this mutating virus is well known in the Klingon Empire, even though most of us are immune to it. Ask Korsal. He might not recognize its genetic structure, but every Klingon knows about the Imperial plague." The screen blanked.

Kirk turned to Korsal. "All right—talk. What's this Imperial plague?"

To his annoyance, Korsal was laughing. But it was the painful laughter of irony. "If that's what our Nisus plague really is, the Klingon Empire certainly cannot use it as a weapon!"

"Why not?" Kirk asked.

"Because the Klingon Imperial race not only is not immune to it, but rejects antibodies from other Klingon blood. Everyone entering the Klingon Empire must be immunized against Imperial plague, lest our leaders be exposed. To them, it is deadly. You have seen how fast the worst strains kill—in the twenty days it takes to synthesize the only cure they can use, most would be dead."

The Imperial race. Kirk knew that the real leadership of the Klingon Empire were never seen in the neutral territories bordering the Federation, although they had been seen back in the days of First Contact. He had seen old tapes of men with gnarled foreheads, who wore their hair longer than the Klingons he was familiar with.

"But why didn't you recognize the plague?" Kirk asked.

"I told you: every non-Klingon entering the empire is routinely immunized. The disease has not been seen in the Klingon Empire for generations, and as Kef said, my field is not medicine. One of your physicians might recognize a case of, say, smallpox —but would you, a starship captain?"

"I suppose you're right," Kirk admitted. He began to relax. "At least we don't have to worry about Borth now; he has nothing to sell. Korsal, I trust you. And I suppose I can trust Kef's enlightened self-interest."

As he was saying it, Mr. Scott arrived with Kevin and Karl. The two boys were bubbling over with excitement, but they sat on Kevin's bed as Scott asked, "Who's Kef?"

"Captain of the Klingon ship whose crew is right now donating blood to stop the plague," Kirk informed him, enjoying seeing his chief engineer flabbergasted.

Scott looked from Korsal to his two sons, then to T'Pina and Beau Deaver by the door. "Saved by Klingons and Romulans. Klingons in Starfleet Academy. Captain, we've not gone through some strange space anomaly, have we?"

"No, Scotty," Kirk assured him, and explained the latest situation. Then he turned to Kevin, who was listening avidly. "You, young man, appear to have a choice again."

"I still want to go to Starfleet Academy," the boy replied. Then, looking at his father, "At least I want to try it."

"Maybe," said Kirk, "by the time you are ready to graduate we'll have a real alliance instead of just an armed truce with your father's people. What's going on on Nisus is certainly contributing to that."

"I hope so, sir," Kevin replied.

Kirk turned to T'Pina and Deaver. "If we do get better relations with the Klingons," he suggested to the girl, "you may be able to find out more about your ancestry."

"Perhaps," she said, but despite her Vulcan control he heard the poignancy in her tone. Beau Deaver put a hand on her shoulder. She did not shrug him off, but turned to look up into his eyes. "Please, Beau, do not do that."

"T'Pina, you *have* a family," the man said. "Who cares about your ancestry? You are complete in yourself—someone I want to know better, if you'll let me."

This time she did reach to remove the offending hand. "I am honored to call you friend, Beau, but with my mother remarrying, I must begin to make my own decisions."

"Have you decided to return to Vulcan?" he asked.

"No. I will stay on Nisus."

"Well, then," said Deaver with a disarming smile, "that will give me time and opportunity."

Dr. McCoy arrived just as T'Pina and Deaver left, saying, "Korsal, you're free to go as soon as you feel fit—same for you boys."

"Thank you, Doctor," said Korsal, getting out of bed. "I will be glad to return to my work. Kevin, those plans we were working on for better safeties for the dam—"

"If we're right, there'll never be another flood like this one," the boy replied, taking his disk from the computer.

Kirk went to McCoy's office, for he had news for the

doctor after he completed checking the Klingons out of sickbay. He found Spock there, studying a diagram on the medical computer. "The cure?"

Spock nodded. "The cure, Captain. It's hemo-globin-neutral; it can be synthesized for either iron-based or copper-based blood." He looked up. "Provided by the Klingons."

"So the IDIC Epidemic spreads," Kirk observed.

One of Spock's eyebrows rose for a moment, and then he realized what Kirk meant. "Yes, infinite diversity may have provided a breeding ground for the disease, but it also provided cures. Not just this one. T'Pina. Korsal. All the people who came to help."

McCoy joined them, hearing what Spock was saying. "It's too bad we won't be staying on Nisus much longer. The additional blood serum will cure all the critical patients left. In twenty days we'll have the synthetic serum, and we can immunize everyone left among the crew and passengers, and get on with our mission."

"I'll be glad to," said Kirk. "I'm ready to dump Sendet and the rest of that crew and get back to our job. Which reminds me—I pulled some strings with Starfleet, Bones, and got Geoff M'Benga assigned to the *Enterprise*. When we leave, he comes with us."

Spock's eyebrows shot up. "You have acquired a physician who has actually studied Vulcan physiology?"

"Vulcan physiology, maybe," McCoy retorted. *"I'm* still the resident expert on *yours."*

"I shall endeavor," Spock said solemnly, "to avoid requiring that expertise."

"An endeavor you've never been very successful with in the past," McCoy pointed out. "Well, maybe

I'll let Geoff practice on you. He says you're a classic, Spock."

"Indeed?" The eyebrows rose again.

"A classic case of procrastination, that's what you two are!" said Kirk, actually only too happy to see Spock and McCoy relaxed enough to snipe at one another again. "I'm tired of orbiting Nisus."

He went to the intercom. "Engineering."

"Scott here." Already. Of course.

"Get those engines ready, Scotty. We break orbit in twenty days. Kirk out." Then he turned to his two closest friends. "Well, what are you standing around for? You've got a serum to synthesize, and I've got a ship to run. Twenty days, gentlemen; twenty days and not one minute more!"

THE STAR TREK
PHENOMENON

THE

≡STAR TREK≡

PHENOMENON

Fabulous books that keep every Star Trek® movie alive for you.

____STAR TREK– THE MOTION PICTURE
64654/$3.50

____STAR TREK II– THE WRATH OF KHAN
63494/$3.50

____STAR TREK III–THE SEARCH FOR SPOCK
64655/$3.50

____STAR TREK IV– THE VOYAGE HOME
by Vonda N. McIntyre 63266/$3.95

____STAR TREK: THE NEXT GENERATION
65241/$3.95

____THE OFFICIAL STAR TREK QUIZ BOOK
55652/$6.95

____STAR TREK: THE KLINGON DICTIONARY
54349/$3.95

____STAR TREK COMPENDIUM REVISED
62726/$9.95

____MR. SCOTT'S GUIDE TO
THE ENTERPRISE
63576/$10.95

Simon & Schuster, Mail Order Dept. STP
200 Old Tappan Rd., Old Tappan, N.J. 07675

POCKET
B O O K S

Please send me the books I have checked above. I am enclosing $_____ (please add 75¢ to cover postage and handling for each order. N.Y.S. and N.Y.C. residents please add appropriate sales tax). Send check or money order–no cash or C.O.D.'s please. Allow up to six weeks for delivery. For purchases over $10.00 you may use VISA: card number, expiration date and customer signature must be included.

Name _____

Address _____

City _____ State/Zip _____

VISA Card No. _____ Exp. Date _____

Signature _____ 775